T0129424

The friendship of four young ladies has created an indestructible bond to protect one another from the perils of love and marriage . . .

After the demise of her friend's disastrous marriage, Mercedes Parsons isn't about to let the widowed Wallflower of West Lane, Lady Aurora Radcliff, undertake another perilous trip to the altar. At least, not before the bridegroom-to-be is thoroughly investigated. If only Mercy could stop her uncharacteristic daydreaming about Wesley Renshaw's charm, his intellect, his dashing good looks. After all, the earl has already set his sights on her best friend! She must keep her wits about her and avoid giving into temptation.

Wesley is both irritated and intrigued by the machinations of Mercy—He cannot let her cleverness and beauty distract him. He needs to marry her friend, Aurora, so he can reclaim his family's ancestral home. A wrong he has hoped to right his entire life. Besides, who is penniless spinster Mercedes Parsons to decide whom he can and cannot marry? Yet while he admires her unwavering loyalty to her friends, he decides it's high time the misguided woman had a dose of her own medicine. Two can play at this spying game. But they are both embarked on a dangerous charade. And it won't be merely Mercy's reputation at risk—or her heart on the line—as Wesley comes to the inescapable conclusion that he has found the right woman at exactly the wrong time.

Visit us at www.kensingtonbooks.com

Books by A.S. Fenichel

The Wallflowers of West Lane
Capturing the Earl
The Earl Not Taken
Misleading a Duke

The Everton Domestic Society
A Lady's Honor
A Lady's Escape
A Lady's Virtue
A Lady's Past

Forever Brides Series
Tainted Bride
Foolish Bride
Desperate Bride

The Demon Hunter Series
Ascension
Deception
Betrayal

Published by Kensington Publishing Corp.

Capturing the Earl

The Wallflowers of West Lane

A.S. Fenichel

LYRICAL PRESS
Kensington Publishing Corp.
www.kensingtonbooks.com

LYRICAL PRESS BOOKS are published by
Kensington Publishing Corp.
119 West 40th Street
New York, NY 10018

All Kensington titles, imprints, and distributed lines are available at special quantity discounts for bulk purchases for sales promotion, premiums, fund-raising, educational, or institutional use.

Special book excerpts or customized printings can also be created to fit specific needs. For details, write or phone the office of the Kensington Sales Manager: Kensington Publishing Corp., 119 West 40th Street, New York, NY 10018. Attn. Sales Department. Phone: 1-800-221-2647.

Lyrical Press and Lyrical Press logo Reg. U.S. Pat. & TM Off.
First Electronic Edition: January 2021
ISBN-13: 978-1-5161-1053-7 (ebook)
ISBN-10: 1-5161-1053-6 (ebook)

First Print Edition: January 2021
ISBN-13: 978-1-5161-1056-8
ISBN-10: 1-5161-1056-0

Printed in the United States of America

Some people meet as children and fall in love with youth and the thrill of the unknown to forge a path. I had that once a long time ago, then it was gone. Yet there is another kind of falling in love that comes to us as adults. We know the risks and see them clearly. We know the obstacles and look beyond them to the possibilities. With eyes wide open, I found the second love of my life and thank God daily for bringing him to me.

This book is for Dave. Thank you for keeping your eyes and heart open.

Acknowledgments

A huge shout out to my editor, Elizabeth May, for being so thorough and making sure this book was great during such trying times. I had moments of doubt, but she never did.

As always, I have to say that the circle of friends I am blessed with have carried me through each and every book. Thank you, Karla, Juliette, Debbie, Chad, Llonda, Naima, Jessen, Tif, Kristi, Gemma, Corinne, Farah, Mona, Robin, Laura, and Maggie. You are my people.

Thanks to so many readers who sent wonderful thoughts during the height of Covid-19 and helped me want to write about romance. You are the spark.

Prologue

Mercedes Heath shook her head. She must have heard him wrong. After all, why would Wesley Renshaw, the Earl of Castlewick, want to dance with her?

The ballroom was loud and awash with activity. The Duke of Breckenridge lived in one of the largest townhouses in London, but it was still enough of a crush that she might have misunderstood the charming earl.

"Miss Heath?" Wesley's light brown eyes sparkled with some amusement only he understood.

"I beg your pardon, my lord?" Mercy tried to be polite, but it came out sharper than she'd planned.

Mercy was tall for a woman, but the earl was still a few inches taller, with the broadest shoulders she'd ever encountered. She had a fleeting thought about what he must do to stay so muscular, but brushed the wayward notion aside. His dark blond curls fell over the golden tan of his forehead, but his bright eyes glinted with browns and golds, or at least she imagined they did. Mercy spent so much time admiring him, that once again, she had missed what he said.

Her aunt Phyllis had urged her to put her spectacles in her reticule and stop hiding her pretty face. She had done so to appease her only living blood relative, but found herself out of sorts with her vision blurred.

However, she saw well enough to note his offered arm, indicating he did indeed wish to dance with her.

As she had missed the opportunity to give some random excuse for why she couldn't possibly dance with him, she placed her hand on his arm and they joined the other dancers.

The conductor tapped his wand and a waltz began. Mercy tried not to notice the missed notes and out of tune second violin, but the sound grated on her nerves.

Wesley placed a hand at the small of her back a bit more firmly than was strictly necessary.

Turning her attention to him, she asked. "Have I been rude?"

His smile sent a shot of attraction from Mercy's head to her toes and it stopped in a few interesting places along the way. "Not at all. You are seemingly distracted. Is the music not to your liking?"

It would be more polite to say nothing or deny any issues with the orchestra, but Mercy didn't care about such customs and she had no reason to attempt small talk with this earl. He was nothing to her. She looked from the ornate arch ceiling with its frescoes to her aunt Phyllis, who watched from the furthest corner of the ballroom before settling her attention back on the handsome man whirling her around the room. "The second violin is out of tune, the pianoforte is being played by a complete oaf, and the flutist has missed no less than two notes of every eight."

"I see." He grinned as if perhaps he did actually understand, but perhaps he was just amused by her in general. That could explain his desire to dance with a girl of no means and few relations.

"I realize I am likely the only one to notice such things and that the duke and his sister have hired one of the most popular orchestras in London." Mercy shrugged as she also knew no one cared what she thought of the music.

A robust couple bounded across the dance floor laughing and smiling as if they were part of a circus. Neither seemed capable of waltzing but neither did they care as they pushed several couples out of their way and headed directly for Mercy.

In one graceful move, Wesley lifted Mercy from her feet and out of harm's way. Her body crushed to his with an embrace that felt almost tender before he released her and in the same instant fell back into the perfectly balanced steps of the waltz. "You are a musician then."

She laughed and it surprised even herself. She rarely laughed in the company of strangers. Girls of her kind were not supposed to show outward enjoyment in public. It was grotesque, in Aunt Phyllis's opinion. But the way he dismissed saving her from a pummeling as if it never happened and took up the conversation without a hitch amused her. "I would not call myself as such, but I do play."

"Yet you hear every nuance. I think you might be being modest." His firm hand on her back guided them easily around the room and sent heat through her in way no other man ever had.

Mercy had no response. If she said she was an accomplished musician, she would be a braggart, and if she denied it, a liar. Remaining silent was her only choice.

"I would like to hear you play some time, Miss Heath." He cocked his strong chin to one side. "I think I would enjoy that very much."

The music ended. "Perhaps you will, my lord."

She turned to walk away, but he touched her elbow. "Will you not stay for the Boulanger?"

It was common for partners to stand up for two consecutive dances. Mercy just assumed he would have had enough dancing with a girl of no consequence and politely let her find her way back to some quiet corner or to her friends. "If you wish, my lord."

He offered his hand and they joined a circle of dancers.

The Boulanger left little time for chatting, but it did give her time to observe Wesley and how he interacted with others. He smiled politely at every woman he partnered, though never so wide as to give someone the wrong impression. When they were once again hand in hand, his eyes sparkled with something tender.

Mercy assumed she was imagining things. With her blurred vision, she could easily imagine anything in the place of the truth. He couldn't care about someone like her. If he showed special regard it was only because he wanted something. In most cases what men wanted from her she was not willing to give. Her wicked body responded to the earl without regard for the fact that he was unattainable. Heat flushed up her neck and face, while parts lower suddenly came alive with desire.

Quashing the thought, she focused on the music, noting every mistake and even a few nicely handled stanzas.

It was rare that Mercy got to dance. Without a title, lands, or a large dowry, she had nothing to offer a young gentleman besides her body and that was not a prize she was eager to give. At most of these affairs she'd find a quiet corner and watch out for her friends, or if the music room was not in use she might closet herself away and putter with finer instruments than she generally had access to.

Moving around the floor to the beat of the music and occasionally coming together with a man who had specifically asked her to dance with him was a rare delight. It was easy to glide around the floor, but she wished she had clear sight so she could see all the nuances of his expression.

His full lips were turned up, but she couldn't tell if the expression touched his eyes. Fumbling for her reticule, she decided that she would put her spectacles back on just as the music ended and catch a glimpse of Wesley's true gaze before it was likely she'd never see him again.

Gripping the wire rim between two fingers she turned toward Wesley.

The final notes were played.

Applause erupted from the dancers.

The man with the paunch on her other side bumped her, pushing her into Wesley.

Wesley's arms came around her before she tumbled to the floor.

The spectacles flew from her hand as she gripped his arm.

A sickening crunch followed.

As the dancers dispersed and the musicians put down their instruments, among the clatter Mercy crouched beside her crushed spectacles. She picked up the twisted frames. One lens was crushed to powder on the wooden floor, but the other was still in the frame with just one crack diagonally across. Mercy put the one lens to her eye. "I suppose it could be worse."

"I'm sorry, Miss Heath. I hope those are not a desperate need."

She had expected him to walk off when the others had, but he'd stayed with her and stood just behind. She drew a long breath and let it out. "I shall survive, my lord."

Firmly he gripped her elbow and drew her back to standing. He studied the crushed wire and glass in her hand. "Do not injure yourself on the glass, miss."

Ladies of worth didn't care if they could see or not. It was more important to be lovely and snare a fine husband with money and power. Mercy preferred to see and to read. She needed to read the music of the masters as much as she required breath. Still, her weakness was too obvious in his presence and heat crept up her cheeks. Plunking the ruined spectacles back in her reticule, Mercy forced a polite smile. "Thank you, my lord. I am uninjured. I enjoyed the dance."

She turned and strode toward the hallway where she could rush to the ladies' retiring room and recover herself.

Wesley stayed at her side. "To whom may I deliver you, Miss Heath?"

Halfway across the wide grand foyer, she stopped and turned to him. "You need not concern yourself, my lord. I am a grown woman and can manage to keep myself safe. My friends and my aunt are here tonight."

Stepping until he was inches from her, his warmth spread through her. "I can see you are upset and only wish to help."

It was impossible he could know her mind. She had practiced the indifferent mask she wore to these events and it had never failed her. The fact that she couldn't afford to replace the spectacles was bad enough. His knowing she was distressed was unbearable. "I am not upset. They are only a meaningless object. You need not worry."

"It is too late for that, Miss Heath." His soft voice brought her head up. Even slightly blurred he was more handsome than was good for her. "I thank you for your concern, my lord. I shall just retire for a few minutes and be right again."

He shifted from one foot to the other, his frown obvious. "Shall I find your friends and send them to you?"

"That is not necessary." Though, she had to admit, it was a very kind idea. "I am fine. It was a vigorous dance and I need to rest."

The air thickened in the moment where he made no reply. He bowed. "As you wish, Miss Heath. I thank you for the dance."

After making a quick curtsy, she tried to think of something to say, but instead rushed away and closeted herself in a small parlor to catch her breath.

Once she had thoroughly inspected her ruined spectacles, she returned them to her reticule with a sigh. Perhaps she could ask her aunt for a few extra pounds to replace them. No. She would see if she could take on a few new music students and earn enough wage to buy a new pair.

That settled, she left the parlor and popped out into the cool night for some air. She was in a part of the house unused by the ball attendees and reveled in the quiet. The gardens were lit and she heard voices on the other side of a tall hedge. Several couples were hidden from her view, but she heard them chatting on the larger veranda that flanked the ballroom. Staying hidden, she circled a baluster and stepped onto a stone path.

It was a perfect night. Mercy took a deep breath. She had to return, but not yet. Her mind bustled with questions about why the Earl of Castlewick would ask her to dance, or care about her broken eyewear or her state of distress. It was all very odd.

Another set of footsteps sounded from behind.

Mercy spun around to find Wesley quickly approaching. "My lord?"

"Miss Heath, when you didn't return, I became concerned." He bowed. She stepped back. "Why would such a thing concern you?"

"I beg your pardon." His tone sharpened.

Keeping her distance, Mercy regretted stepping so far from the safety of a crowd. "I mean you no offense, my lord, but why should my state of being be of any concern to you? I am nothing to you save a dance partner.

To be honest, I'm still trying to fathom why you asked me to dance in the first place."

It was rude. She should have kept her questions to herself, thanked him for his attention, and walked away. Yet she wanted to know and had little to lose.

A man in his position might have walked away or become affronted and given her a setting down. Wesley smiled. "I asked you to dance because you are a lovely woman and I thought it might be a pleasant way to spend part of the evening. As for my concern," his face grew serious, "I should have protected you better during the dance and after. What happened to your belongings should never have occurred."

He felt responsible. How odd. Mercy hadn't met many men of his ilk who were so solicitous of their dance partner's feelings. He likely wanted to steal a kiss or more and had followed her to get her alone. Mercy feigned patting her hair, but pulled a long hatpin she kept tucked in her elaborate bun. "My lord, I appreciate your attention." It was difficult to not sound sarcastic. If necessary, she would jab him and run. "You may rest assured, I am in no immediate danger. I just wanted some air."

The way his laugh rolled around the garden and caught on the breeze brought nothing but delight. "I think the weapon is a fine idea, Miss Heath. I shall instruct my two sisters to have exactly such an item placed in their hair for balls, trips to the theater, and the like."

Mercy raised her brow and smiled, but didn't sheath her weapon against overly amorous admirers. "You might tell them picnics and walks in the park are better suited to several pins in one's stays or actual hats. One never knows when man of means will try to take advantage of a woman below his station. Of course, your sisters have your title to protect them."

She had no need for spectacles or better lighting to see that her words had angered him. His fists clenched at his sides and his shoulders went rigid. "I have no intention of taking anything from any woman, regardless of her station, that is not offered freely."

"Then you had better go back to the house, my lord, before someone sees you and me in the garden alone and I am ruined. Or do you intend to marry me, should we be discovered?" She made a scoffing sound that was not very ladylike.

The moon shone on him like a god of old as he crossed his arms over his chest. "I have no intention of marrying you, Miss Heath. Though I have to say your candor is refreshing after so many inane hours of debutantes who connive to have my attentions."

"Conniving is not really in my nature. And in any event, I am not of your station. I am only Miss Heath, an orphan whose father had no title and whose lands were entailed elsewhere. If not for my aunt's kindness, I would be someone's governess or worse. You may be sure that I have no designs on a man like you." She carefully and deliberately put her hatpin back into her hair without poking herself.

"I'm not sure I like the way you say, 'a man like me.' In fact, I didn't like any of what you just said." He scowled.

"And yet it was all true."

Giving her a nod, he said, "Good evening, Miss Heath."

She made a quick curtsy and rushed back toward the house.

* * * *

Mercy played the pianoforte in the West Lane music room. She knew the piece from memory and would have to endure it played by her student later in the day. Playing it herself beforehand was a small indulgence.

Ignoring the bang of the doors and the scratching on the music room's door, she played on.

Tipton stood several feet away with a package in his hand and a bland expression.

Stopping play, Mercy sighed. "Yes, Tipton?"

He approached. "Miss Heath, this just arrived by special messenger for you." Tipton placed the package, wrapped in thick brown paper, on the pianoforte. With a bow, he turned and left.

She wanted to continue playing, but too curious about the package, she reached for it. Who would send her anything?

Removing the note from beneath the package, she opened it.

Miss Heath,
Consider this a small apology for my lack of attentiveness.
Regards,
Castlewick.

Heart pounding, Mercy opened the box without tearing the thick paper. Inside lay a case covered in the finest kid. The soft leather was usually used for expensive gloves. However, in the case lay a pair of wire-framed spectacles.

Mercy gasped and stared at them.

"What is it?" Aurora said from the doorway. "I heard the music stop and came to check on you. Have you an admirer?"

"No," Mercy said too quickly.

Aurora's golden hair caught the light and her pale blue dress flowed around her as she approached the pianoforte. She studied the spectacles. "Who would send such an unusual and thoughtful gift?"

The Wallflowers of West Lane did not lie to one another. Since she had nothing to hide, Mercy handed the note to Aurora.

One perfectly curved brow rose above her clear blue eyes. Aurora said, "Why would the Earl of Castlewick send you replacement spectacles?"

"I haven't the faintest idea. Perhaps he truly felt responsible for the ruination of my other pair." Mercy took them from the case and put them on. The sheet music before her came into view with perfect clarity. Her heart soared. "Better than my old ones, but I can't accept them."

Aurora waved a hand. "You did nothing wrong and if it makes his lordship feel better, I see no harm in keeping the glasses, which you need and would not be able to buy for yourself for many months. Unless you have changed your mind about either letting me buy you a pair or asking your aunt?"

Shaking her head, Mercy said. "I have not changed my mind, but to accept such a gift from a man…What will he want in return?"

Aurora tapped her lip with her index finger. "I suggest you consider it a loan. You can write back to his lordship and tell him you appreciate his gesture but must pay him back in full within some set time frame of your choosing."

It made sense. Mercy did need the spectacles. After several distracted hours of wondering why he had done it, she finished with her last student of the day and sat down to write Wesley a note of thanks and terms for the loan.

Once she'd handed her mail off to Tipton, Mercy pushed her new spectacles up on her nose and settled into the ladies' parlor with a book.

Chapter 1

Mercy sipped her tea and listened to Faith's tale of finding a mouse in the grand parlor of her new home at the Breckenridge townhouse. Faith had only been a duchess for a few months, but from the sound of it, she was making a singular impression.

"Several priceless items were broken, but really it couldn't be helped." Faith put down her cup, took a biscuit from the platter on the low table, and nibbled a bite. One wild curl escaped her bun and hung in her eyes. She blew a puff of hair to try to move it out of view.

Poppy, who had also married less than a year before, ate her fourth sweet and giggled. "Why didn't you just call for a footman to handle the mouse?"

With a sigh, Faith put her biscuit on the edge of her saucer. "I panicked. Besides, plenty of footmen, maids, and the butler, Dumford, all rushed in. Lady Hatfield was up on her chair screaming as if a murderer was brandishing a sword. I didn't know what to do. I took off my slipper and chased the poor horrified rodent."

"How did the vase and statue get broken?" Aurora's blue eyes sparkled with mirth, but she sat calmly with her hands folded in her lap.

"That silly mouse ran right under Lady Hatfield's chair. It was really quite remarkable. She is a woman of some girth, but she leaped over the Queen Anne and landed on the settee. It would have been a move worthy of applause had not her size and forward motion caused the settee to slide across the rug and smash into the table holding those items.

"Poor Dumford tried to save the statue as it was of Nick, but alas, his haste toppled the harp in the corner and that went right through the window." Faith shook her head and more disobedient curls escaped.

Mercy gave up trying not to laugh. Her eyes teared and her stomach ached with the image Faith painted. "Good lord, where was the mouse with all this going on?"

With a shrug, Faith picked her tea up. "We lost him in the commotion."

Poppy, who had never pretended to take the entire story seriously, laughed openly and had to catch her breath to speak. "And what of Lady Hatfield?"

Faith narrowed her eyes and frowned. "I will not be inviting her back. Not that I believe she would ever return, but the silly screaming caused such a scene and all over a tiny mouse."

"What do you mean? Once the mouse disappeared, surely she calmed." Aurora sat straight as a proper lady despite the fact that it was only the four of them having their Tuesday tea. She never let her guard down, at least not in years.

"She didn't stop," Faith continued. "She screamed and fussed, bringing half the neighborhood out. You would have thought the world was coming to an end. Word reached Nick at his meeting in Parliament and he rushed home, thinking I was in some danger. I really have no tolerance for such histrionics."

"That does seem a bit much," Aurora agreed.

Poppy made her best effort to calm herself and catch her breath. "How did you get her to stop?"

"Dumford called Doctor Milne, who gave her a sedative. It was quite a mess."

Mercy regained control of her laughter, took a sip of tea, and said, "I'm glad becoming a duchess has not left you bored, Faith."

Faith, who had remained stoic through the entire telling of her story, cracked a wide grin. "Lord, that's the last thing it is. Tuesday tea is the only time I've had for myself all week."

"I'm glad you still make time to come." Aurora's voice was soft and a bit wistful.

Mercy and Aurora were the only Wallflowers still living in the house left to Aurora by her horrid but thankfully dead husband. Leaning around the back of the chaise, Mercy squeezed Aurora's hand. "We shall always have each other, no matter what else happens in our lives, Aurora. You never have to worry the Wallflowers will abandon you."

With a hesitant smile, Aurora nodded. "I know, but you must admit, the house has gotten very quiet this last year."

A commotion in the foyer turned all of their heads.

"I don't care what her ladyship said, I will see my daughter regardless of what day of the week it is." Lady Jemima Draper, the Dowager Countess of Marsden, and Aurora's mother scolded Tipton before pushing through the doors of the ladies' parlor.

The Wallflowers all stared.

Tipton stood just behind Aurora's mother. "Her ladyship, the Dowager Countess of Marsden, is here to see you, my lady." He made a hasty retreat, closing the doors as he went.

Standing, the Wallflowers all turned and curtsied.

"Hello, Mother. This is a surprise," Aurora stepped forward and kissed her mother's cheek. "I don't recall our having an appointment today."

"Aurora, I insist you fire that butler of yours. He meant to turn me away. How dare he think to do such a thing?" Jemima huffed and sat in the chair Aurora had vacated.

Aurora sighed and sat on the chaise next to Mercy as they all resumed sitting. "On Tuesdays, Tipton is instructed to turn all callers away as it is my special tea with my friends, Mother. I'm sure you can understand."

"I most certainly do not. I have rights to enter this house whenever I choose. You and your...friends will not stop me." Lady Draper had the stiffest posture Mercy had ever seen. It was a wonder her slim back didn't snap from the rigidity.

Another sigh from Aurora. "Mother, would you care for some tea? This has gone cold, but I can call for a fresh pot.

"I would not like tea." Her tone was still scolding. "I have news and it cannot wait. You may want to send these women away."

The corners of Aurora's eyes narrowed. "Of these women, one is a countess and your daughter-in-law, and another a duchess, Mother. Try to have a little respect for my friends, as you should to all people regardless of title."

Mercy had to hide her amusement behind a cough and her hand as Aurora had gotten quite good at putting her mother in her place. A scoff pushed from Jemima's full lips and she waved a dismissive hand. "If you won't send them away, then they shall have the honor of learning your good fortune firsthand."

Mercy's stomach tightened with warning that whatever Jemima Draper believed was good fortune was likely unpleasant news for Aurora.

A small tick in Aurora's jaw indicated she thought the same. "What is it, Mother?"

"The Earl of Castlewick is going to court you and, I should think, shortly after that, marry you."

All the air rushed out of the room. Mercy had no breath and when she scanned her friends, Aurora's fair skin was sheet white and her hands drew into fists in her lap. "I..." She shook as she drew in a long breath. Her voice was steady, but with the same scolding undertone her mother used. "I have no intentions of ever marrying again nor will I allow any man to court me. I would think you know that, Mother."

"Nonsense. You will allow him to court you. You are too young and beautiful never to marry again. It has been a year since Radcliff left us. You have much to offer a man of means like Castlewick."

Mercy thought of Wesley Renshaw's expressive brown eyes and touched the frame of the spectacles he'd sent her to replace her broken pair. She'd paid him back for the gesture, but treasured the thoughtfulness of the gift all the same. What had started as worry for Aurora turned to dismay for herself. Her feelings about a couple of dances and kind looks from an earl amounted to very little. It wasn't as if an earl would ever return her amorous thoughts. Mercy swallowed it down and focused on her friend.

"Mother, I may have a great deal to offer a man because I have land and money, but I would lose all of that should I marry. Why would I do such a thing?"

Jemima stood and circled the room. She wore a severe russet day dress that covered her from the top of her neck to her feet. The style was out of date and made her look far older than she was. In fact, at only forty-three, she appeared old and mean. The pretty items strewn around the Wallflowers' favorite room made her look even more unpleasant.

Mercy wanted to pull her out of their sanctuary and lock the door. Aurora didn't want to remarry and even if she had, why did it have to be Wesley who asked? Of all the eligible bachelors in London, why him?

Standing at the window, the glow of sunlight pushed aside Jemima's disguise and her beauty came into focus. A few wrinkles around her eyes and a strand or two of gray in her golden hair, but Aurora was the image of her mother and both were classic beauties. "I wish it, Aurora. I want grandchildren and a legacy for your father. It seems your brother and Penelope will not obey me in this area, so you must do your duty by me."

Poppy stuttered. "I...I...Your son and I have only been married six months, my lady. We have refused nothing."

"By now you should be increasing." Jemima waved her hand in dismissal of Poppy. "You failed with your first husband, Aurora. Since he is dead, we shall assume it was his failing. A second husband with good breeding is what you need. This family needs another generation. You would have your cousin Templeton inherit when your brother dies?"

Poppy gasped.

Faith went to her and wrapped an arm around her shoulders. "No one is dying."

"Dear lord, mother. You should really monitor your mouth. Rhys is healthy and his wife is sitting in the room. Have you no care for the feelings of others?" Aurora took a breath. "I will think over your news. Lord Castlewick may pay a call if he likes, but I have no intention of allowing him to court me. That said, his interest is flattering, and I shall let him down myself."

A slow smile played on Jemima's lips.

Mercy's gut twisted again.

"Very well. I'm sure he will call within the week." Jemima turned and stepped toward the door.

Tipton opened it, without the need of being called. He held out the dowager's hat and pelisse.

She accepted the outerwear, pinned her hat in place, and grinned back at her daughter. "I'm sure you will find his lordship as charming as I do. You need protection, Aurora. No woman as young and solvent as you should be without male protection."

When no one replied, she said, "So sorry I can't stay to tea. Good afternoon, Aurora, Poppy, Your Grace, Miss Heath."

Like the tidal-wave she was, the dowager swept out just as quickly, leaving disaster in her wake.

Mercy glanced from Poppy to Faith. The three of them avoided looking at Aurora, but the silence couldn't last. Mercy wanted to scream, anyone but him, but she could see how Wesley might be a good match for Aurora if the lady were interested in such a thing. Of course, Aurora's aversion to remarrying did not make him any more suitable for Mercy. "What do you want to do, Aurora? Shall we discourage his lordship?"

Aurora studied her hands in her lap. "I can't imagine what Mother is thinking."

"That it would be an advantageous marriage with property." Poppy never minced words. It was one of the things Mercy liked best about her fearless friend.

Rolling her eyes, Aurora finally looked up. "She knows another marriage is the last thing I want. I have funds enough to live well for the rest of my life. I don't need a man to protect me. What might Lord Castlewick have said to make her think he was worth my time?"

"I doubt he had to say much more than 'I'd like to court your daughter,'" Faith said. "We all know she has been crazed to have you married from our school days. It's why you were the first of us to marry and at such a young age."

"She didn't even mind that your father married you to a monster," Mercy added.

The four of them had been sent to Switzerland for finishing school. Spirited youths, they had presented difficulties for their parents. For their crimes, at fifteen they had been shipped off for three years to the Wormbattle School for Young Ladies. It turned out to be a blessing as they had met during the travel to Lucerne and been the closest of friends ever since.

In the final weeks of their exile, Aurora had received a letter from her parents informing her she would be married just a few weeks after arriving in London. The Earl of Radcliff was a fine match on paper, but in reality he was a vicious monster. An incident at a Gaming Hell cost Radcliff his worthless hide. Aurora was lucky to have escaped marriage with her life.

"Perhaps he's just very charming." Faith shrugged. "You danced with him, Mercy. What was your impression?"

"That was months ago." Mercy avoided the question.

The three of them continued to watch her.

Mercy drew a long breath. There was no avoiding her friends. "He was a good dancer and careful to keep me out of harm's way when an overzealous couple nearly barreled over me. His conversation was substantial and interesting. I'm not sure what you want me to have gleaned from one dance." She finished with a huff of frustration. Speaking about two dances that had kept Wesley Renshaw on her mind for months was not good for Mercy's wellbeing and in the context of his courting her friend, it was not good for her heart's sake either.

"He did replace your spectacles that were broken during the dance." Aurora bit her thumb.

"Did he?" Faith sat up straighter and pinned Mercy with her gaze. "You never said anything."

Mercy tucked her feet under her on the chaise and gave a shrug. "What was there to say? He felt responsible for my other pair breaking and sent a new pair. I sent him a note of thanks and had my solicitor pay him back from a portion of my allowance each month. It would have been improper to accept such a gift."

"I see your point," Poppy said. "That does not negate the fact that it was a kind gesture on his part. You must have made quite an impression on him, Mercy."

A laugh bubbled up inside Mercy and came out as a snort. "So much of an impression that he'd decided to court my friend."

Aurora was still on the end of the chaise and turned to face Mercy. "I hope you don't think I encouraged this behavior. I hardly spoke to him." Mercy took her hand. "Of course not. I'm sure his lordship has his reasons. Perhaps we should find out what those reasons are and then dissuade him from his folly. If that is what you want, Aurora."

"I most certainly don't wish to be courted by the Earl of Castlewick, or anyone else for that matter. I will tell him so when he comes to call and that will be an end to it." Aurora gave Mercy's hand a squeeze and firmly nodded her head.

Poppy frowned. "We should find out what it is he really wants. Not that you are not a worthy prize on your own, Aurora, but he hardly knows that. He must need something you can offer."

Heart shriveled like an apple left out in the sun, Mercy saw no point in wishing for a different life. She had to live the one she'd been given. "Faith, your husband knows his lordship quite well. Can you ask him what might have attracted Aurora to him?"

Pulling a sour face, Faith said, "If I must, but Nick doesn't like our Wallflower meddling after the mess he and I ended up in after our investigation of him and my subsequent trapping him in the country."

"It was hardly our fault that Nick had enemies who came after him." Poppy stomped her foot.

"No," Faith agreed, "but he still doesn't like it. If we can't find the information out on our own, I will ask Nick. Until, we reach an impasse, let's keep him out of it. Maybe Rhys knows something, Poppy?"

"I'm not sure how acquainted Rhys is with Lord Castlewick, but I will ask him. I think he secretly loves our schemes. Besides, he'll want to investigate anyone who wishes to marry Aurora." Poppy crossed her arms over her chest and narrowed her eyes in thought.

Aurora stood. She paced a few feet away before turning toward them. Her hands were fisted at her sides. While her dress, hair, and features were all perfectly in order, there was an undercurrent in Aurora's eyes of fear and determination. "I have no intention of marrying anyone...ever! I will make that as clear to his lordship as I am making it to the three of you. There is no amount of charm that will persuade me to let another man control me for as long as I live. Once was quite enough. My mother will have to live with disappointment."

"Then we will see to it you are not put in that position," Faith said. "Men can go to many extremes within society to get what they want. We should prepare to do battle if necessary."

Mercy's heart stopped, then pounded out a staccato drumbeat. "You don't think he would do something foolish to gain Aurora's hand, do you?"

Faith shrugged. "I don't know him as well as you, Mercy. What do you think?"

"I suppose it's possible that he made the gesture with my spectacles just to get into Aurora's good graces. I don't know." Her stomach tied in knots. She hated the idea that Wesley would have used her to get close to Aurora, but it would explain his attention to a woman of no means.

Faith opened her mouth to say more, but Poppy put a hand on her shoulder, stopping her. Poppy rounded the table and sat next to Mercy. "You liked him, Mercy?"

"I like the attention he paid me, but I knew even during the dance there was no possibility of more than a fleeting association with a man like him for a girl like me. I never held out any hope for more." There was enough truth in the statement that Mercy didn't feel she'd lied to her friends. "In fact, as you and Faith are both married now with much to do in your own lives, I will volunteer to rid the Wallflowers of Lord Castlewick."

Poppy made a line with her lips that said she wasn't totally convinced.

Faith gave a nod and smiled.

Aurora's shoulders relaxed in relief before she called for more tea.

Mercy wished she could run to her room and have a silent cry before she took on her upcoming task for her friend.

Chapter 2

The Earl of Castlewick's Townhouse
London

Wesley frowned at his cousin as he finished dressing. "Why are you here, Mal?"

Malcolm Renshaw was the only child of Wesley's uncle. They had grown up together and become good friends. But the constant badgering over the properties was driving Wesley mad.

"I am here to make sure you have everything you need to secure Whickette Park." With his arms open palms up he gave the appearance of someone who was about to give a sermon.

"I shall do all in my power to convince Lady Radcliff to marry me, as you well know. What I want to know is what good you think it will do *you*?" Wesley pulled on his green velvet coat with the help of Dooley, his valet.

Besides his cousin's blue eyes, the two men had a similar look and could pass for brothers. Malcolm ran his fingers through his hair. "You might die without a son and I might inherit."

He said it so banally, Wesley laughed. "Good to see you're always hopeful, cousin."

"Might it not be that I want our family to have back what grandfather lost just as much as you do?" Malcolm flopped into a chair by the wardrobe.

"You have been a great help to me, Mal. I know you want what is best for our family, but your father's entailments have been recovered. I have done right by your side of the family. I'll take care of my own business from here on. My father asked me to do this before he died. I only wish he had lived to see the estates all returned to the Castlewick title." The last few years of his life had all been about this one request from his father. Taking care of his sisters would have been enough responsibility, but when his father lay abed asking for the impossible, Wesley knew his life was no longer his own.

He swallowed down the memory. Giving his appearance one last look in the glass, he told Dooley to have his horse brought around.

Dooley narrowed his gaze at Malcolm, made a bow to Wesley, and left them.

"I have to go now. You can show yourself out, Mal." Wesley stared his cousin down until he relented and preceded him downstairs.

"Come by my house and tell me how it goes." Mal accepted his hat and gloves as Peters opened the door.

"I most certainly will not." Wesley took his own hat from the butler. "Thank you, Peters. I have several errands to run today after paying calls. I shall not be home for dinner. My sisters have informed me they will be walking in the park later. See that two footmen follow them and Mrs. Manfred."

"Very good, my lord." Peters saw them both out before closing the door.

Wesley mounted his horse and petted his silken black coat. "Good boy, Brutus."

"Will you not even bid me a good day, cousin?" Malcolm laughed as Wesley guided his horse away from his townhouse.

Wesley waved a hand. "Good day, Mal. Try not to get into trouble."

It was a short ride through neighborhoods to West Lane and the residence of Lady Radcliff. He made sure to think only of her blond hair and blue eyes. He made a mental note of how lovely she was when she smiled. Aurora Sherbourn was a lovely woman and would make him a fine wife, along with making it possible for him to do right by his family. It was the right thing to do.

At the West Lane townhouse, Wesley tugged his coat into place and took a deep breath. He had a lot to lose if his charms didn't work. She would have him or he'd have used stronger measures to obtain his goal.

He ran his hand along his smooth jaw and banged the knocker.

The butler opened the door. Slightly portly, he narrowed his eyes on Wesley. "May I help you?"

There was something both sarcastic and benign in his question. Wesley thought in a house where women were the primary residents, this was the perfect butler. "The Earl of Castlewick to see the lady of the house."

With the barest raise of his brows, the butler took Wesley's card and fully opened the door. "My lord, if you would wait in the grand parlor, I shall see if my lady is available to receive you."

Wesley followed the butler to a large parlor with both austere furniture and a rather whimsical touch with lace and pale curtains. Wesley walked to the window and touched the satin-trimmed in lace. The pink was light enough to be mistaken for white, and the hue appeared slightly out of place with the dark browns and greens of the furniture.

"We are in the midst of redecorating this room, my lord. The curtains are new." Tall and slender, Mercy Heath glided into the room. Her strawberry blond waves were carefully put into a loose bun with curls framing her face on either side. She watched him with direct regard and those green eyes could undo any mortal man. Her peach day dress swayed along her slender hips and made his mouth water. Once inside, she stopped and eased into a curtsy.

"They do seem a bit more feminine than the other furnishings." Wesley bowed. "How do you do, Miss Heath?"

Mercy glanced at the curtains before retuning her frown to him. "I'm afraid Lady Radcliff is not at home just now. My aunt is just arriving to take tea. Would you care to join us?"

He should be disappointed. He tried to gather up a good bit of indignation at postponing his intentions. But spending an hour with Mercedes Heath sent a thrill through him just as dancing with her had so many months ago. "I would be delighted."

The hint of something that might have been happiness flashed on her face, then was gone. "Please follow me. We always take our tea in the ladies' parlor."

Knowing that he might see her at West Lane hadn't prepared him for the actual event. She was even more beautiful than he remembered and he found himself wishing he'd never set eyes on Mercedes Heath. Stepping beside her, he longed to place a possessive hand at the base of her back and guide her through doors. Wesley kept his hands to himself with some difficulty.

"I'm glad you have come, my lord. I wanted to thank you for your thoughtful gesture." She touched the frame of her spectacles.

"You said as much in your letter. You did not need to repay me, Miss Heath. It was entirely my fault you lost your other pair." The memory of receiving bank notes from her solicitor each month tightened his jaw.

She stopped in the foyer outside a pair of doors and turned to face him. "I think you take too much on yourself, my lord. It was very thoughtful of you to send the new ones, but I could not accept such a gift. It would not have been proper. As a loan, it was very kind."

Preferring her to have accepted the gift would not make her statement less true. It had been impulsive to take her loss as his own. The idea of her not being able to read her music had kept him awake at night and he felt he had to do something about it. "They look very well on you."

A warm blush crept up her cheeks. "Thank you."

He assisted with the door and they entered the ladies' parlor. Appropriately named, it was feminine but not simpering. There was a classic elegance to the way the blue and butter colors blended and comforted. With a large window facing the street, the ladies would always know if someone was approaching.

Seated in a Queen Anne chair, a woman whom Wesley presumed was Mercy's aunt narrowed her eyes before widening them. Her hair was mostly gray with hints of red from younger days, though her skin was free of wrinkles. The same green eyes that Wesley had admired in Mercy scrutinized him from her aunt's face.

"Your lordship, may I introduce my aunt. Lady Phyllis Mattock. Aunt Phyllis, the Earl of Castlewick," Mercy said formally.

He bowed. "Lady Mattock. I believe I knew your husband. My father and he went to Eton together, if I'm not mistaken."

"My husband spoke very highly of your father, my lord. I understand you have increased your lands in the last few years. I think your father would be pleased about that." Lady Mattock appeared not to be the kind of woman to make small talk. She didn't speak of the weather or gossip around town, but mentioned his very serious recovery of lost lands as if it were common knowledge.

"I hope he would be, my lady. It is my goal to restore the family estate to what it once was."

Mercy sat on a chaise just as the tea arrived. The maid placed a large tray with the tea and treats on a low table set between the arrangement of seating. A long chaise, the Queen Anne chair, and its match flanked a settee.

Wesley joined them, sitting on the other chair. He accepted a rose-painted cup and saucer from Mercy and sipped the warm, strong brew. Since the ladies were so free with their comments, Wesley said, "I understand that you live here with Lady Radcliff, Miss Heath."

"That is correct, my lord." She stared at him with cautious eyes.

"Are you her ladyship's companion then? I admit, I have never quite understood the arrangement." He wanted to keep her off balance. He didn't know why, but her paying back his gift had made him uncomfortable and he was bothered by her cold assessment of what was meant to ease her way. Mercy glanced at her aunt, who shrugged and sipped her tea.

Turning her attention back to him, she spoke softly and with little emotion. "Lady Radcliff and I went to school together. We are friends. When her husband died, three of us moved here so that she wouldn't be left all alone. The other ladies have married and moved away. I am still here."

"What will you do when her ladyship marries again?" A hint of shame washed over him.

A slow smile warned of danger. "Lady Radcliff has no intention of ever marrying again." She lifted a hand stopping his rebuke. "However, in the unlikely event that she should change her mind, I will hope my aunt is kind to me and will allow me to return to her house."

Lady Mattock looked from one to the other, her brows raised. "My niece is a fine young lady. Don't you think so, my lord?"

The springs of some trap had pulled tight, but there was no way to avoid answering. "Miss Heath is a charming young woman."

"Indeed. May I ask, what brought you to West Lane this afternoon, my lord?" Lady Mattock asked.

There was no avoiding a direct question. "I came in hopes of seeing the lady of the house."

"You intend to court Lady Radcliff?" Lady Mattock brushed a long hair from her cheek and tucked it back behind her ear. "How interesting."

"Is it?" He wanted to look over at Mercy and see if she was displeased by the idea of him courting her friend. Not that it mattered, but part of him wanted her to care. If his needs had been different, he might have courted her. She was without title or connections. She would make a man a fine mistress, but he couldn't very well marry her friend and make her his mistress. His mind had taken a turn. He'd never thought to have a mistress after marriage, at least not until he'd danced with Mercedes Heath. Yet, he knew she would never allow such a relationship. Not with him, not with anyone. She would likely die a spinster rather than do anything as outlandish as sully her reputation. When he'd received the note from her solicitor explaining the remission of funds for the spectacles, he knew any chance of time with Mercy under the covers was unlikely.

"I have a box for the symphony tomorrow night. My niece and her ladyship will be attending with me. Would you care to join us, my lord?" Lady Mattock watched him unblinkingly. "It would afford you time to get to know the lady and I will chaperone my niece, of course."

A war raged inside Wesley. He needed to get to know Aurora Sherbourn but time spent with Mercy was dangerous for him. It didn't matter, he told himself, pushing aside his stupidity. "What a splendid offer, my lady. I would be happy to join you. How fortunate that I have no other plans." He made a mental note to cancel the dinner plans he'd made with his cousin Malcolm at Whites.

Putting down her tea, Lady Mattock clasped her hands together and almost smiled. "Perhaps I will invite a few more friends to join us and we'll make a fine time of it. What do you think, Mercedes?"

"You always have the finest ideas, Aunt Phyllis." Mercy sipped her tea and let the sarcasm drip from her sour grin.

Wesley left as soon as it was appropriate to do so. He needed to see Aurora Sherbourn and not dally with Mercy. Liking her was beside the point. Aurora was his goal and a silken voice and a pair of green eyes was not going to alter his course.

* * * *

Mercy knew the day would come when Wesley Renshaw would call at West Lane and she also knew he would not be coming to see her. Still, it had been a thrill to take her first look at those broad shoulders while he examined the new curtains in the grand parlor.

"I expect you to behave in front of Lord Castlewick, Mercedes." Aunt Phyllis had a gleam in her eyes that could only mean trouble.

"I always behave. Besides, Castlewick came to see Aurora and has no interest in me. I would very much like to know why he's so interested in Aurora, though." Mercy said the last mostly to herself.

Aunt Phyllis shook her head. "Didn't you listen to the man? I thought I taught you better than this, Mercedes."

Thinking back over the tea and everything Wesley said, Mercy couldn't remember anything that gave a hint to why Aurora should be his choice for the next Countess of Castlewick. "I suppose you will have to continue my education. He didn't say anything about Aurora other than he'd come to call on her."

"No." Phyllis's voice was singsong. "But he did say what interests him in general. He wants to pull his family estate back together. Did you know that young man's grandfather was in so much debt he had to ask the king if he could sell off his lands to stay out of debtors' prison?"

Something shuddered inside Mercy. "But he seems so solvent."

"He is. Once they had the funds, his father, still quite young himself, took over the running of the estates and finances. His father managed to keep from going to debtors' prison and didn't lose any more lands, but I have heard that this current earl pulled the family back into good standing. He's bought back much of the estate land over the last three or four years." Phyllis took a biscuit from the tray and dipped it in her cooling tea before eating the sweet.

A thought niggled in the back of Mercy's mind. "Aunt Phyllis, where is the property entailed to the Earl of Castlewick?"

"I believe it is in Cheshire."

The niggling turned to nausea. There was no sense caring that she now knew with reasonable certainty that Wesley's interest in Aurora had to do with a certain piece of property she owned in Cheshire. He had never been for her anyway, but she had hoped his intentions toward Aurora were less cutthroat.

Aurora had been given the land in Cheshire by her brother, Rhys. The property had been Aurora's father's part of the betrothal and marriage bargain with Radcliff. Considering all Aurora had suffered as the Countess of Radcliff, making a gift of the Cheshire property was the least her brother could do.

The front door opened and closed. A moment later, Aurora breezed into the parlor. "Aunt Phyllis, how good to see you."

All of Mercy's friends had taken to calling Phyllis aunt when in private. It was an affirmation that they were sisters by choice, if not by blood.

Aurora kissed Phyllis on the cheek before sitting on the settee. "How was tea?"

"Interesting," Phyllis said.

"Oh?" Aurora's eyes widened.

Mercy sighed on the inside but kept emotion from her voice. "Lord Castlewick paid a call. He'll be joining us at the symphony tomorrow night."

"Oh dear. Well, it makes no difference," Aurora began. "I have no intention of marrying him or anyone. He will be disappointed."

Worry rumbled inside Mercy. If a man wanted something badly enough, he would go to any lengths to obtain it. Knowing what he wanted was a start. She needed to find out how important it was to Wesley so she could rid the Wallflowers of him.

"Tell me, Aurora." Phyllis grinned. "Would you happen to own land in Cheshire?"

Damn. Why did her aunt have to be so clever? "Aunt Phyllis, that is none of your business."

Aurora gaped from one to the other. "I do own a large piece of property that was part of the marriage agreement between my late husband and my father. When Radcliff died, my brother gave it to me."

Aunt Phyllis clapped. "That's it." She stood and called for Tipton.

The parlor door opened. Tipton stood awaiting instructions.

"I'll be leaving now. Please gather my things, Tipton."

"Yes, my lady."

"I will see you both tomorrow night. I will come collect you and we can go to the theater together, if that is agreeable." Phyllis's joyful demeanor made Mercy uncomfortable.

Mercy rose and kissed her aunt on the cheek. "Please don't do anything that I shall regret, Aunt Phyllis. I can see that you're up to something."

With a pat on the cheek, Phyllis beamed. "I have your best interest in mind, my sweet girl. I shall do nothing untoward."

Doubts riffled through Mercy, but there was nothing more to say as Phyllis rushed out of the house.

Aurora waved her goodbyes. As soon as Mercy's aunt was in her carriage and rolling down West Lane, she turned to Mercy. "What is going on?"

Shaking her head, Mercy sat. "My aunt is up to something, but more importantly, I know why Castlewick is so keen on courting you."

"Oh? Well, out with it." Aurora took a treat from the tray.

"That property is part of his family's lost lands. Aunt Phyllis tells me he has been trying to put back what his grandfather lost. I would guess there is some longer version of the story, but you know she'll not tell it until she's ready." Mercy shrugged.

Aurora's grin assured she was not upset by the news that it was land rather than adoration that motivated Wesley. "But we can be positive Aunt Phyllis knows every detail and is just biding her time. She is such a treat."

"I'm not sure that is the word I would use," Mercy said. "You are not upset about his lordship's lack of sentiment?"

"Heavens no." Aurora bit into the biscuit. "I'm glad it's something that can be dealt with rather than his being enamored. I would hate to break his heart, but I have no qualms about ruining his hopes. Besides, if it's the property he wants, perhaps he can buy it. I have no use for it."

"You are always so sensible, Aurora." The notion eased the pounding of Mercy's heart. All of this could be settled without her having to spend too much time with Wesley Renshaw. "I know I will never secure his attentions, but I don't think I would have liked for you to marry him."

Aurora patted her knee. "Not to worry."

"I think I shall go and play a while. I have little Lady Alice Pinkering coming for a lesson in half an hour."

Cringing, Aurora stood. "I will closet myself on the opposite side of the house and write some letters. Be sure to close the music room door."

They laughed as they went to different parts of the house.

Chapter 3

The theater's golden domed ceilings and grand arches were perfect to conduct sound, while the rich red curtains kept down the echoes an overly large hall might endure. Every wall and alcove were draped in red velvet and it would have been easy to hide away. Mercy considered the idea of getting behind a curtain and settling in for the evening.

Poppy and Rhys stood with Aurora, who told them about Lord Castlewick's intentions of courting her.

"So, he wants to marry Aurora to gain some property," Poppy whispered. "Well, that's not so bad."

"Wouldn't you prefer to hear he had seen her beauty across a ballroom and was smitten?" Rhys said, giving his wife a quick squeeze around the waist.

Mercy didn't like either scenario. Of all the women in England, why did Aurora have to hold some bit of dirt that Wesley wanted?

With a nudge of her elbow, Aurora got Mercy's attention. "You look sour and his lordship is coming over," she whispered through clenched teeth. "What's gotten into you?"

It was a good question. Mercy set her face into the slight smile and dull eyes that she'd perfected at the Wormbattle School for Young Ladies. She had learned in her three years away that she didn't have to be mild and good, but it was easier if she appeared as if she hadn't a care in the world or a thought in her head. The lesson had made her life much easier over the years.

Aunt Phyllis rushed over. "Lord Castlewick, I'm so glad you could join us. You know Lady Radcliff."

Wesley bowed. "A pleasure to see you again, my lady." His gaze turned to Mercy. "Miss Heath, I'm happy to see you again so soon."

"My lord." Mercy curtsied and avoided meeting his stare. Whatever she saw there would either be disappointing or lead to that emotion later on. Her function was to dissuade him from Aurora and nothing more. The fact that she could think of nothing worse than Wesley and Aurora as a married couple only made her task easier.

The silence extended a bit too long and Mercy studied her aunt.

Phyllis grinned too wide but recovered herself a moment later. "My lord, may I introduce Lord and Lady Marsden?"

Wesley bowed to Poppy and shook Rhys's hand. "Marsden and I went to Eton together, though I was a year ahead. I was delighted to hear of your marriage. Congratulations to you both."

"Thank you, Castlewick. I was very sorry to hear of your father's passing. I hope you received my note. He was a good man." Rhys said.

The slight lines around Wesley's mouth deepened and a haze of sorrow passed across his eyes. "Thank you. We buried him in Cheshire. I know it's not popular these days, but the family plot is there and it was what he wanted."

Mercy wished she could have given him comfort. It was clear that despite gaining a title, Wesley missed his father.

A bell signaled that the patrons should find their seats. Mercy kissed Poppy on the cheek before the couple went to their own box. Without looking at Wesley, she followed her aunt up the stairs to the box she had secured for the performance.

Aurora walked beside him. "Did you attend Parliament today, my lord?"

"No. I had some personal matters to attend to and no questions were coming up for vote. It's been rather quiet this session. Are you much interested in politics, Lady Radcliff?"

"I read the papers, my lord. It is good to stay informed."

They arrived at the box and a footman pulled back the curtain.

Aurora stepped inside with Aunt Phyllis.

The outline of two men within the box held Mercy back. Her aunt was up to something and that meant trouble.

The slightest touch on her upper arm let her know Wesley was too close. His heat spread through her like a warm, familiar quilt. "What about you, Miss Heath, are you interested in politics?"

It was all too much, the fact that Wesley wanted to court Aurora and Aunt Phyllis's schemes to find her a husband. She snapped her gaze toward him and met those alluring eyes. "What does it matter what my interests are?"

"Have I offended you, Miss Heath?" Those eyes that had looked tenderly while they danced opened wide.

She sighed. "No. I apologize. It seems my aunt has several suitors here for my inspection. Excuse me, my lord." She stepped into the box.

The two shadows belonged to Lincoln Baker, a dim-witted man but a great lover of music, and Wallace Colby an extremely tall man who was quite smart and also enjoyed hearing Mercy play. They were both gentleman with land but no title and they both had a liking for Mercy. Either would be a suitable match and neither interested Mercy in the least.

She made her curtsy and greeted each man before taking her seat and waiting for the darkness of the theater to swallow her up.

The conductor, dressed in black with a crisp white cravat, approached the podium. Everyone applauded. He tapped his baton on the wooden stand. Musicians took note, as did the audience. The theater shimmered with anticipation.

Mercy let her aunt's constant interference float away with the first notes. Mozart's Concerto in C began with a harp and flute and Mercy was lost. By the third piece, tears flowed freely down her face.

Soft linen pressed into her hand at her lap. She closed her fingers around it and raised it to the corner of her eye before daring to look at Wesley to her left.

Between the emotion that filled his eyes and the music, Mercy's faced flushed hot and her heart pounded. Unable to breathe, she stood and rushed from the box.

* * * *

The fact that Baker and Colby were there as suitors to Mercy shouldn't have made Wesley's blood boil, but it did. That they both got up to chase after her had his fists balled up. It took all his will to keep his seat and not give both men a sound thrashing.

Lady Mattock raised a hand to stop their pursuit. "She becomes emotional from the music. Give my niece a few moments, gentlemen, and she will return."

Aurora smiled and Wesley must have looked as distressed as he felt because she leaned in and whispered, "It is true. Mercy feels music very deeply and can become overwhelmed."

The assurance of normalcy didn't make him feel any better. When she hadn't returned after several minutes, he eased from his seat and slipped from the box.

Sconces lit the hall but the larger candelabras had been put out during the performance, which kept down on light and saved candles. It took a moment for his eyes to adjust. A few feet away he made out her shape where she leaned against the wall, his handkerchief clutched to her chest and her head back. The way her body arched and her full neck was exposed set him on fire. He wanted to taste that neck and every other inch of her elegant body.

"Miss Heath, are you all right?"

She straightened. "Go back inside, my lord. I am fine. Just some silly female emotions."

Drawing closer until he was merely an inch from her, he said, "Does that statement usually work?"

She drew a shuddering breath, but her green eyes flashed, still wet with tears. She was the most kissable woman he'd ever seen. "Always. Men believe women all full of nonsense and my confirmation gives them ease."

Unable to resist, he used his thumb to brush moisture from under her eye and pressed the thumb to his lips, taking in her essence. He'd turned into a fool, but she tasted of salt and promises and he wanted more of her. "Shall I tell you what I see?"

Wide-eyed and staring at his lips, she nodded and pressed her back against the wall.

Pressing his body against her tall slim form, he reveled in every curve. "I see a woman who is special but who puts on a mask every day to please the world, and I wonder when she pleases herself."

"Why should you care, my lord?" There was a pleading tone to her usually strong voice, but for what he didn't know.

Rubbing his lips against hers, he drew in her breath and gave his to her in a slow sensuous kiss. He struggled to catch his breath. "I don't know, Mercedes, but I do care. I most decidedly care a great deal."

He had never longed for any woman with so little concern for propriety. In fact, he didn't remember any female, girl or lady, stirring such desire within him. There was no doubt he wanted Mercedes Heath. He indulged his hands in the feel of her hip and the slight curve to her waist and higher.

Her breath came in short gasps, and he delved inside her mouth and found a warm, soft heaven where he wished he could spend eternity.

No experience in his life had prepared him for the jolt of urgency in that moment. Heart pounding and body thrumming, he wrapped his arms around her and pressed her full length into his. He longed for her to know how critically his need gripped him.

She kissed him back, her tongue swirling with his in the mating dance. A soft sigh was like a musket ball from her throat directly to the space deep in his chest. He'd long thought that part of him dead to such emotions.

Voices just out of sight made him take stock of the fact that they were not in private, but he couldn't gather the strength to stop.

She pressed lightly on his chest with one hand and drew her mouth away. "Will you take me here against a wall, my lord? And then what? Go on to court my best friend?"

A bucket of cold water would not have been more effective. Wesley backed up but remained close enough to feel the heat rising from her sweet body. "Forgive me, Miss Heath. I was overcome."

He must have truly lost his mind. All the work he'd done to secure his family legacy and it could all be wiped aside by an indiscretion with a woman who should mean nothing to him.

"Perhaps you too were overwhelmed by the music, my lord." The tears were gone from her eyes, leaving passion and anger in their wake.

"I'm certain that was it." Lies of this kind hurt no one. At least, that was what he told himself. His ridiculous heart thumped a different story.

She bit her lip and a shadow passed over her eyes. Had he hurt her too? An instant later the emotion was replaced by a bland expression and she patted her hair into place. "I will return to the box. You might wish to wait a few minutes before taking your seat."

Wesley hated the flat tone of her voice and the way she appeared to dismiss the mingling of their souls in a kiss that rocked him on his heels. He regretted never touching her hair and finding out if it was as soft as it appeared, but she was right and he did intend to court and marry her friend. Any other scenario was not an option.

Aurora Sherbourn would be his wife and Mercedes Heath could never be anything to him.

As if she read the thought directly out of his mind, she nodded once and turned her back on him.

His hand itched to grab her and do exactly what she predicted. Take her hard and fast against a wall in the theater full of people. It was impossible and wrong. Not only wrong because it was not his destiny, but because Mercy deserved better. She was not going to be anyone's mistress. She would likely marry Mr. Landon or Mr. Colby and have a parcel of children who would all play and sing like angels.

Perhaps one day he would hear her play. Surely there was nothing wrong with wanting to hear a reportedly good musician show off her skills. Yet even that seemed untoward somehow.

Wesley pressed his head against the wall and called himself a dozen names, the worst of which were stupid, selfish, and defiler of innocents. How had he come to such a pass?

By the time he'd pulled himself together, people were talking and moving around for the intermission. Wesley acted as if he were just returning to the box as the others stood and stretched.

"I thought we'd lost you, my lord," Lady Mattock said.

"I apologize, my lady. I met an old friend in the lobby and lost track of time. The music sounded wonderful even from that vantage point."

One curved brow raised on Lady Mattock's forehead but she just returned his smile and said nothing.

Mr. Colby tugged his coat down over his stomach and adjusted his cravat. "It really is quite good, but Miss Heath is a superior musician on both harp and flute."

Mercy met Wesley's gaze for the briefest moment before a warm blush crept from her neck up her cheeks. She shook her head. "You are too complimentary, sir. These are the finest musicians in all of England."

They silly argument continued, with Mr. Baker chiming in and agreeing with Mr. Colby.

Wesley wished he could touch her cheek and see if it warmed with each blush. Instead, he turned to Aurora, who grinned and gawked at the people milling about below. "You are very quiet, Lady Radcliff. Did you enjoy the first half?"

She continued her perusal of the crowd, spotted Lord and Lady Marsden across the theater in their box, and waved. "I enjoy the music very much, my lord. Mercy is correct when she says these are the finest musicians to be assembled in all of England."

"And is she also correct when she implies that she is not as talented?" It was dangerous to speak of Mercy to Aurora, but no other topic interested him.

Facing him, Lady Radcliffe studied his face from his brow to his chin, then returned her gaze to his eyes and cocked her head. She really was extremely pretty in the way society loved. Her light golden hair was shiny and perfectly coiffed and her blue eyes held intelligence. Neither tall nor short, she had a pleasing figure and straight, white teeth.

He should be thrilled that the woman who now owned his ancestral lands was not only available but pretty as well. His heart knotted like a stone and he had to force himself not to clutch at the organ in his chest. It was just as well. He couldn't let a tall reed of a woman dissuade him from his course.

"I speak as someone who adores Mercy, of course, but the gentleman is correct. I feel safe in saying that anyone who has heard her play any of the instruments she excels at would be hard pressed to deny her extraordinary talent." Aurora continued her inspection of his face.

"Have I dirt on my face, Lady Radcliff?" Wesley rubbed his jaw.

Her smile made her even prettier. "No, my lord. I'm just taking my measure of you."

"And what have you discovered?"

"It's too soon to say really. My mother says you wish to court me." She spoke plainly and without emotion.

Taken aback, Wesley choked and had to recover himself. "You are blunt, my lady, but not incorrect."

"I think you should know immediately that I have no intention of marrying now, nor will I ever consider it again. My mother should have informed you of that." Aurora's sky-blue eyes never wavered from his.

This was going to be harder than he would have wished, but it changed nothing. He would have Aurora for his wife no matter what he had to do to accomplish it. Charm would be a good start. "Your good mother did not mention your aversion to marriage, my lady. However, perhaps we might start with a friendship and then you can thwart my attentions at a later date."

Her grin was quick and her laughter gone before anyone could enjoy it, most of all herself. "If it is friendship you seek, then I am willing to oblige, my lord." She offered her hand like a man might during a business agreement.

These women who called themselves wallflowers were a treat. He liked them more than he had liked any women save his sisters. He took her hand and shook it. Her grip was firm and sure. "I appreciate your honesty, my lady."

Turning her hand, he bowed over it as if to kiss her, but did not touch his lips to her skin. Somehow, the notion of touching his lips to another woman after kissing Mercy nauseated him, as if it might wash away the essence of her and he didn't want that. Not yet.

He glanced up as he rose from his bow and found the lady still studying him as if he were the subject of some scientific experiment.

The signal that the music was about to start up again was a welcome respite from her inspection. He took his seat with Mercy to his right and Aurora to his left. A slow sad violin played in the darkness before being joined by a cello's low tone. They seemed in conflict, just as he was seated between a woman he wanted and the one he needed.

By the time the symphony had concluded, ever nerve inside Wesley shook with frustration and rage. He wanted to run from the theater and not look back. However, he had a goal and he would pursue it to the inevitable end. "Lady Radcliff, why is it that you and your friends call yourselves wallflowers? It is clear to me that not only are you lovely but only one of you is left unmarried."

The theater was crowded and spilled out onto the street, where they waited for Lady Mattock's carriage to find its way to pick them up.

Aurora exchanged a smile with Mercy, who shrugged.

"An old moniker from our schooldays. We still meet, every Tuesday for tea at West Lane and started calling ourselves the Wallflowers of West Lane." Aurora smiled.

It took every bit of his will to keep from looking at Mercy. Was she as fond of the name and these women as Aurora? He imagined she was and he longed to see the warmth of expression in her eyes and a genuine grin on her extraordinary lips.

Oh Lord, why had he thought of her lips?

The carriage thankfully arrived. Aurora accepted his hand up. "I suppose I will see you at my mother's dinner party, my lord."

"I have accepted the invitation and am very much looking forward to the event."

With a nod, she entered the carriage.

Mercy jumped in behind her, barely allowing his hand to graze hers. "Good night, my lord."

"Miss Heath." He wanted to grab her and hold her. He longed to tell her he'd never been so attracted to anyone in his life and wipe that look of disgust off her face that she'd given him in the hall before she walked away. Her thinking he was trying to seduce her as if she meant nothing but a source of pleasure rubbed him raw from the inside out.

She'd said none of what rolled around in his mind, but his guilt implied it might all be true.

Handing Mercy's aunt up into the carriage, he met her glare. "Thank you for the invitation tonight, my lady. It was a singular night." At least that wasn't a lie.

"I agree, my lord. I am pleased you have become part of our society and know we shall meet again soon." The wicked twist of her lips said she knew more than she said.

Had Lady Mattock seen him nearly defile her niece in the hallway of a public theater? Surely not. She would have demanded he marry the girl on the spot. He held his expression soft and bland and hoped he pulled it off. "Good evening, my lady."

The carriage rolled away and Wesley watched until the night obscured his view. He shook off the last thoughts of marrying Mercy instead of Aurora. It did no good. Though still the daughter of a gentleman, she was beneath him. She didn't have what he needed and Aurora did. There was no help for it.

Wesley climbed into his own carriage and thought their being close friends was some kind of punishment, which he richly deserved.

Chapter 4

She had lost her mind. That was the only explanation Mercy had for how long she had been sitting in front of the glass staring at her reflection and wondering if she should stay home for the night.

Because spending an evening in Aurora's mother's home with Wesley at the dinner party was foolish. Still, the idea of not going gnawed at her. She'd fussed with her hair for a half hour after Jane finished with it and changed her gown three times. Now she couldn't seem to make herself get up and go downstairs where her aunt, Faith and her husband, Nick, and Aurora were likely enjoying a chat and a sherry until the time came to leave.

The knock at her door told her a Wallflower was about to enter. In school, they had started a special system of three knocks, a pause, and one knock for knowing it was one of them wishing to enter. She didn't turn when the door opened. "Is everyone waiting?"

Faith stood behind her. Her wild curls were already making an attempt to escape the elaborate style her maid had probably spent hours on. She pushed one brown lock back into place and it immediately popped back out. "No. They are fine, but you are never tardy so I came to check on you."

"Why did you say you were coming up here?" The idea of everyone thinking something was wrong made Mercy nauseous.

"To fix my hair, but of course, it's not possible. Why don't you tell me what's troubling you and save me the time it would take to wring it out of you?" Faith's grin made her golden eyes crunch up and sparkle.

It was senseless to evade Faith's questions as she meant what she said. She would find a way to drag the information from Mercy even if it took weeks. Turning from the glass, she faced her friend. "You must keep it between us. I don't want Aurora to hear of this."

"Why ever not?" Faith's eyes were wide as saucers.

"The other night at the symphony, I became overwhelmed by the music and the company and stepped into the hallway to catch my breath and contain myself." It was even harder than she imagined to tell her tale. A light sheen of perspiration popped out on her skin, and she felt the flush just thinking of Wesley.

Faith took Mercy's hand and pulled her over to sit on the divan near the fire. "You are often moved by music."

Sconces on either side of the mantle and the other lamps in the room gave good light to the pale green and lavender room though the hearth was dark in the warm weather. "

"It was more than that. Somehow being near Lord Castlewick enhanced my emotions." Mercy's heart lodged in her throat while she waited for Faith to give her the sound berating she deserved.

"Oh." Faith frowned but then looked up with a calm expression. "If you have an interest in his lordship, why would you not want to tell Aurora about it. If by some chance she decides to marry him, it would make it very hard on you, Mercy."

Everything Faith said had kept Mercy up for several nights. "It gets worse."

"Does it?"

Mercy nodded. "His lordship came into the hall to check on me. At least, I think that is why he followed me." It was impossible to go on. Mercy swallowed several times to clear the emotions welling up as if the events had just happened.

"What happened, Mercy?" The sternness of Faith's voice said she would not accept anything less than the entire truth.

"He kissed me."

Faith stood. "In the hall? What kind of a man does such a thing? We should go to Aurora immediately and tell her he is not the kind of man anyone of us should be courting. Her mother should be told as well."

Horror welled inside Mercy. She rose and gripped Faith's hands. "No. He may have initiated the kiss, but I did not attempt to stop him. I think he is a good man, though I'm sure it is Aurora's property he is after. Many people marry for such things. If he could make Aurora happy, I cannot stand in the way. They might be a good match."

Mercy struggled to catch her breath and it came in great gulps until no air would pass and panic set in.

Forcing her back to sitting, Faith put her face just an inch from Mercy's "Slow, dearest. Slow down. One breath at a time."

With small success, Mercy tried to follow the directions to breathe but it did little good and the room started to spin.

Faith handed Mercy the guitar she kept in the corner of her bedroom. Aunt Phyllis had discovered the instrument while traveling in Spain and brought it back for Mercy.

Smooth wood pressed into her hand and the weight of the guitar fell on her lap. Instinctively, Mercy strummed with her thumb and pressed the strings between the frets. Sensual cords filled the room as it came back into focus. She played part of Mozart's Requiem, which she had converted for her Spanish instrument.

Calm washed over her. Putting the guitar aside, she peered at Faith, who once again sat beside her. "I'm a terrible person."

"No. You are a wonderful person." She said it as if it were a matter of fact and not her opinion. "What makes you say that despite his kissing you in a darkened hallway, Castlewick is a good man?"

It was a fair question but the answer was complicated. "I can only tell you that if he felt as I did on that night, in that moment, nothing could have stopped that kiss." Heat rose up her cheeks with the exquisite memory.

Faith sat back and examined Mercy with her head cocked to one side. "You didn't try to stop him." It was not a question. "You kissed him back."

"I couldn't stop myself, let alone him." Shame mixed with the wonder of her recollection. She wanted the moment to be pure and beautiful, but circumstances covered it with filth.

"Why not tell Aurora that you want him for yourself and let her mother go to Bath to calm her nerves?" Faith's concerned expression had eased into raised brows and curiosity.

It was a ridiculous suggestion. "The Earl of Castlewick is not going to marry Miss Heath with little money or connections. Have you lost your mind? He might think to make me his mistress if he didn't wish to marry Aurora, but even a man would see how that would never work."

Anger rippled through Faith's golden eyes and she straightened her shoulders. "You are no man's mistress, Mercedes. How can you even think such a thing? You will marry whom you wish when you wish and if you wish. If Castlewick loves you, he should marry you. This is not up for debate."

"Well, he doesn't love me. He barely knows me. It was just the passion of the music in the dim corridor. I'm sure he's already forgotten all about his little slip with a girl of no consequence."

"You know, Mercy, I love you like a sister, but when you speak of yourself so meanly, I want to shake some sense into you."

"I am nothing but good sense, Faith. If I marry, it will be to someone like Mr. Colby who is uncomplicated and loves music. We shall live modestly, but well enough, and my aunt will come visit often. I will still be able to come to tea with the Wallflowers and all will be well." Mercy's heart beat out a miserable staccato that only she could hear.

"You could marry an earl, become a countess, and still have tea with us and your aunt would be delighted," Faith countered.

"It does no good to live in a fantasy world, Faith. My only relationship with Wesley Renshaw would be as his mistress. In which case, I would lose all my friends and my aunt would disown me." The notion of being Wesley's mistress, to be used and discarded in a few years, made her feel sick again despite her desire to be in his arms. "While I'll admit that the kiss was extraordinary, I am not overcome with silly ideas. He is just a man and I'm a little embarrassed to see him again so soon. That is why it has taken me so long to come downstairs." Mercy stood and brushed out her skirt before checking her hair in the glass. "Shall we join the others?"

Faith slipped her arm through Mercy's. "You are wrong about something, Mercy."

"What is that?"

"The Wallflowers would never abandon you no matter what choices you make. Though I think I know you well enough to safely say you are not going to settle for less than a spectacular lover who meets all your needs."

Mercy went with Faith arm in arm downstairs. Would Wesley be a spectacular lover? Shaking her head, she brushed the idea aside. She would run him off for Aurora, if need be, but she would keep her distance emotionally.

That was that.

Lifting her chin, she knew she could do what had to be done.

* * * *

The worst part of his pursuit of Aurora Sherbourn was undoubtedly her mother, the Dowager Countess of Marsden. Of course, it had been through her ladyship that Wesley had gotten in the door to meet Aurora. Still, her constant spouting of her daughter's talents, along with the strange way she also told the lady's flaws, had become tedious.

He had arrived on time and only Rhys and Poppy Draper had arrived before him. Lord Marsden was Aurora's brother and a good fellow. His wife was funny and straightforward. She reminded him of Mercy. He brushed the thought aside. He had convinced himself the kiss had been a fluke and would never happen again. It had been a response to the music and nothing more.

"I don't want you to think Aurora is willful, my lord. My late husband and I sent her to the Wormbattle School and Miss Agatha banished all signs of disobedience." The dowager glowered at Poppy and bared her teeth in something like a smile, but scarier. "Look at my daughter-in-law. She is every bit a countess and she went to the Wormbattle School as well. All signs of bad behavior gone."

Rhys went into a fit of coughing that Wesley thought might be hiding laughter.

Patting her husband's back and making no attempt to hide her own amusement, Poppy said, "Thank you, my lady. You are too kind and free with your compliments."

Even Wesley had trouble keeping a calm facade when sarcasm oozed from Poppy's words.

Oblivious, Jemima Draper gave a condescending nod.

"Mother, you needn't prop Rora up so much. Lord Castlewick can see for himself that she is a wonderful girl." Rhys pored two brandies and handed Wesley one. "You will need this before the night is over."

Raising his glass in thanks, Wesley sipped. "Lady Radcliff and I had a moment at the symphony with Lady Mattock. It was a very pleasant evening."

A deep frown creased Jemima's brow. "We are charitable with regard to that family because Lady Mattock's deceased husband was knighted and Aurora went to school with the niece, but that is all."

Poppy's eyes narrowed and she stepped forward.

Rhys took his wife by the arm and held her in place. "Mother, you know that is not entirely true. You call it charity, while for Poppy and me it is a deep and binding friendship with Mercy and her aunt."

While Poppy physically relaxed, her eyes still burned with fury.

"I found the evening with all three ladies filled with entertainment." Wesley hoped to diffuse what was obviously an ongoing family dispute.

Luckily whatever the lady of the house was about to say was interrupted by the arrival of a large crowd. The Duke and Duchess of Breckenridge were followed by Aurora and finally Mercy and her aunt.

The overdecorated parlor wasn't large and the influx of guests made the excess of expensive furniture more obvious. Two footmen came and removed a large settee with rolled arms and a thick gold cushion to give the party more room.

Wesley watched Mercy as she greeted Poppy and Rhys and made a polite if cool curtsy to their hostess. He longed to go to her and make sure his behavior at the symphony hadn't irreparably damaged their ability to remain cordial, but she kept her distance, making her way to a corner where all four ladies of the Wallflowers gathered with their heads close together.

They were like four flowers, each different yet all perfectly suited to the bouquet.

Aurora's mother called in a tone one might use to address the servants. "Miss Heath, it will be some minutes before dinner is served. Time enough for you to play for us."

It was a struggle to keep his place. Wesley's jaw tightened until his teeth ground together and he had to make an effort to unclench his fists. How dare that woman treat her guest with so little respect.

"Mother, you really should wait until after dinner to show off Mercy's talents. She's not a musician for hire." Aurora kept her voice even, but there was no mistaking her censure.

Mercy's smile was warm and a touch of amusement lit her eyes. "I really don't mind at all."

Rounding to the corner where a pianoforte had been placed with barely enough room for the bench between the instrument and the wall, Mercy sat and opened the cover from the keys.

From the first note, Wesley's world crashed down around him. She did more than play or even play well. Emotions poured from Mercy into the keys in a way he had never heard before. It was no wonder Colby and Baker were in love with her. The vibrancy of one note melded with the subtlety of the next until everyone in the room was drawn nearer to her. It was incredible there weren't more love-starved men crammed into the theater box to pay her homage.

"What do you think now, my lord?" Aurora had stepped beside him as he flocked to stand on the worn brown rug placed in a sitting area near the pianoforte.

"Magnificent," he said before he had time to modify his reaction.

"I first heard her play at school and she was a wonder, but she's so much better now. And pianoforte is not even the instrument she loves best." Aurora sighed, closed her eyes, and listened. Her face filled with contentment.

It took an effort not to ask what Mercy's preference was. He longed to hear more and as he glanced around the room, every expression eased with a sense of the peace rolling from her music.

Even her ladyship smiled as she listened.

It was a magnificent gift to convey music in such a way that everyone in hearing was transported to their own personal bliss. What other emotions could Mercy produce with her skill?

A tall butler cleared his throat from the doorway.

Mercy's fingers stilled.

Everyone turned as if in a dream.

"Dinner is served," intoned the butler.

The ornate dining room was like the parlor in that it had also been overdecorated, with too many candles, gilded mirrors, stern paintings of old men, and extra chairs filling every corner.

For the small dinner party, the long table had been set for ten despite there being only nine of them.

"Mother," Rhys began, "it seems we have an extra place."

She laughed and pulled open her fan, waving it like a flag and causing two candles on the table to snuff out.

The footman rushed over to rekindle them.

"Not at all," Jemima Draper said as they all took their seats. "Mr. Garrott said he might be a few minutes late."

Poppy gasped. "Decklan Garrott is coming to dinner?"

Jemima frowned. "Don't look so shocked. He has just secured a very nice parsonage in Sussex and just because you didn't prefer him doesn't mean another lady wouldn't be charmed by his light manner and secure profession."

Smiling behind her napkin, Aurora looked as if she might burst into a fit of giggles.

Wesley leaned in to whisper, "Have I missed something relevant about Mr. Garrott?"

Eyes sparkling with mirth, Aurora kept her voice soft so that only he would hear as Poppy and Rhys had a rather animated discussion with Jemima. "Mr. Garrott was rather set on wooing Poppy before she was married. He followed her like a lost puppy at balls. I think this is going to be a very entertaining evening, my lord."

"I feel honored to have landed myself with such a lively group, my lady." All thoughts that courting Aurora would be a tedious task with boring evenings and inane conversation had fled him from the moment he saw Mercy. Being in her company breathed life into him in a way no one ever had before. Even more surprising was the intrigue over each member of this Wallflower family, driven both by blood and by choice; they all made contentious but interesting company.

"Has your mother invited this Mr. Garrott as a match for Miss Heath?" It shouldn't bother him. Mercy was not his, nor would she ever be. Yet his appetite left him instantly and he gripped the linen napkin he'd just placed in his lap.

Aurora gave the slightest shrug while her gaze locked with his. "Perhaps. It could be she just wanted an even number of guests and Mr. Garrott is a good choice if one wishes to annoy Poppy."

A harried-looking man with brown hair and eyes stumbled into the dining room in a black suit and badly tied white cravat. "Sorry to be late."

The butler narrowed his eyes beside the man. "Mr. Garrott," he intoned.

"Yes, Wick. We can see that." Jemima scolded the butler for doing his job.

Mr. Garrott bowed several times before he took the empty seat beside Mercy at the far end of the table.

With Aurora as his dining partner, Wesley should have been thrilled. He could spend the night charming her, and he could already tell that he liked her. Beautiful, smart, titled, and with the land he needed, she was everything he wanted in a wife.

As the squab was served with a warm brown sauce, Mercy laughed and Wesley's attention was drawn instantly away from his quarry. He didn't know Garrott, but the man had entered the room with no grace, bowed too much, and seemed ridiculously out of place next to the stunning Mercy, who did everything exactly right. She sat straight with her back away from the chair, cut dainty pieces of bird, and took little bites, never eating all of any course. Never once did she speak too loudly or become animated in any way. Throughout the meal her expression remained serene while seeming to show interest in whatever Garrott said.

She was the perfect picture of what a lady without means should be, but Wesley knew passion stirred inside her soul and he hated to see it bottled up so tightly. Reminding himself that Mercy was none of his business and he should be paying more attention to his own dinner partner didn't stop him from attempting to hear what was said at the end of the table.

Aurora whispered, "Did you not like the pork, my lord?"

A footman took his untouched plate away. "I became distracted, I'm afraid. Forgive me, I have been a terrible dinner partner."

"Not terrible, just quiet. Is anything amiss?" Aurora asked, as if she might already know the answer.

Surely, Mercy wouldn't have told her friend about the incident at the theater. Good lord, had she done that, all was lost. No. If she had informed Aurora of his bad behavior, this conversation or any would not be happening, or at the very least it would be less polite.

Forcing a smile he hoped was full of irresistible charm, he said, "It is nothing, my lady. Forgive me."

At the end of the table, Mr. Garrott's voice boomed. "Miss Heath, you are a delight."

It took all of Wesley's will to keep focused on Aurora and not turn to find out if Mercy liked being complimented in such a public way. He guessed not but couldn't look. His jaw tightened, but he kept his attention with the correct woman.

Aurora's eyes flitted over his shoulder, down the table, where Mercy sat, then back to him. She raised a brow and her lips turned up in a sweet smile. "You are forgiven."

"Thank you." It was more difficult than he would have believed to speak politely to one woman while wishing, without any sense of right or wrong, to be in the company of another. This madness had to stop.

Chapter 5

It did no good to refuse when someone asked her to play. She knew it bothered her friends when their parents asked, but Mercy loved to play. If she refused, Aurora's mother would call her too proud or arrogant. For a girl without fortune and only an aging aunt to protect her, it was best to remain liked among the *ton*.

The look on Wesley's face when she risked a glance at him before dinner had nearly made her lose her place in the music. His eyes locked on her and there was a serenity within him that she hadn't seen before.

Why did he pay her so much attention and why did she care? He knew she would never be his mistress. In fact, she would never be disposable to any man. She had seen it many times; a man took a mistress who was young and lovely—actresses, opera singers, or ladies of a lower station and little means. Then after a few years, the men tired of their lovers and if the girl was lucky she was given a small pension to live off.

Of course, she lost any friends she might have had before and after the affair. That was no life for Mercy. However, her job was either to rid Aurora of his attentions or at least determine his character. Perhaps his interest in her might be a good way to do just that. A knot formed in her chest and rose to her throat before she swallowed it down.

"Miss Heath," Aurora's mother clapped as if stating of her name would not be enough to gain her attention.

It was demeaning, but Mercy drew in a breath, turned and smiled. "Yes, my lady?"

"I recently acquired a very special violin." She brightened as if she were very proud of her acquisition. "It belonged to an Italian master, perhaps you've heard of him. Stradivarius?"

Mercy's heart stopped.

Stepping in, Rhys said, "I think the violin is made by the Stradivarius family. Mother purchased it from a woman in Paris to add to her collection of instruments she cannot play."

It took several gulps of air before Mercy was able to form words. The idea that she was in the same house as an instrument of that class had her near to fainting. "May I see it, my lady?"

A wide smile pulled at Jemima's lips. "I'm so happy you asked. I have been told you can play and these old string instruments must be played from time to time or they will ruin. I thought to ask you to come by from time to time and play this one." She turned to the group. "Come into the music room, everyone. This should be something quite extraordinary."

Mercy followed close behind despite the fact that Aurora's and Rhys's mother had never admired her for more than her musical talent. It didn't matter. To have the opportunity to touch a Stradivarius was worth swallowing a year of pride. She gripped her skirt with both hands, crushing the light green fabric.

The music room held a great many fine instruments. From time to time, Mercy had been asked to play the harp and a beautiful cello that each stood in opposite corners. In the center of the room under a glass case was the violin. Its red wood and sensual arch called out to her, but she forced her hands to remain at her sides as she stared down into the case. "It's perfect."

Aurora touched her arm. "You don't have to play if you don't want to, Mercy. Mother may need someone to use this, but it need not be tonight."

"I would very much like to play it." Her voice hardly sounded like her own with its rough edge.

Rhys lifted the glass, but Mercy just stared down at the masterpiece.

In the kindest voice Mercy had ever heard from the lady, Jemima said, "It's all right, Miss Heath. You may pick it up. I know you will not let any harm come to it."

"Never." Mercy would almost give her own life before she would let anything happen to a violin of that quality. She touched the strings, wrapped a hand around the neck, and lifted it from its wooden cradle. Taking up the bow with her right hand, she ran it lightly across the strings while the violin was still close to her chest.

It took a moment to tune the keys with care for the perfect tone. Mercy's heart soared when she found it. A flash of the kiss at the theater and the lips that had set her soul aflame burst into her mind. She closed her eyes to avoid looking at Wesley.

With a shuddering breath, she tucked the finest instrument she had ever held beneath her chin and let Vivaldi's "Summer" from the Four Seasons pour out of her. The subtle sounds drew a sigh from several in the room.

Venturing a glance for Wesley, she found him leaning against the door jam. His eyes locked with hers, but his expression was stoic even as fire lit his eyes.

The music lifted and rose from the perfectly made violin, filling the room. She closed her eyes and allowed the masterpiece to sing out.

Lost in the music, Mercy floated in the world of sorrow and hope, where possibilities were endless and limitations didn't exist. It was a world made by an artist and a composer who lived long before she was born, but had gifted it to her in that moment. A perfect moment.

As she drew the bow across for the final strains, her heart sank and she opened her eyes.

Her closest friends smiled back at her.

Jemima held her hands together under her chin.

Aunt Phyllis beamed with pride.

The only change in Wesley's expression was the sorrow she detected in his eyes. Otherwise, he remained unmoving.

Despite her bright smile, Faith wiped a tear from her cheek and began the applause. Everyone joined in and rushed forward to congratulate her. Wesley remained near the door.

"Rhys, will you lift the glass, please?" Mercy didn't want to risk anything happening to the violin.

Complying, Rhys helped her secure the instrument. "You were wonderful," he said.

"I can take little credit for what comes from such a work of art." Mercy's cheeks heated and her heart slowed to a normal beat for the first time since learning the Stradivarius was in the house.

Everyone ignored her comment and preceded to tell her how wonderful she was.

"Miss Heath, you have made me very happy," Jemima exclaimed with more respect than she'd ever shown Mercy before.

"I am honored to have played such a violin, my lady. Thank you."

Beaming, Jemima said, "Cake and other treats will be served in the parlor."

The guests all followed their hostess out of the music room.

Aurora squeezed Mercy's arm. "Are you coming?"

It was all too much. "I'm going to step into the garden for a moment, if you don't mind. I'm just a bit overwhelmed."

"Are you all right?" Aurora's blue eyes narrowed as she studied Mercy. Giving Aurora a quick hug, she said, "Of course, I'm fine. You know how I am when faced with such an emotional experience. I'll just get some air and be in the parlor in a few minutes."

Aurora nodded and left her.

In the garden, a cool breeze had swept away the heat of the day. Roses bloomed along a wall and scented the air.

"What is it about you, Miss Heath, that keeps me following you into the dark?" Wesley asked from the shadows.

Any sense of calm she sought in the garden evaporated with his nearness. "I cannot tell you that, my lord."

He stepped into the moonlight. His honeyed hair glowed angelic while his dark eyes bore into her with intentions that felt anything but saintly. "I have things I must do and people who depend on me."

With no idea what he was talking about, she stared a long time. "That could be said of all of us."

Stepping closer, he crowded her against the bricked edge of the veranda. "You don't understand."

The knot she'd swallowed rocketed to her throat again and a swarm of bees bumbled in her chest. "No, I don't believe I do. What do you want from me, my lord?"

With a touch so light she might have imagined it, he caressed the side of her face. "There is nothing I want that I am entitled to, Mercedes."

The words and his lover's tone did not match and the sound of her name on his lips stirred something inside her as volatile as playing "Summer" had. How could she survive such a night? "Then perhaps you had better go back in the house, my lord."

He closed his eyes and leaned in enough that only a breath of space separated them. "Is there any way you might call me Wesley?"

Blood rushed to her head and filled her ears. He was too close and she should push him away, but she was caught in his trap. "Why would I do that?"

Opening his eyes, he looked younger and more vulnerable. "Because it is my name and I long to hear it from your lips."

Too much temptation drew her close. "And what happens after that? What happens to all the people who are counting on you for the things you say you must do?"

Pain etched lines around his eyes and shapely lips. He stepped back. "You're right, of course."

Mercy drew a deep breath to clear her head of both desire and disappointment. She was familiar with both, but never had a man shaken her resolve so thoroughly. "It is only the music, my lord. You will recover your senses soon enough."

He crossed his arms over his broad chest. "You play with such abandon and live with such restraint. Is it intentional or have you cultivated this over time?"

"I cannot control my emotions when faced with music and to play a Stradivarius is a great boon." She kept her voice under tight control.

Head cocked, he stared and frowned. "You know that woman used you to impress her guests?"

"I know." Mercy had known for years that her ability to entertain and her friendship with Aurora was the only reason she and her aunt were invited to such evenings.

"Yet you play on command just the same. She treats you little better than a servant and invited that clergyman to woo you as some kind of example of where you stand in comparison to her daughter. How can you bear it?" His fist and jaw clenched until his teeth scraped.

She could hear his unchained anger, but his concerns warmed her even though she found it confusing. He must know as well as Aurora's mother that she was beneath him in rank. "Aurora is my dearest friend. She, Faith, and Poppy have always treated me like an equal despite my lower station. One cannot expect to be treated by everyone as an equal when I am clearly not. What would you have me do, make a scene, refuse to play?"

"Yes," He gave a sharp nod.

The anger emanating from him and the easy way he would have her toss aside her narrow hold in her friends' company lit a fire inside Mercy. "That would be foolish and my friend would have to deal with censure from her mother. Not to mention that playing that violin was a highlight of my life in a way you will never understand. Do not dare to judge me, sir. You hardly know me and know nothing of what my life is and will be."

Like a snake attacking his prey, Wesley's arm sprang out and gripped her around the waist. He dragged her close, eyes flashing.

She gasped, not sure if she should push him away or cling to him.

His tight grip eased and his gaze softened. "I think you are magnificent in many ways, Miss Heath...."

There was more behind his tender expression, but he let her go and stepped back. "Forgive me for my rudeness. I'm happy that you were able to play tonight. It is selfish of me, but I have never heard or felt anything like it."

How it was possible he didn't hear her pounding heart, she didn't know. It sounded like a full parade in her ears. "I'm glad you enjoyed it."

After a long hesitation, he nodded, turned, and left her in the garden.

Mercy stared after him and had to tell herself to close her mouth. His ever-changing moods worried her and she'd need to know if it was only in her presence that he ran hot and cold so erratically.

Strolling back to the house, she made sure he was inside a full ten minutes before she reentered and found her way to the parlor, where everyone chatted and sipped sherry or brandy.

Avoiding the hostess was paramount in Mercy's mind after the things Wesley said. It shouldn't matter, but she didn't want him to see her as a servant. He approached Aurora, who watched the gathering from a safe vantage near the fireplace.

With a long breath, Mercy strode across the room to join them and make sure Aurora wasn't left alone with him.

"Lady Radcliff, I wonder if I might call on you tomorrow. I have something to discuss that might be of interest to you." Wesley's smile was easy but didn't touch his eyes.

"I have no engagements tomorrow." Aurora's voice caught, but she plastered a dull look on her face.

Mercy stepped close to them. "I too shall be home tomorrow," she said with more glee than was appropriate.

His frown didn't make him less handsome and it was very annoying that he was beautiful despite his annoyance at her feeble attempt discourage his attentions to Aurora.

"Then I will see both of you tomorrow." He narrowed a gaze on Mercy before giving Aurora a smile and excusing himself.

A low laugh bubbled from Aurora. "You are about as subtle as a horse in the parlor, Mercy."

"I'm trying to keep him away from you so he'll get the hint that you're not interested."

Aurora shook her head. "Perhaps we should go and see this property in Cheshire. It seems he's going to a lot of trouble over a plot of land that I know nothing about. I might like to settle there if it's nice."

"Do you want to marry Lord Castlewick?" Mercy's voice was low so that only Aurora heard her. Her heart tightened into a stone and breathing was not easy.

"Lord, no. I just think it's worth a trip north to see what all the fuss is about." She patted her perfect hair as if it might slip out of place. Of course, not one strand ever did.

The stone eased but didn't go away. Mercy said, "We are going to Mr. Arafa's home in a few weeks. Perhaps we can travel from there to Cheshire. It should only be a few days from there."

"That is an excellent plan. Mother will want to accompany us," she ended on a sigh.

"I'm sure Aunt Phyllis will wish to come as well," Mercy added.

"Your aunt is always welcome. She is the only parent we Wallflowers have that seems to care more for us than for titles and parcels of land."

Mercy loved her aunt. When her parents had died, Aunt Phyllis had taken her in. She'd only sent her to the Wormbattle school because her husband had demanded they travel for a few years. When Sir John Mattock had died, Aunt Phyllis had wanted Mercy to come home. By then Mercy was fond of school and had good friends. She'd only gone back to London for a few weeks before returning to Switzerland. "Aunt Phyllis is quite fond of all the Wallflowers and would do anything to see us happy, true parent or not."

"She will keep Mother in check as well. It could be fun." Aurora smiled.

"I will discuss it with her this week," Mercy said.

Aurora pulled a face. "I think I shall wait until the last moment to tell Mother. She's already put out by the notion of attending Mr. Arafa's house party." Aurora put her sherry glass down on the mantle. It was half full, but she never finished a drink when they were in public. Aurora was very keen on being in control at all times. After being married to a monster for three years, it was little wonder she'd grown used to being on guard.

"I assume you told her she need not go." Mercy took up Aurora's glass and downed the remaining sherry. "It's not as if you require a chaperone."

After a long sigh, Aurora nodded. "I told her, but she thinks I am wasting my beauty on a silly notion that husbands should be good to their wives."

"Good Lord, she didn't actually say that, did she?" The way some women thought always baffled Mercy.

"Of course, she did. You would have thought that years of bullying by my father would have shown her that was no life for anyone, but she can only see what is proper in society's view." Sorrow laced Aurora's sharp words.

"You remaining a single widow is perfectly acceptable if you wish," Mercy countered, trying to think of some way to rid them of her ladyship for the house party.

Aurora pulled her shoulders back. "Even if it were not, I have no intentions of ever marrying again. Not Lord Castlewick or anyone else, no matter how kind they seem."

"Then we shall discourage his lordship from his quest." The tightness in Mercy's chest eased. The idea of spending time with Wesley after Aurora became his wife hurt her more than she would have thought. Now the man just had to be deterred. She didn't care who he eventually married, but it would not be her friend and that was all that mattered. "I am so looking forward to Mr. Arafa's brand of society."

Geb Arafa was an Egyptian living in England. He had a small castle in the country, which was where the house party was set to take place. The castle had some difficult memories for Faith and Nicholas, but they said they would not be bothered and needed to make new memories to fill those parts of their minds.

"Do you know if Faith is bringing the puppy?" Aurora asked.

Faith joined them with Poppy. "Rumple is hardly a puppy anymore. He weighs more than me. It's lucky he's of a good nature or he could tear the entire house down. I had planned to bring him. Do you object, Aurora?"

"No. I was just curious about how much similarity you will wish to have with your last visit to Parvus." Worry darkened the blue of Aurora's eyes.

Poppy threaded her arm through Faith's and gave her a squeeze.

With a shrug, Faith's gaze was steady and sure. "You will all be there and Mr. Arafa. It will be nothing like before. That was winter as well. It will be a lovely time and a bit crowded too." She laughed.

"Oh, Aurora, perhaps you can convince your mother the castle is too small and she should stay home." Mercy meant it as a joke.

Aurora cocked her head. "I doubt that will work. I think she's rather curious about Mr. Arafa. Many of her friends speak of him with both fascination and disdain."

Rolling her eyes, Poppy scoffed. "Those people hate anyone who isn't just like them. Meanwhile, Geb Arafa is a better man than most and a fine friend to have. Half of London goes to him for artifacts and then speaks badly about him behind his back. I, for one, am pleased to call him my friend."

Rhys sauntered over and pressed close to his wife. "Who is your friend, Poppy?"

"Mr. Arafa." Poppy briefly leaned into Rhys before straightening.

Rhys's blond hair gleamed in the candlelight. He grinned. "A fine fellow."

A laugh from across the room drew Mercy's attention to where Wesley and Nick were standing by the window talking. His laugh filled the room with warmth and Mercy longed to hear the sound again. She liked the way his eyes crinkled in the corners when he laughed. It made her think he did so often, if not in her presence.

"Miss Heath," the dowager called. "Won't you play for us again. I hate to see the pianoforte go unused with all these people clamoring for entertainment."

Wesley's smile fell and his eyes narrowed on her.

Part of her wanted to rebel and tell the dowager countess what she could do with her pianoforte, but she just gave a nod and went to the instrument. It was where she was most comfortable anyway. Though she was also at home with the other Wallflowers.

"A fine idea, my lady," Mr. Garrott exclaimed with a clap of hands.

Poppy murmured, "Fool" under her breath.

Mercy lifted the cover off the keys and rested her fingers on the smooth ivory. Without bothering with sheet music, she played a Beethoven piece that had come to her attention a few years earlier. She wanted to play it on that violin too, but of course one could not play both at once. She laughed at herself. A nice flute would be fine too. She would practice it on hers when she arrived at home.

"This piece is on the sad side too, Miss Heath. Do you only play music that moves one to tears?" Wesley placed one strong hand on the top of the pianoforte, his tanned skin a stark contrast to the white paint. What did he do to retain such a tan?

She didn't miss a note as she shrugged. She'd been so caught up in her own notions of music, she'd not seen him approach and didn't know how long he'd been watching her musings. "This is not so much sad as tempered. It has its bright spots and is quite lively with other instruments in accompaniment."

"Is that what you were just thinking about?" His smile was enough to send her body up in flames.

It annoyed her that he'd read her mind. "My thoughts are my own, my lord. I may be the entertainment, but I am still a lady and have much to keep to myself."

Something flashed in his dark eyes that might have been shame. "I meant no disrespect, Miss Heath. I would never have you play for the amusement of others unless it was your wish, nor would I deprive you of your privacy."

Mercy wanted to leap up and assure him that she'd overreacted. She hated seeing him distraught and that she was the cause of it burned a hole in the stone where her heart had once been. If she ceased playing, all attention would be on them. As it was, the rest of the people in the room were quietly speaking in small groups as the evening wound down. Continuing her play, she said, "I should not have reacted so meanly, my lord. Please forgive me. I suppose our conversation in the garden had drawn my attention to her ladyship's use of my skills. I hope you will forgive me."

A myriad of emotions flew past those eyes that she admired more than she should. "It is I who should beg forgiveness."

With them both contrite the round of apologies might never cease. Mercy bit her lip to hide a smile. "Perhaps we might acknowledge our mutual sorrow and move forward, my lord."

His full grin sent her stomach flipping and a warmth through her. Adjusting herself on the bench only worsened her situation and she drew her attention to the keys rather than continue to gaze at him.

A true gentleman would have walked away, but Wesley tortured her. "Have I discomposed you in some way?"

"No." Her answer came too quickly. She sucked in a long breath. "If you remain here, my lord, our hostess will make a scene that will surely embarrass us both. Perhaps you might leave me to my playing now?"

Mercy kept her eyes on the keys.

"As you wish, Miss Heath." His voice was a cold whisper.

From the corner of her eye, he retreated toward where her aunt and Aurora's mother sat. Focusing on her music, she was determined not to show emotions that would serve no purpose.

Chapter 6

The idea of going to visit Aurora as he'd indicated gave Wesley a sinking stomach. She was a lovely woman, smart and clever from what he'd seen, but there was a good likelihood that Mercy would be at the West Lane townhouse as well. He didn't think he could survive another encounter with her so soon.

He shook off these unhelpful thoughts and, having risen early, rode to Jaffers Fencing Club to see if he might work off some of his frustration with a good match. The clash of steel as he entered was familiar and he longed for this type of club, where there were no women. Not that all women were distracting, but lately he could not seem to avoid the Wallflowers of West Lane and one in particular was on his mind all the time. Unfortunately, it was not the correct one.

Determined to focus on something else, he strode through the door and scanned the long hall with its raised rows. Early morning sun shone through the tall windows, each one throwing shards of light that highlighted the dust like a thousand stars dancing.

Of the three risers, two were in use. Each held a pair of gentlemen engaged in a fencing duel. The battle on the right was quite beautiful as both men were skilled. The two on the left were in danger of harming each other even with the blunted tips due to their clumsiness. The one farther away caught his opponent in the upper arm and his white blouse immediately stained red.

Wesley winced.

The injured man's sword clattered to the floor as he gripped his wound.

"It was bound to happen." Nicholas Ellsworth said from behind Wesley's shoulder.

Turning, Wesley nodded. "Those boys have no business sporting up there." Several men climbed the platform to offer assistance and a proper scolding. Nick and Wesley watched the scene for a few moments before Nick said, "Would you care for a match, Wes? You've been away from Jaffers too long." Wesley grinned. "I imagine with your new and happy marriage; you are not here often either." He took off his coat and donned the protective vest handed to him by one of Jaffers' valets. He took hold of a mask to keep his face safe and gripped his foil in his right hand.

Nick was already suited up for the duel and they walked to the empty platform. "It is a sacrifice I am more than willing to make. I have been trying to get here in the mornings lately to get some exercise. I don't wish to grow fat along with happy." His beaming smile spoke volumes more than his honest admission.

"I'm pleased for you, Nick. Truly, I am. But would you mind if we didn't speak of your wife or any of her friends for the next hour?" They reached the top of the platform and put on their masks.

A low chuckle came from behind the screened helmet hiding Nick's face. "The Wallflowers of West Lane can vex even the saintliest of men. You have my word. I shall not mention them until our duel is complete and even then, I'll keep my peace if you wish."

"I'm no saint." Wesley took his *en garde* stance.

The fury that had welled up inside Wesley for the months since he'd met Mercedes Heath poured out of him like a geyser. All thoughts of a friendly match set aside, Wesley slashed left and then right until he'd backed Nick to the edge of the platform.

Heaving, he raised his arm for the killing blow, but felt the dull thump of Nick's blade hit his ribs hard enough to wake him from his rampage.

"What's gotten into you, Wes? You're never this reckless." Nick walked back to the center and took up a ready stance.

Wordlessly, Wesley followed but didn't bother with the courtesy of the salute. He plunged forward and was immediately swept aside by Nick's deft move and another touch that would likely leave a bruise on his back.

Even under the shadow of the mask, Nick's cocked head begged to question Wesley's stupidity.

Forging forward, Wesley lunged.

Nick spun to the side, easily avoiding the blade. He slid his foot out and toppled Wesley. Nick's knee pressed Wesley's sternum and his dulled blade was pressed to just under Wesley's throat. "Care to talk about it?" Nick asked mildly.

Breathing was only possible in gasps. Beaten handily because he acted like a fool, Wesley sighed. "I doubt talking will help my predicament."

Nick stood and offered Wesley a hand up. "Let's go to the club and see if something can be done. At the very least, you'll be able to get whatever it is off your chest."

Taking Nick's offered hand, Wesley nodded.

The ride from Jaffers Club to Whites gave Wesley time to breathe and remind himself that Nick and he had been friends since their first week at Eton. Nick was not the problem.

He accepted a cup of tea from a footman once they'd seated themselves in a quiet corner of the men's club. The dark woods and deep red and woodsy green fabrics gave him some relief from the fact that wherever he turned, his sight seemed to light on a willowy redhead with the greenest eyes he'd ever seen. At least in Whites she would never be admitted.

Sighing, he sipped the tea and let the sun streaming in the large windows warm him.

A low chuckle from Nick brought Wesley out of his blissful state. "Sorry," Wesley said. "It's just so perfectly peaceful here."

"Care to tell me where it is not so peaceful?" Nick exaggerated the word "not." Holding his teacup in one hand and his saucer in the other, he stared over the rim at Wesley and raised one brow.

"I have every intention of courting and marrying Lady Radcliff." Wesley emphasized this determination by placing his cup with a snick into the saucer on the low table separating them.

"And that is why you behaved little better than those two whelps we saw fencing when you walked in? Because you intend to marry and it has put you in a foul mood?" Much more carefully, Nick placed his cup and saucer on the table.

"I have had some difficulty getting to know the lady. I had a plan to charm her and then propose, but it would seem she is not easily charmed." Wesley tugged on his waistcoat.

Nick huffed and his blue eyes sparkled with amusement. "You mean that you have spent more time charming her friend than you have her." Nick held up a hand, stopping Wesley's denial. "The Wallflowers, as they like to call themselves, are a tight group. They won't let you in easily. If you really want Aurora, you'll have to tread carefully. She is not inclined to marry again."

"I plan to change her mind." Liking the confidence in his own voice, Wesley went on. "I can be very persuasive when I want something."

Nick sat forward, his mouth drawn in a stern line. "I am very fond of both Aurora and Mercy, Wes. Do not toy with them. If you mean to separate those women, you will fail. The bond they share is stronger than you or me. Be sure of what you want, for when you get one Wallflower, you get them all in one way or another."

"Are you telling me you can't control you wife, Nick?" The idea that the Duke of Breckenridge had been brought low by a woman half his size was unfathomable.

A wry smile tugged at Nick's mouth as he sat back against the high-backed chair. "I have no need to control Faith. She is perfect as she is and trying to change her would make us both unhappy. Why do you want to marry Aurora?"

Surprised by the sudden change of topic, Wesley stuttered for a moment. "I...She..." He pulled himself together. "It's a good match. We are of equal status and she would be safe as the Countess of Castlewick. She has lands and titles that will give me connections. Why else do people marry?"

Nodding, Nick called for more tea. "I see. Yes, on paper the match is a good one. I'm certain the lady's mother would be delighted by the marriage. You would gain some very nice lands left to her by her first husband. It all seems to make sense."

"It makes perfect sense." A wave of nausea made Wesley decline the footman's offer of more tea.

Nick picked up his full cup and sipped. "They why do you keep seeking out Mercedes Heath?"

"I do nothing of the sort." His pulse tripled at the mention of his affinity for the woman, ruining all his plans.

There was Nick's slow grin again. "A good friend of mine, Geb Arafa, is hosting a house party in a few weeks. You should join us. Geb will be delighted."

"I assume all the ladies will be there." Wesley couldn't get a single moment alone with Lady Radcliff in London. Maybe in the country it would be different.

"Of course, all the Wallflowers of West Lane will be in attendance."

Wesley could secure Aurora's affections with a few weeks in her company. It was a perfect scenario. Even as he told himself so, the image of green eyes and hair the color of a sunset after rain forged its way inside him. He held back the wave of excitement and pushed away his anger at himself for lacking control. "I know Mr. Arafa. I'll speak to him myself if that's all right with you."

"Of course." Nick raised that brow again as if in a dare.

Calling for pen and paper, Wesley posted a quick note of apology to Lady Aurora and explained that he would not be able to make their scheduled meeting at her West Lane townhouse. He decided his plan was better suited to the country setting.

Nick excused himself to speak to someone across the room. When he returned, he said, "May I ask you something that is none of my business, Wes?"

"You may ask." Warning bells went off inside Wesley's head.

"It's about Miss Heath. Is it her lack of title that keeps you from pursuing her? Because, if that is the case…"

"That is not my reason. Lady Radcliff suits me better. We each have something to bring to the marriage. It will be an amicable match." Wesley's gut tightened painfully. What he wanted and what was the right thing to do never seemed to match up. Why should the finding of his bride be any different?

Both of Nick's brows rose high on his forehead. "I'm sure that's true. However, the lady you speak of is not interested in marriage and Miss Heath is quite fascinating in her own right. She is not as mild mannered as she appears."

"What does that mean?" Wesley shouldn't have asked. He shouldn't have cared.

Nick shrugged. "Someday, if you have the opportunity, perhaps you might ask the ladies about the death of the Earl of Radcliff. Personally, I've never had the nerve to find out the entire truth."

Surely his mouth was agape, Wesley didn't know what to say or what his friend meant.

"The fact is Aurora has declared she will never marry." Nick put his cup down.

"Then I must change her mind. I'll not be talked out of it, Nick. Aurora is the woman I want. You cannot dissuade me."

Head cocked, Nick studied him for a long beat. "I wouldn't dream of trying to alter your decision."

For once, Wesley didn't take the bait. He changed the subject to matters of the House of Commons.

* * * *

His sisters were bickering in the parlor when Wesley arrived and he was about to skirt past the room and avoid coming between whatever they disagreed upon today. After his parents had died, he had taken on the task of raising his sisters. They were twins and rarely left each other's company. Wesley had hired Mrs. Manfred to keep an eye on them and it had all turned out well enough.

In the formal foyer with the dark woods of a masculine home, Peters took his hat. "Mr. Renshaw is with the ladies, my lord."

His cousin had been coming around far too often. "How long has my cousin been here?"

"Over an hour, my lord. The ladies have both played for him and Mrs. Manfred has ordered tea twice." Peters's droll tone gave no indication of emotion.

"It might be time to gather his things." Wesley didn't care for the notion that his cousin might be wooing one of his sisters. They were too young to fend off his charms.

Peters bowed. "As you wish, my lord."

At the door to the parlor, Wesley took a deep breath and put on a mild expression. He and Malcolm were friends, but that didn't mean he wasn't after something. Inside, his sisters sat together on the cream damask sofa, whatever they had been arguing over now a distant memory.

"Wesley, you are home early." Ester rushed across the dark red and cream rug and kissed his cheek.

"I changed my plans and thought we might have a nice afternoon together, but I understand tea has already been taken." He patted her soft cheek and smiled. His sisters were a great joy to him. Both were sweet tempered and full of life.

"How nice," Charlotte said without standing. "I'm sorry we did not wait, but we thought you would be gone most of the day."

"Do not trouble yourself, Charlotte." Wesley turned to Mrs. Manfred, who sat on a small gray chair near the windows. He gave her a nod of greeting before facing Malcolm, who stood by the hearth and grinned. "Renshaw."

"Castlewick." Malcolm tipped his chin down. "I came to see you, but since you were out, I was charmed to spend time with my young cousins."

"Not so young." Ester frowned and sat next to her sister.

"You are both fine young ladies," Wesley said. "Someday you will be happy to be called young."

"How did it go with Lady Radcliff?" Malcolm asked.

"How did what go with Lady Radcliff?" Ester asked and sat on the edge of the cushion.

Equally excited, Charlotte's blond curls bounced around her heart-shaped face. "Are you courting Lady Radcliff? I have heard many of the ladies speak of her beauty."

"I heard she had a very bad marriage before her husband died." Ester took up the story.

"Her husband was killed in some dispute." Charlotte gushed with excitement.

"Enough." Wesley held up a hand and hoped it would bring peace. "I have not begun to court her ladyship. I will not have you engaging in gossip. If I do court her, you will be the first to know and won't you feel bad if you'd been talking behind her back?"

Like a pair of surprised doves, his sisters stared at each other for several seconds. Finally, they calmed and gaped at him. As if by some silent agreement, Ester spoke. "We were only repeating what we have heard, Wes. I'm sure if you should choose to marry the lady, we will adore her."

It was impossible to stay annoyed with them when they smiled politely and looked at him so innocently.

Malcolm coughed to hide his chuckle. "So, tell us how the courting is going."

Even Mrs. Manfred's bright brown eyes were alight with curiosity and she'd put aside her sewing ring.

"Thank you, Mal. I'm so glad you came by." He stared down his cousin, who grinned back at him. "I'll have you know that today I went to Jaffers to fence and then to my club with an old school chum. I didn't see her ladyship and none of this is any of your business."

"You didn't see her?" Malcolm stepped away from the fireplace. "You told me you would see her."

"I spoke to her at the theater, and dined with her last night at a party thrown by her mother, but decided against today's visit." He didn't know why he felt the need to defend his actions.

"She is the key to getting back what was lost." Mal's face turned bright red and his eyes narrowed.

The ferocity of his cousin's response made the hair on the back of Wesley's neck stand up. "Calm yourself, Mal. You wouldn't wish to upset my sisters."

Reining in his temper, Mal smiled at Charlotte and Ester, who sat wide eyed, clutching each other's hands. "My apologies, ladies. I forgot myself."

"Indeed," Wesley agreed. "Have you finished your tea?"

Malcolm drew in a long breath and bowed. "Of course, I shall call another day, cousin. Ladies, it was a pleasure as always."

There was no conversation in the foyer and Wesley imagined Peters had been awaiting the exiting guest with hat in hand.

Once the front door closed, Wesley prepared himself for the barrage of questions that was bound to pepper him.

"What on earth caused Mal to get so upset?" Ester asked.

"He was furious." Charlotte stood her hands fisted. Her yellow day dress swirled around her legs as she strode over to Wesley. "Why was he angry?"

In a similar dress of periwinkle, Ester approached more cautiously. "I've never seen him so emotional. He's always been so charming. Did you anger him, Wes?"

Wesley adored these girls. "You need not worry about Malcolm's state. He was angry at me because he wants me to marry Lady Radcliff and is not happy that I have delayed."

"Are you in love with Lady Radcliff?" Charlotte cocked her head to the left.

"Of course, he is." Ester cocked her head to the right. "He would never marry someone he didn't love."

"Shall we sit?" Wesley needed a moment to clear his head. He didn't wish to lie to his sisters and he knew they would not like what he was about to say.

Mrs. Manfred gripped her sewing ring and came to join them on a settee in front of the fireplace. She had a keen instinct for when his sisters might need her council. "The world is not always as clear as we might like, girls," she said.

"Thank you for that, Mrs. Manfred." Wesley sat in an overstuffed chair covered in pale blue fabric and faced his sisters on the sofa.

Two pairs of brown eyes quite similar to his own stared at him as if terrified over what he might say.

"I like Lady Radcliff, but as yet I do not love her. She is beautiful and clever and owns property that our family must recover." Impressed with how easily the words came out, Wesley could only hope his young sisters would understand.

Charlotte blinked. "You plan to marry her for her property?"

"I must recover what our grandfather lost. Luckily, Lady Radcliff is a very nice woman whom I think you will both be very fond of." It was heart-crushing to voice these things to Charlotte and Ester, who idealized him and the world.

Ester sighed. "We understand, Wes. If she is a good person, I'm sure she will come to love you. I still don't understand why Mal was so enraged though."

"That is puzzling," Charlotte agreed.

"I'm not all together sure myself," Wesley wondered if his cousin believed a quick marriage would give him some opportunity to court one of the twins. "He seems very focused on my marrying sooner rather than later."

All the times Malcolm had shown up at the house over the past six months suddenly seemed like a threat to the people he'd sworn to protect. "I think you should keep your distance from Malcolm."

"Why would you think that?" Ester asked.

"He may have a notion to court one of you and I'll not have that." Worry and anger settled heavily in the pit of Wesley's stomach.

Mrs. Manfred sat up straighter. "He has always been a perfect gentleman, my lord, and I have never left the girls alone with him or any man other than yourself."

"You do an excellent job, madam." He thought of Mercy's ability to defend herself. "I recently met a lady who keeps a hatpin tucked in her hair when she attends balls and other events. She uses it against the unwanted advances of men. It seemed a worthy precaution."

The twins giggled.

Ester asked, "Was it Lady Radcliff who kept the hatpin?"

Their quick joy made him happy. "No, a friend of her ladyship shared the information with me, though I suspect her ladyship may be similarly armed."

The look he got from Mrs. Manfred was not particularly flattering, but Wesley just gave her a grin and she blushed and turned away.

"Oh, Charlotte, we must begin to keep our hatpins handy. You have that one with the lovely large pearl. It will look very fine in your hair." Ester bubbled with glee at the idea.

Charlotte grinned. "We shall go immediately and assess our assortment of weapons."

They ran from the parlor chattering and happy.

Mrs. Manfred rose and made a curtsy. "I rather like the idea, my lord. This lady must be quite something."

Wesley rose. "I have met some extraordinary people these last few weeks. I should inform you, I will be traveling out of London soon. A house party in the country. I assume you can manage here."

"Of course, my lord." Mrs. Manfred gave him a smile and went after the twins.

Wesley went to his office to send a note to Geb Arafa to secure his invitation to the house party. Mr. Arafa had always been very accommodating and friendly. It was unlikely he would refuse. Still, he spent an hour crafting just the right letter before deciding to ride out to the gentleman's home and discuss the matter in person.

Chapter 7

Mercy arrived with all the Wallflowers a few days earlier than Aurora's mother and Aunt Phyllis. It was nice to be without the judgment or Mercy's need to impress for a while. The salon's fire burned low as the rain had finally stopped and left them with a cool summer day.

Like a mother hen, Mercy kept an eye on Faith and Nick to make certain neither one appeared to be suffering any ill effects of being back in the castle where they were tortured by a group of French spies bent on revenge against Nick.

Tall and elegant, Nick bent low to kiss Faith's hand. The two stood by the window, smiling at each other as if they hadn't a care in the world.

Perhaps Mercy was looking for problems where there were none in order to avoid her own thoughts that seemed always to come back to a certain earl whom she had no business thinking about.

"Miss Heath, when is your aunt arriving?" Geb Arafa sat in a large overstuffed chair with gold and light blue upholstery. His dark jacket was in the English style and suited him nearly as well as the Egyptian clothes he often wore.

Mercy tugged her mind back to the people in the room. "She should be here any time. She is very much looking forward to meeting you, Mr. Arafa."

Geb was a friend of Nick's first. He sold information as well as artifacts from the east. He might have many secrets, but he smiled as if he hadn't anything to hide. "Ah, yes. I am a curiosity to the English gentry."

A shot of worry sliced through Mercy and she opened her mouth to defend her aunt.

Aurora said, "Lady Phyllis Mattock is not like the other socialites you have met, Mr. Arafa. You will find her genuine. If she dislikes you, there will be no doubt in your mind about it."

The Wallflowers and Rhys laughed.

"My aunt is very frank, Mr. Arafa, but as Aurora said, she is not like most of our contemporaries. She will judge you on your own merits and nothing else." Mercy was sure Aunt Phyllis would like their host. He was charming and quick witted as well as loyal. They were all attributes her aunt admired.

Mr. Arafa smiled. "I'm glad that when she wrote asking if she could bring an additional guest, I said it would me my pleasure to host whomever she wished. I would not want to get on the bad side of a woman who all of you ladies admire so."

"What?" Mercy blurted before she could contain her shock.

Poppy rushed in with her usual candor. "Who on earth could she be bringing and why? I thought it was just to be Wallflowers and family."

Geb raised both hands helplessly. "I had the same thoughts but when Nicholas invited Lord Castlewick, I assumed it would be permissible for Lady Mattock to bring Mr. Colby."

Aurora's eyes were wide as saucers. "Lord Castlewick," she groaned.

Eying her husband, Faith crossed her arms over her chest. "Nick, you didn't?"

With a shrug, Nick said, "He's all the four of you talk about. I assumed having him here would expedite whatever scheme you're about. Besides, I quite like Wes. He's been a good friend to me and I see nothing wrong with balancing out the abundance of women I'm constantly surrounded by."

"Here, here," said Rhys.

Poppy turn on him. "Don't tell me you had anything to do with this, husband."

Hands up in defeat, Rhys said, "No. However, Nick does make a valid point about the lack of men in our immediate circle."

Mercy couldn't stop the wave of amused hysteria that washed through her. It began as a grin that she couldn't push away and morphed into a giggle that shook her entire body. "It's just all too ridiculous."

"Miss Heath, are you all right?" Geb sat across from her and leaned his elbows on his knees.

"Please don't tell me Lincoln Baker will be here as well." The thought of another of her admirers with whom she had no interests had amused tears streaming from her eyes.

Poppy began to laugh heartily with Mercy. "Or perhaps Decklan Garrott will be joining us."

"I say we invite every man who has ever taken an interest in a Wallflower to stay the fortnight." Faith sat next to Mercy and wrapped an arm around her while they waited for their amusement to be spent.

Aurora covered her mouth to hide her growing delight. "Indeed. That would be a relaxing time away from town."

Rhys stood. "We may as well leave them alone. They will not say a single reasonable thing while we're in the room until this episode has passed."

Geb rose and followed the two married men from the salon, leaving the Wallflowers of West Lane alone.

It was a few minutes before any of them could draw enough breath to speak. Finally, Poppy took a long gulp of air. "What shall we do?"

Shaking her head, Mercy shrugged. "Nothing has changed. We shall convince Lord Castlewick he cannot marry Aurora, and I will avoid poor Mr. Colby despite my aunt's continued attempts to find me a husband."

"You really can't like him?" Faith took Mercy's hand and gave it a squeeze. It would make her life easier if she could like Mr. Colby. He was smart, moderately wealthy, and a gentleman. He loved music and he was not bad looking. However..."I don't love him and never could," Mercy said. "Believe me, I wish he thrilled me in some way."

Aurora sat next to Poppy and sighed. "Perhaps it is not so important to love them as to tolerate, Mercy. You might even admire Mr. Colby. Would that not be worth having your own home and the opportunity for children?"

"I find that surprising coming from you, Aurora." Mercy held back the jolt of disappointment. Wallflowers never pushed marriage where there was no love. "Why would you say such a thing?"

Poppy narrowed her gaze on Aurora. "I agree with Mercy. When did you decide that love was unnecessary? I can assure you; I would never have married your brother or anyone else had I not been helplessly in love."

Fussing with her lace on her light blue skirt, Aurora kept her gaze down. "You might be happy. There is no rule that says one must love to find contentment."

Mercy's heart pounded against her ribs. "Do you wish for me to leave West Lane, Aurora? Is that why you are advocating I marry where I do not love?"

Aurora's golden blond hair quivered around her face as she stared, mouth agape. "No!" Reaching forward, she took Mercy's hand. "I love having you with me and wish heartily all four of us still lived together." She released her grip and clutched her fingers together. "It is only that I don't wish to be selfish. It occurred to me that you might be thwarting interested men because you worry about leaving me alone. I would never wish that. You should have your own house and a family."

Relief flooded Mercy and she let her shoulders relax. "I am perfectly content at West Lane. I don't think Aunt Phyllis would object to my staying with her either. I have options, which is more than most women in my circumstance can say. I will probably marry one day and Mr. Colby is not a bad option."

Pressure built behind Mercy's eyes, but she swallowed down the flood of doubt and disappointment.

Faith sighed. "I think we should enjoy our fortnight in Parvus and not let the whims of men deter our good time. Let Lord Castlewick do as he might, Aurora will ignore him or cast him off."

"Mr. Colby is mild mannered enough to push aside any advances on Mercy's time." Poppy crossed her arms over her chest and lifted one hand to force a wayward hair out of her eyes.

Nodding, Aurora wrapped her arm around Poppy's shoulders. "You are right. I have no intention of accepting any offer and his lordship will eventually have to come to understand that, as will my mother. We will have a lovely stay here and then make a quick trip up to Cheshire and see what all the fuss is about. After that, I will go back to my life in West Lane and Mercy can decide if any of the men vying for her attention are of interest."

Mercy laughed a bit too loud. "All the men...I hardly would make it sound so grand, Aurora."

Poppy cocked her head. "There are at least three that we know of, Mercy. You have choices beyond West Lane or being a companion to your aunt."

Her three dearest friends stared at her expectantly, but she had no good response. At least not one that made logical sense in her circumstance. "I will think about my options, but I see no need to marry. I'm happy at West Lane and I certainly don't love Mr. Colby, Mr. Baker, or Mr. Garrott. They are gentlemen, that is true, but none of them do I regard with any particular affection."

Faith sighed. "You shouldn't have to settle."

"Everyone settles," Aurora said.

Faith's eyes softened as she made a futile attempt to put her wayward curls back into the chignon. "You are speaking from your own experience,

Aurora. You had little choice but to marry where your father ordered. We were very young and had no way of knowing what a monster Radcliff would be. Mercy is not in your situation. Her aunt would never force her to marry and we can protect her if need be. I would like to see all four of us happy rather than married to men we cannot like."

"That is easy to say since you have a husband who loves you and is kind." Aurora's tone was even, but fire lit her bright blue eyes.

Reaching across the gap, Faith offered Aurora her hand. "You are right, of course. That doesn't make it less true though, does it, Aurora?"

Aurora took Faith's hand in both of hers. "No. I'm sorry. And, Mercy, I owe you an apology as well. You shouldn't marry where your heart cannot follow. I think all this interference in my life by Mother and Lord Castlewick has put me in a bad temper."

Poppy put her hand on top of Aurora's. "Not to worry. Wallflowers always protect each other."

Mercy topped the pile with her own hand. "That's right. No one will ever harm one of us again."

"Never again," they all repeated.

* * * *

"I'm not angry, Aunt Phyllis. I just don't know why you brought Mr. Colby to Parvus. It was supposed to be a quiet retreat for friends." Mercy sat by the writing desk in the room assigned to her aunt.

Geb had recently decorated all the rooms at Parvus, giving them a fresh, cozy feel. The curtains in Phyllis's room were the color of a peach sunrise and went very well with the cream coverlet. The furniture was simple and elegant, with the bed, a nightstand, the writing desk and chair, and one overstuffed chair facing the fireplace.

"He is a nice man who seeks me out at every opportunity to ask after you. He loves music and I am convinced he loves you quite ardently. This was the perfect opportunity to see if you might gain some affection for him as well." Aunt Phyllis supervised her maid's care of her dresses.

There was little point arguing. Her aunt had her best interest at heart. "I'm sure he does not love me. He loves the music and perhaps loves to listen to me play, but he doesn't know me well enough to determine if he has those deeper feelings."

The wrinkles around Aunt Phyllis's eyes deepened as she reined in her grin. "Then this will be a fine time for him to get to know you better.

And—that means you and the rest of the girls are not to run him off at any opportunity the way you have with poor Lord Castlewick."

Mercy's mouth opened to argue, but Phyllis held up a hand to stop her. "I know your game, niece. Don't deny it. It does you a disservice to fib. Besides, I don't know why anyone would object to Castlewick and Aurora. They are a fine fit socially."

"Aurora does not wish to remarry and that is enough of a reason." Mercy stood and crossed her arms over her chest. She might let her aunt dictate her behavior, but she would not allow her to bully Aurora.

A softening of her aunt's eyes told her the argument was at an end. "Then Aurora should tell him so. If she breaks his heart, then at least she didn't also waste his time."

Mercy's scoff escaped before she could stop it. "Castlewick does not love Aurora. He just wants that land she owns and she is a convenient means to obtaining it."

"How can you know what is in the man's heart, Mercedes?" Phyllis dismissed her maid, Ann. "Do you know more of him than I am aware?"

Oh lord, she'd said too much without thinking. "No. I only know what I've seen and deduced the rest. Besides, men like Wesley Renshaw think they can have any woman they want. He is on some kind of conquest to win Aurora and has used her mother to get closer than he ever should have. The dowager will be able to tell all her friends that Aurora landed not one but two earls in marriage. She lives for such things."

Phyllis sat on the edge of the bed. "Jemima Draper can be a bit shortsighted, but I don't think she means any harm. She only wants her daughter to be protected, just as I want that for you."

It was best to steer away from her own safety. "Aurora is a rich widow. She is perfectly safe. She has land and a house in London. She has no need for a husband and certainly not another one who cares more for his own needs than hers."

"You cannot know what his lordships needs are, Mercedes. You might gather more information before you judge the man so harshly." Standing, Phyllis brushed out her skirt. "In the meantime, give Mr. Colby a chance. He really does dote over you."

Mercy stifled the long sigh building in her chest and stood. "I will be polite, Aunt Phyllis. I promise no more than that."

"And you won't avoid him for the entire fortnight?" Phyllis's brows rose high over her piercing green eyes.

"Since I hate to disappoint you more than I can say, I will give Mr. Colby some of my time." Mercy kissed her aunt's cheek. "But don't get the idea that I'll marry him, Aunt. I will just be polite to him as he has come all this way and he does seem sincere in his enjoyment of my music." Ann had placed Phyllis's jewelry on the table to be put away. Mercy fingered the broach that had been in her father's family for generations. A round diamond sat in the center with more to create a starburst. Small sapphires punctuated each tip. "This always makes me think of my parents."

Next to her, Phyllis sighed. "It makes me think of my parents as well. Mother wore it each year to the country ball they would throw. She gave it to your father when he married and your mother wore it often. She loved it so."

"I have never seen you wear it, Aunt." Mercy scanned her memory of some time when she had seen the bauble on her Aunt.

"No. I have never worn it. I do so like to have it near though. A reminder of those we have lost." She gave Mercy's shoulder a squeeze and crossed to the wardrobe, where Ann had hung three gowns to be examined. "Does one dress for dinner here?"

Mercy turned away from the jewels and swallowed the emotions that thoughts of her mother and father always conjured. "Yes. Of course. You will find that Mr. Arafa embraces most English customs, though without all the judgment."

Patting her graying hair into place, Aunt Phyllis flashed a smile. "What does that mean?"

"Only that if you choose to arrive at dinner in your dressing gown, he would still treat you like an honored guest."

A deep rumble of laughter reminded Mercy of her youth and all the good days she'd spent with her aunt. "I hope you are not warning me that you will be dining in your nightclothes."

Mercy's face warmed. "I will wear my green gown. I'm not daring enough to shock anyone."

"Oh, I don't know. You may not be at the level of the English housekeeper who wears a turban, but you are interesting in your own right."

Frowning, Mercy wasn't sure what her aunt meant. Unwilling to open up some topic she might regret, she focused on the first comment. "Do you mind Mr. Arafa and his unusual household, Aunt Phyllis?"

Phyllis touched the silky cuff of her russet gown. "On the contrary, my dear. I am intrigued by the way things are done here. The very tall butler is particularly interesting. I have never seen a man so tall or a servant who made one feel as welcomed. Perhaps it is his voice, but I felt sure I would be safe in this home as long as the butler was present."

"Kosey is devoted to Mr. Arafa and a very fine musician as well."
Mercy had played a duet with the butler and she liked him too. She could
see what her aunt meant. He did give off an air of capability.

"Indeed. How singular to have a servant who can play. This will be quite
a house party I think." Phyllis sighed. "I must rest for an hour before dressing
for dinner. Will you come and collect me when it is time to go down?"

Giving her aunt another hug, Mercy said, "I'll collect you at six thirty.
We all generally gather in the salon before dinner."

"Very good. Send Ann back in, please, my dear. Oh, and you look a bit
pale. It's a fine day. If you will not rest, you might get out in the fresh air."

Mercy nodded as she left the room.

Ann waited in the hall and curtsied to Mercy before going to
tend her mistress.

The mirror on the landing proved that Aunt Phyllis was quite right.
She did look wan. Too much time indoors and in carriages over the last
few weeks. Rushing back up to her room, she gathered a light shawl and
determined to take her aunt's advice.

Chapter 8

Wesley arrived at the small castle while most of the guests were resting. He'd spoken to Mr. Arafa for half an hour before excusing himself to settle into his room. Once in the well-appointed bedroom, he'd been restless. There were several hours before he'd need to dress for dinner. He'd been cooped up in a carriage for several days and he hated to sit alone in his room. He searched the house for some company, but finding none he opted for a bit of exercise.

The gardens were managed but wild. Not at all in the style of most English homes.

A hunched man with a wheeled barrel rounded the corner and stopped to stare at him.

Wesley wasn't accustomed to servants staring, so he stared back. "May I help you, good man?"

"You look like a lord of something to me." His voice was rough and direct.

"Castlewick," Wesley said on a laugh.

The man bowed. "Well, my lord, what do you think?"

"About what?"

"My gardens, of course."

"They are not what one would expect of an English home, but I can see while it all looks quite wild there is a specific order to it as well. I'm fond of wild roses and the evergreens are likely a wonderful staple in winter. The mugwort is a nice touch, but the nightshade seems a bit out of place." In so short an exploration, that was as much as Wesley could report.

Having abandoned his cart, the man studied the blooming plant and then Wesley. "I thought it would give a bit of color to the area, but you may be right. I'll think about moving it to the east side of the garden where it might make more sense."

"You are the groundskeeper I presume?"

"MacGruder, my lord. You have a keen eye for gardening."

"I enjoy a well-thought-out plan and I see you have a great deal of time invested here. I hope to explore more today with the weather being so fine." Wesley eyed the path where it disappeared around a wild rose bush that sprawled over a trellis.

With a nod and a grunt, MacGruder took up his cart again and stomped off to the west end of the garden.

Sorry to lose even the company of the gruff gardener, Wesley sighed and walked deeper into the gardens.

The rain that had slowed his travel left behind a bright blue sky and a fresh new world dotted with droplets that caught the light.

Like fairies in a dream, two figures walked along the ridge; one in white and one in blue. Immediately, he knew one was the tall lithe shape of Mercy Heath in the white day dress. The light hair of the other made it likely Aurora walked with her.

His skin tingled with the memory of touching Mercy and his heart pounded. Anticipation and dread warred inside Wesley. Pulling back his shoulders he started up the path to his future. Aurora Sherbourn would marry him, there was no question in his mind about that. Mercedes Heath was not what he wanted or needed, he repeated to himself for the hundredth time.

A footpath led him up the hill to where he had seen the ladies. Along the west side of the garden a wildly kept hedge jutted and curved to block the wind like a lush green rock formation. At the top of the ridge he surveyed the sprawling farmland that stretched as far as he could see in a patchwork of plots, each rich with summer growth.

The hills rolled in every direction and a large manor house shone in the sun several miles to the north. The village bustled the same distance toward the east. Parvus was a small castle, but the grounds and views made it a very desirable parcel to own. Geb Arafa had done well to secure the place.

"Lord Castlewick?" Aurora's soft inquiry brought his attention to his right.

"Lady Radcliff, Miss Heath." He bowed.

The ladies curtsied.

"When did you arrive?" Aurora asked. Her hands were clasped in front of her with her elbows bent and her expression was of only mild interest. She appeared the perfect example of an English lady.

He had to force himself not to look too long at Mercy, whose hands were white from gripping them and the stiffness of her arms forced her modest bust to the edge of her dress's neckline. "I only arrived about an hour ago. I was greeted by our host and then shown my room. However, after days of travel in bad weather, I was anxious to get out in the sunshine and obtain some exercise."

Mercy drew in a breath that sounded a bit ragged. "We are happy for the fine weather as well. It has been dreary since we arrived a few days ago."

"May I walk with you ladies or are you in confidence?" He loved the sound of her voice and had to push his attention back to Aurora.

"Please, join us," Aurora said. "We had planned to venture into town as we have already been around the gardens."

"That is a fair walk, my lady. I think it's five miles at least." Not minding a long walk, he wanted to make sure the ladies knew what they were in for.

A slow smile pulled at the lips he longed to kiss again. Mercy said, "Faith is not with us, so the walk will not daunt us, my lord."

Aurora laughed.

"I feel I am missing the joke, ladies." He liked to see them laugh. They were usually guarded in his presence. Letting them pass him so they could walk the path to the road into town, he bowed.

"Faith hates walking." Mercy pulled her shawl more securely over her shoulders. "It is no great secret. We used to walk and climb the mountains in Switzerland and she would complain constantly. Once we returned to England, we often teased her about her dislike of the diversion."

"May I ask what each of you did to be sent to a school so far away?" He'd been more than curious about what someone as sweet as Mercy might have done to deserve such a punishment.

Aurora's smile took a wicked turn. Her blue eyes flashed with memory. "I will only tell my own tale, my lord, but I was a very willful youth who did not always listen to a very strict father. He hoped sending me away to Lady Agatha Wormbattle's school would make me a proper lady."

"It seems to have worked?" Every time he had seen Aurora, she'd been the model of propriety. So much so that he couldn't imagine the disobedient child she spoke of.

Mercy frowned, but kept her attention on her hands and the road.

"I would say, I have learned to hide my personality better. If Lady Agatha taught us anything, she taught us that." Aurora's smile never wavered but the joy left her eyes.

"And what of you, Miss Heath? Were you sent away for lack of obedience?"

"No, my lord. My aunt took me in when my parents died and when she remarried her husband felt it best to send me to school while they traveled."

"I'm sorry." He was a cad for bringing up what must be a difficult memory for her.

"No need," she waved a hand. "Going to Lady Agatha's was the best thing that could have happened. If I hadn't gone to Lucerne, I would never have met Aurora and the others. My life would be very dull without my friends."

The ladies linked arms affectionately and walked slightly ahead of him.

"I suppose all things happen as they are meant to," he said, but wondered if he believed it. If he did, then he'd have to think his attraction to Mercy was meant to be and that made no sense.

"Perhaps," Aurora said on a sigh. "But sometimes the things that happen seem far too harsh, my lord."

There was no way to ask her what she meant without inquiring about her marriage and he didn't feel he knew her well enough for that. She must have been far more devastated by her husband's death than he'd previously considered. Having never met Radcliff, he assumed the general consensus of his bad character was true. The rumors his sisters had heard might be just that. Perhaps she had loved him despite what others said about him. "I suppose that is true, my lady."

Mercy watched him as if looking for something to censure. He stared back, waiting for some indication of what he might have done or said to offend her. A moment later, she blinked and turned her attention back to the road ahead. "You must understand, my lord, for ladies who have no ability to change their situation our fate is in the hands of others. Not everyone has our best interest at heart."

Trying to read between the lines was giving him a headache. "I am certain there are a great many things about being a lady that I cannot fathom, Miss Heath. However, you must also accept that everyone has obligations they must meet and those do not always align with what we might want."

"I believe men do not understand because they do not care to." Mercy pressed her lips together as if forcing herself to say no more.

"It is also possible that women are reluctant to share information with my sex and thus we are all doomed to ignorance on the topic."

"Oh touché, my lord." Aurora laughed. "Though I doubt you really want to know the troubles we face."

They had separated so he stepped between them and offered each an arm. "I am your servant. I would be elated to have you ladies enlighten a poor ignorant man such as myself."

Giving each other a long look, they shrugged and took his offered arms.

Mercy said, "I will tell you something, but please know I do not share this for the purpose of gaining sympathy. I insist you accept my tale for its educational value."

"Agreed," he said too quickly. His heart beat anxiously to hear anything about her.

"My parents were warm and kind. Father was a landed gentleman though the lands and monies were entailed to a cousin. When they died, I was fourteen. The cousin came to collect his new home and told me I had a choice. I could leave or be a servant in his house. Even at that age, I knew the way he leered at me would lead to something sordid. Thankfully, before I had to make a decision to be homeless or ruined, my aunt came to collect me." She spoke calmly and with only the slightest hint of emotion, but suddenly the depth of emotion when she played made more sense.

"Your cousin is a pig, Miss Heath. He was not obligated to care for you, but he had no rights to you either. If he had been a good man, he might have waited a few years and offered for you." Wesley's sense of justice beckoned him to find her ass of a cousin and thrash him bloody.

Mercy shuddered. "What a horrifying notion, but my aunt agrees with you."

"I am grateful your aunt was able to take you out of a bad situation." He had no right to his gratitude and should have kept the thought to himself.

Aurora patted his arm. "She is safe, my lord. Though we do appreciate your outrage. Mercy's is not that unusual a story. You must realize a lady's fate is often in the hands of some man. Before Mercy's deplorable cousin, her life was in her father's hands. Had he lived to see her married, his obligation would have been passed to her husband."

"You are also protected by these men, my lady. You have no obligations to keep the financial end of a fortune going. You do not worry over the family honor. All of those concerns are left to the men." It was too soon to divulge his family history even when he wished to.

"Not all men care about the safety of their wards, wives, sisters, and mistresses." Aurora kept her chin high and stared straight ahead, but her posture stiffened.

"No. I realize there are men who would take advantage of the people whom it is their responsibility to protect. Miss Heath's cousin does not sound like a caring man. I would have been sorry to see you fall under his control, Miss." Anger surged through him with more ferocity than was wise on a casual walk to town.

"You would never have met me if he had, my lord. Perhaps in a parlor one day, you would have heard a sad tale about a girl gone bad." She rolled her eyes. "I would have been the destitute orphan of Mr. Heath. People would have blamed me for my fate. No one would have tried to help me. What choices did I have at fourteen years that would have left me a lady in the eyes of society? You would have heard the tale, blamed my father or me for my fate, and never given me a second thought."

He wanted to deny it. With every fiber of his being, he wanted to tell her she was wrong and he would have cared very much for her fate. However, he was not foolish enough to defend a position that never occurred. "I hope I am a better man than that, Miss Heath. I hope one day to prove that to all of you ladies. I am the caretaker of my sisters and would hate to think of them falling into disreputable hands. It is fortunate you do not need rescuing and even if you did, I believe you would prefer to save yourself."

Aurora threw her head back and belched out a loud laugh. "Oh my, that is truer than you know, my lord. I think you very brave to have spoken it aloud."

Unable to keep his own amusement hidden, he chuckled with her. "I'm happy to have any rise in my character in your estimation, my lady. I hope bravery is something favorable in your eyes."

She smiled and winked at Mercy, who was not at all amused.

The village of Lambly with its quaint houses and stores came fully into view.

"This is lovely." Mercy released his arm and rushed forward.

He missed her closeness immediately. His mind plotted ways of bringing her back to him, but he held his tongue.

Aurora remained at his side. That was what he wanted. He had to convince a very pretty, wealthy woman to marry him. It was not a terrible task. So, why did his heart sink?

"Mercy is very fond of new places. She'll want to investigate all the shops before we return to Parvus." Aurora grinned after her friend.

"And you, Lady Radcliff, do you enjoy new places?"

She shrugged on a long sigh. "I don't mind, but I wish I had the enthusiasm that Mercy displays when she thinks a discovery is to be made."

They walked to where Mercy peered in a store window.

"Look at this, Aurora. It's a hat shop and isn't that the most charming little bonnet?" Mercy had put her spectacles on and pointed to a lavender confection with perfectly folded silk, with larger folds incremental to its left side, where a long pheasant feather sprang from behind an amethyst.

"How unusual to find such a work of art in this village." Aurora went to the door.

Wesley opened it for her. When Mercy made no move to join them inside, he asked, "Will you not come inside, Miss Heath?"

A forced smile pulled at her lips for barely a second before she stepped inside the shop.

Aurora bought the bonnet and several other "very clever" items before they left the shop. "Was there nothing that you fancied, Miss Heath?"

"It is a lovely shop." She took her spectacles off and put them in her reticule. "I have no need for anything at this time. I do enjoy looking."

He offered his arm and once she took it, they followed after Aurora, who had rushed to look in another shop across the street. "You only wear your spectacles on occasion, Miss Heath?"

"They were very expensive and I worry I will break them, so I only wear them when I really need or want to see something clearly." Her smooth cheeks pinked.

Guilt tightened his chest. "Had I sent you less expensive eyewear, would you wish to see the world around you all the time?"

Her throat bobbed as she swallowed several times. "I appreciate you sending them and allowing me to pay you back over time. I could never have afforded them on my own."

Stopping, he faced her. "I wanted you to have them to wear, Mercy. It would have pleased me if you had accepted them as a gift."

She nodded. "I know, but what would accepting such a gift have said about me, Wesley?" She exaggerated his name.

"No one would have had to know." He lowered his voice. Despite her making sure he knew she didn't approve of the use of their Christian names, he loved hearing her say his name. "I should have taken better care."

"In my experience, my lord, someone always knows. Besides, you and I would have known, would we not?" She stared at him; her green eyes filled with questions.

"And you would never wish to be on such intimate terms with a man like me." Sarcasm escaped despite his desire to keep their relationship light.

Pulling her gaze away from his, her voice was tight. "Our intimacy will always be reserved to friendship. As you know, it can never be more than that. Accepting an extravagant gift is out of the question."

"Miss Heath, would you then be willing to accept a less expensive pair of spectacles that you might be comfortable wearing every day, from a friend. It would give me great ease of mind to know you had your sight at all times."

She looked everywhere but at him. "It is not necessary. I can manage as it is and I quite love the pair I have."

The fact that she had not said no gave him a jolt of hope that erroneously went right to his heart. He tried to quash the feelings, but the more he tried, the harder they pushed to the surface. His decision made, he said, "May I ask why you were not wearing the old pair when we danced last year?"

Blinking, she looked up at him. "I have been told to not wear them at social functions where my aunt feels I might attract a suitor."

Wesley took her reticule from her, pulled it open and removed the spectacles. Carefully he placed them on her nose and wrapped the side pieces around her ears. Soft tendrils of hair tickled his fingers and her skin was silken, but he forced himself to only touch her where necessary to let her see. "You are just as lovely with them on, Miss Heath. Perhaps it is time to defy your aunt on the subject. There is much to see in the world. I should hate for you to miss any of it."

Bright pink, she studied his face from his forehead to his chin and then back to his eyes. "You are too bold by far, my lord."

"Perhaps, Mercy, but as your friend, I am quite in earnest. Do not sacrifice your sight for someone else's idea of beauty." A cart rumbled down the street, waking him from the appeal of being so close to her. He stepped back. "Shall we join Lady Radcliff? It looks as if she has found a book shop.

Mercy's eyes sparkled and her lips bowed. For the barest moment she showed pure happiness.

The effects on Wesley both mentally and physically had to be hidden quickly. If they had been alone, her smile alone would have forced him to pull her into his arms and claim those lovely lips. As it was, he fisted his hands and turned away.

She rushed across the street and he followed more slowly, trying to decide if it was his compliment or the notion of a book shop that had brought her such outward joy.

Lord, the woman was going to be the death of him. As determined as he was to abandon her for the woman he had to marry, he still wanted her painfully.

They would be friends and nothing more. Aurora was the woman he would marry. His family honor depended on it.

Chapter 9

Mercy had always liked her soft green gown. It matched her eyes and made her feel pretty. She worried that after the wildly flattering complement from Wesley, she might be feeling a bit too pretty.

Of course, he hadn't meant it when he'd said she was just as lovely with spectacles as without. No man wanted a lady who appeared studious or mousy she thought as she pushed her frames up her nose. Giving herself one last look in the mirror, she ran her hand along the pearl beads that trimmed the low neckline of the gown.

Popping her spectacles into her reticule, she went downstairs. She had promised her aunt she would spend time with Mr. Colby and she intended to honor that promise even if she had no intention of allowing the man to court her.

In her head she knew Mr. Colby was a good catch for her, but her heart wouldn't agree to be wooed by someone she had such pale feeling for.

Yet at the bottom of the stairs stood the man himself. Tall and slightly awkward, Wallace Colby smiled at her. "Miss Heath you are a vision."

His legs were a bit thin in his breeches and his coat was poorly tailored for his wide shoulders and narrow waist, making him look as if he might be wearing someone else's clothes. But his blue eyes were kind and he waited expectantly for her to speak. "Mr. Colby, how nice to see you again. It was kind of Mr. Arafa to invite you."

"Indeed, he seems a fine fellow, considering. Though I'm certain your aunt had a great deal to do with it." He offered his arm.

Mercy cringed. She took his offer to see her into the salon. "You might leave the word 'considering' off the next time you speak kindly of our host, Mr. Colby."

Patting her hand as if she were some child he'd inadvertently offended, his smile didn't waver. "You know what I mean."

"Unfortunately, I know exactly what you mean, sir. I just do not care for your way of thinking." It was getting harder and harder to keep her word to her aunt.

"I think much the same as the rest of society." He stopped at the salon's threshold.

"Indeed." She faced him, taking her hand back. Keeping her voice to a whisper, she added. "That does not make the attitude right. You might have considered your feelings on the subject before you accepted an invitation to the man's house."

"I wished to see you. Does that not gain me any of your good opinion?" It was the first time she'd noticed the way he spoke as if she might not be smart enough to understand his meaning. Did he think her an imbecile?

Perhaps this was how Mr. Colby dealt with adversity. If she felt inferior, it would be difficult to continue defending Mr. Arafa. However, she did not feel daunted by his wisdom, just bored by his prejudices. "I see my aunt. If you will excuse me, sir."

It was worth dealing with Aurora's mother, who sat with Aunt Phyllis, in order to get away from Mr. Colby before she said something regrettable.

"Aunt Phyllis, Lady Marsden, how good you both look." Mercy kissed her aunt's cheek.

Lady Marsden said, "I see you arrived with Mr. Colby. He seems a very nice young man. You are quite sought after, it would seem, Miss Heath."

Forcing her smile into place wasn't easy, but Mercy managed it. "Mr. Colby has a great love of music. He admires my playing."

"Perhaps he admires a bit more than that, my dear." Lady Marsden's grin was too wide and too pleased with her innuendo. "You could do far worse. He has money enough to make you comfortable."

"We are not courting, my lady, but thank you for your concern after my future." Mercy made a quick curtsy and rushed toward Faith and Nick.

"Are you all right?" Faith whispered and leaned close.

"Can I never be in a room without someone trying to marry me off to some sod who I haven't the slightest interest in?"

Nick's sympathetic eyes shifted behind her. "Mind your tongue, the sod approaches."

Mercy straightened her back and turned to face Mr. Colby.

"Miss Heath, I fear I have offended you." His cheeks were red and doubt creased his eyes.

Unable to stop the sigh waiting in her gut, Mercy let it roll out of her. "Not at all, sir. You could never offend me."

Since she cared not a whit for him, this at least was true.

"I am so relieved." His grin wide, he continued. "In that case, perhaps I can persuade you to play for us."

In the corner by the window sat a very pretty harp, alongside a small but beautiful pianoforte.

Nick cleared his throat. "Miss Heath has not even had any refreshment. Perhaps she might entertain you after she's had a sherry with my wife and me."

"Of course, Your Grace." Wide-eyed, Mr. Colby backed up a step. While he was as tall as Nick, he did not hold the same commanding presence as the Duke of Breckenridge.

Mercy liked having friends in high places. While she believed Nick would be a good friend even if he were a street vendor, it was handy to have a duke on one's side. "I would be happy to play the harp after quenching my thirst. Mr. Arafa, where did you find such a lovely instrument?"

Geb rounded the sofa carrying a glass of sherry, which he handed to Mercy. His own religion didn't permit him to drink, but he always saw to the happiness of those around him. "It was a gift from a Frenchman before all the war. Perhaps you have heard of him, Jacques-Georges Cousineau? He is a fine harpist and developed several changes for the harp, as I understand it."

Mercy's mouth was agape and she forced it closed. "He's a virtuoso, sir. It must be quite a story of how you earned such a gift."

Laughing, Geb shrugged. "I shall tell you some time, Miss Heath, when we are not in company as it is a long story."

"I would like that very much."

He bowed. "Then it shall be my pleasure. It is a story I think you will enjoy as you have a keen appreciation for music."

Faith hid a snicker behind her hand before sobering. "Mr. Arafa, this is our first time here in warm weather. The gardens are magnificent. Nick and I took a turn before we came to meet the party. It really is wildly charming."

"I am pleased you still think so, Your Grace, after the events of last winter." Worry darkened Geb's already dark eyes.

With a warm smile, Faith sipped her sherry. "I will not lie to you, being here has conjured some bad memories for us, but it has also reminded us that this is where we fell in love. Besides, none of what happened was your fault. If anyone was to blame, it was me."

"I must take my part in it too," Nick said. "It was my past that came back to haunt us."

Confusion flashed across Mr. Colby's face, but his gaze flitted to the harp and whatever he'd wanted to ask fled his features. "Have you enjoyed enough sherry to play now, Miss Heath?"

His voice carried to the dowager. "Oh yes, do play now, Miss Heath." Her eyes narrowed on Mercy.

Aurora said, "Mother, Mercy might like to relax before dinner with the rest of our party."

From the other corner, Rhys and Poppy stopped their conversation with Geb's butler, Kosey. Frowning, they turned to the scene being made.

"I see no reason why she can't play for us," Lady Marsden scolded her daughter.

Mercy felt Wesley enter without looking at the doorway. He sucked up all her air in a way that she couldn't help notice. Taking the easy way out, she forced a smile and placed her glass on the table. "It would be my pleasure to play such a lovely instrument." Then her wicked side kicked in. "Maybe Mr. Kosey would be willing to accompany me on the pianoforte?"

A cough from Nick hid his amusement. He whispered, "You are pushing your luck, Mercy."

The most delightful surge of joy flooded her. "Indeed, I am." Smiling at her friends, she waggled her brows at them.

Faith and Nick laughed.

Kosey stared for a long moment. "It would be my delight, Miss."

The look of amused censure on Aunt Phyllis's face did not stop Mercy from crossing the room and taking up the small chair behind the harp. "It has been some time since I've practiced the harp. You will forgive me if I'm slightly off."

Hands on her hips, the Dowager Countess of Marsden stalked over. "You cannot possibly think to play alongside a servant."

"Mr. Kosey is an accomplished musician, my lady." Mercy said.

The countess drew close, leaving only the large harp between them. "It is unseemly and I cannot be present for such a display."

The anger that had stewed in Mercy's belly for so many years bubbled up to the surface. She narrowed her gaze on the insufferable woman and kept her voice low. "My lady, you have often treated me little better than a servant, demanding I play for you on command whenever you wanted to make sure everyone in the room knew I was not as good as you. You have embarrassed me on more occasions than I can count. Tonight is no exception. If you leave the room, your daughter and son will be embarrassed by *your* behavior, not mine.

With a barely audible huff, Lady Marsden straightened and walked to the other side of the room, though she didn't leave.

Mercy hadn't seen Wesley move, but she noticed him now a few feet away, leaning casually against the window casing. One side of his mouth pulled up in a grin.

Running her fingers along the cool strings produced a warm lovely sound. "Mr. Kosey, will you pick a piece? I will follow you."

With the composed nod of a butler, Kosey began to play a piece written for the harp by a Frenchwoman named Marie-Elizabeth Cléry. It would showcase her skills far more than his, but his adaptation for pianoforte was inspired.

By the time they played the last note and Mercy placed both hands on the harp strings to cease their vibration, the room was completely still and Mercy's cheeks were wet with tears.

Breaking the trance, she smiled and patted her cheeks.

The room erupted in applause.

Wesley handed her his handkerchief. "You do live dangerously, Miss Heath. May I escort you." He offered his arm.

Patting the soft linen under her eyes, she dried her face. She offered the cloth back, but he declined to take it. With a smile, she gripped it tightly. "Would you give me a moment, my lord."

Nodding, he straightened but did not move away.

Mercy turned to Kosey and stepped close to where he stood behind the pianoforte. "Mr. Kosey, I owe you an apology."

"It is not necessary, Miss Heath." His white teeth shone in a brief smile.

Determined, she pressed forward. "I think it is. I used you to make a point to a few small-minded people. I fear this does not make me much better than those who have used me for similar gains."

Dressed as he was in a white livery and the addition of a white turban around his head, he was by far the tallest person in the room. His serious gaze held hers. "I think you needed to make that point this evening or the rest of your time here at Parvus you would not be content. I am happy to have been the tool with which you shook the foundation of ignorance."

A lump tightened Mercy's throat. "You are too kind, sir."

He bowed.

Wesley cleared his throat. "Miss Heath, may I escort you now?"

With a slow nod, Mercy turned and took Wesley's arm. Almost immediately her three friends pulled her away. The feel of his fine coat under her fingers remained with her even as she left to refresh herself before dinner.

They closeted themselves in Mercy's bedchamber. Flushed but happy, Mercy fixed a lock of hair that had come lose from her coif.

"Even Mother was impressed, Mercy. I think you made your point." Aurora sipped a glass of wine.

Faith took the glass from her and downed the rest. "Goodness, but you do make a stir. I mean, Mercy, you who are always so proper. What were you thinking?"

"That I'm tired of feeling like I'm second best to everyone else in the room." It was the most honest thing she'd ever said or even thought.

Poppy knelt in front of her. "Oh, sweetheart, I hope you don't think that really. We love you. I think of you as my sister. How can that be second?"

Her tears reappeared and Mercy used Wesley's handkerchief to dab them away. She tucked the fine cloth in her reticule and took Poppy's hands. "I know. I think of you all as sisters as well. But over the years, when it is not just the four of us, I have let people like Aurora's mother, Lady Agatha, and Mary Yates make me feel lesser."

Aurora hugged Mercy around the shoulders. "My mother is not fit to judge you. She doesn't even care that I have no interest in marrying. She would have her own daughter be miserable as long as it made her look good in the eyes of society. You should never let her make you feel anything, Mercy."

Faith joined the huddle. "Lady Agatha is long in our past and Mary Yates is left to her own misery. We should feel sorry for her. You are far and away superior to either of them."

Mary Yates was the schoolmate who had dubbed them Wallflowers. Last year they had come into contact with her and she was just as wretched as ever, but Faith was correct that she was also far more pitiable with only her miserable parents for company. "I know you are right. I'm sorry for going too far tonight."

Poppy laughed and squeezed her hands. "Too far? Pish. I thought it perfect and your playing was so beautiful. I would have paid real money to see her ladyship dab tears away from her eyes and I didn't have to spend a farthing. Even she can't help but be mesmerized by how wonderful you are."

"And you never need apologize to us," Aurora said.

"That is certain," Faith added.

Standing, Poppy winked. "I would love it if we could beg off dinner and stay up here all night, but we must return. I can't abandon my husband to his mother for dinner."

Faith smoothed her gown. Her curvaceous form filled it magnificently despite her small stature. "Yes, we must return."

Mercy swallowed down the mass of tears her friends' love locked inside her. "You three go down. I'll be down in a few minutes. I just need to gather my wits to face Aunt Phyllis."

Aurora nodded. "If it helps, your aunt did not look off-put by what happened."

"Thank you." Mercy stared into the mirror until the door, closed leaving her alone. "I'm a fool." She knew she should have played the good girl and kept peace between herself and Lady Marsden, but her temper got away from her tonight. Mr. Colby was likely shocked and would not wish to court her anymore. That was not so tragic, but her aunt would be disappointed in her. Closing her eyes, she took a long breath in before standing and returning to the party.

At dinner Mercy was seated between Rhys and Wesley. She should have been much lower at the table, but it seemed Geb didn't care about such customs and had randomly seated his guests.

Unsure of herself, she spoke only when spoken to through the first two courses. The young chef at Parvus was excellent and Mercy kept her attention on the sumptuous food.

The table was animated with talk of plans for the next day when the fish was set before them and Wesley spoke for her ears only. "Are you all right, Miss Heath?"

"Fine, thank you, my lord." Her heart pounded too quickly.

"That is the second time your emotions overcame you while playing. Does this not disturb you?" He allowed his tone to return to normal conversation.

"I'm sorry if it distresses you, my lord. I am used to the emotional effects of playing a fine piece of music."

Rhys leaned in. "Those of us who have been lucky enough to hear Mercy play for many years have grown to admire exactly how much of herself our girl puts into her music."

"Indeed." Wesley's frown might have bothered Rhys if he hadn't been distracted by the succulent fish plate before him.

It was best to keep her attention on her food and avoid the unsettling emotions Wesley's attention had on her. If she spent too much time with him, she might do something even more ill-advised than playing with Mr. Kosey in mixed company.

"Miss Heath?"

"Yes, my lord?" her pulse pounded in her ears.

"I noticed you have not worn your spectacles this evening."

"I have no need to wear them for dining." Still, the idea that he thought her pretty circled around her heart.

"Yet, I imagine it might be nice to see what one is eating. I know I enjoy seeing everything in my world." He sighed as if disappointed she'd not taken his advice.

Turning toward him, she smiled. "Thank you for your attention, my lord."

"What are the two of you speaking about?" Lady Marsden demanded.

Without losing a beat, he turned to her and grinned most charmingly. "I was wondering why Miss Heath does not wear her spectacles."

A low laugh that held no humor gurgled from Lady Marsden. "The lady is vain, of course."

Aunt Phyllis cleared her throat. "I do not find my niece to be any vainer than any other woman."

While Mercy appreciated her aunt's defense, she couldn't stomach being spoken about as if she were without voice. "I'm afraid it is vanity that keeps my eyewear tucked away unless needed in company. I do wear them more often when at home with only Aurora."

"My fault, I'd wager," Aunt Phyllis said. "In my efforts to have the most respectable men court my dear niece, I have often asked her to remove the spectacles."

"I think they look very fine on you, Miss Heath." Mr. Colby spoke around a full mouth of food. It was the first time he'd made eye contact with her since she'd arrived back from her room. She had a hope that he'd been so appalled by her playing alongside Kosey that he might have given up his pursuit.

She could not be so lucky.

Everyone at the table was staring at Mercy.

"If it is important to all of you, I will wear my spectacles." Reaching into her reticule, careful not to let the handkerchief Wesley had given her be seen, she retrieved her eyewear and put them on.

One by one the group went back to their conversations and eating. Mercy surveyed the table. It was the first time she'd ever been at such a big table with her spectacles on.

"What do you think, Miss Heath?" Wesley's tone was private.

A bubble of nervous laughter tumbled from her. "I think not seeing was very isolating even when in a crowd."

He nodded. "I cannot tell if you prefer to join the group or preferred the isolation."

"Nor can I just yet, my lord."

His smile was intimate, just for her. Mercy wished she could tuck that away with his handkerchief and keep it to look upon later.

Chapter 10

It seemed that Aurora did not like to play cards and so sat with Faith on a small settee against the wall. The room that was generally used for Mr. Arafa's office had been converted into a card parlor for the evening. There were two tables set out for those who wished to play.

Two small chairs faced the settee, arranged for conversation, and Wesley joined the two ladies there. "May I sit with you?"

Faith smiled. "Of course, my lord. That was a very good thing you did at dinner."

"I'm not sure I know of what you speak, my lady." It was a small lie.

Aurora patted her perfect golden hair as if it might have dared slip. "I'm certain that is not true. We have tried for years to coerce Mercy into wearing her spectacles in company without any success. You have managed it in one night."

He wished it had not been so obvious. "I bullied her. I doubt she is as grateful as you two ladies seem to be. Though I appreciate your saying so."

"You must understand," Aurora began, "Mercy is not overly vain. She just wishes to please everyone."

Time to get to work. "And what of you, Lady Radcliff? Do you make a habit of pleasing those around you?"

Sitting back, Aurora studied him. "We all have our roles to play, sir. You must know that."

"Of course. Even an earl must play his part for society's sake. But you hardly seem overly concerned with the opinions of others."

"I have a title and money to protect me and if my contemporaries were to stop inviting me to balls, it would not forlorn me. I would always have my friends." Aurora's grin fell on Faith.

Faith clapped. "It doesn't hurt either that two of those friends have married rather well."

They all laughed.

A ball of white fur shot into the room, followed by a boy of perhaps eleven or twelve. The boy shouted, "Rumple, no!" The dog bounded over to Faith and leaped into her lap with a vigorous attempt at licking her face.

Faith managed to protect her face. "Rumple, down." The dog complied but put one paw and his nose on her leg. His fluffy tail wagged furiously.

The boy had stopped a few feet inside the door. He pulled his cap from his head and worried it in both hands. His brown hair was tousled, but he was clean faced and pink cheeked. "I'm very sorry, my lady. He got away from me and he's gotten much faster since you were here in winter."

"That's all right, Jamie." Faith laughed and petted the dog. "Leave him here with me for now. I'll have a footman take him out before we retire. You should go to bed. It's quite late."

Jamie made a half bow and ran from the room.

"That mongrel should not be allowed above stairs." Lady Marsden's complaints had become expected even in so short an acquaintance.

Aurora frowned in her mother's direction before turning back to him. "Do you like dogs, my lord?"

"I do, my lady. I had one very much like this when I was a boy."

As if he knew he was the topic, Rumple leaped over to Wesley for attention.

"Your mother is right about one thing." Wesley scratched the dog behind his ear, earning him an occasional lick and a sound thrashing of tail to his calf.

"What is that?" Aurora's blue eyes were wide.

"He is a bit of a mongrel. I've never seen such a mismatched group of characteristics on a dog."

Rumple put his head on Wesley's thigh and stared up at him with large, brown, doting eyes.

Faith laughed. "He is odd, but we adore him. He turned up at the West Lane house last winter and I've had him since. He's only a puppy. Not yet a year."

Already as tall as to pass a grown man's knee, Rumple would be a good-sized dog. "He's a bit coddled for the hunt. Will he chase off intruders for you?"

"He is quite protective," Faith said. "But even if he were useless, we would keep him. He was here with us when we needed a friend. We'll not abandon him."

"My mother thinks only pure-blooded animals should grace the parlor." The tone of censure in Aurora's voice spoke much more than her words.

"If that were the case, most of us would need to show ourselves the door." He leaned back against the chair's cushion and watched her.

Aurora nodded, though her eyes narrowed on him. "Indeed, we would."

Rumple trotted away to find Nick and reclined with his head on the duke's feet.

"I have said something that troubles you, my lady?" Wesley asked.

"Not at all."

Faith sat up straighter. Her petite height and curvaceous figure made her both adorable and seductive. The fact that she was a duchess made her even harder to overlook. "You say all the right things, my lord. I think that is what troubles us."

"Are you looking for flaws in my character then?" He looked from the duchess to Aurora.

Aurora was as lovely as any man could hope for. Blond hair, blue eyes, with perfect gentle curves and lovely skin. She spoke with intelligence and never said more than was appropriate. He liked her, and yet...

"You might save us the trouble and tell us what is wrong with you, my lord." Mercy said from just over his shoulder.

Despite his determination to focus on Aurora and thwart his attraction to Mercy, his pulse sped at her closeness. He stood. As she rounded the chair to take the last seat in the grouping, he couldn't keep his eyes from her graceful form.

"I'm as flawed as the next man, Miss Heath." He waited until she sat and then he did as well. "Besides, I'm certain you ladies have discerned all there is to know about me and my family already."

Faith pursed her lips in an attempt to look put out rather than amused, but it didn't work. "We know what is common knowledge, my lord."

"Your Grace, I'm sure you then know that my grandfather lost most of my family lands rather than go to debtors' prison."

Aurora said, "And you have managed to prosper enough to buy back most of what was lost."

A knot formed in his gut. "Most. Yes."

"And I have the last of it." Aurora sighed, not meeting his gaze.

"That is my understanding, my lady." There was little point in lying. These were intelligent women and not to be trifled with.

Mercy asked, "Will you then offer to buy Aurora's property?"

The way her green eyes begged him to consider the option was more than tempting. It was a foolish dream to desire to gaze into those eyes as the sun set and then again upon a new day. He blinked to break the spell she held over him. "I cannot afford to buy the property even if her ladyship were willing to sell."

"I have never seen the land." Aurora's light tone cut into his malaise over what he could not have.

He focused on what his duty demanded. "Have you not?"

"No. We go from Parvus at the end of our stay to see what all the fuss is about. It seems it was a fair price for my hand in marriage. My father was very keen to have it."

"How did the property come to you, my lady?" Wesley had seen records showing Aurora owned his ancestral lands, but he had no idea how that transaction had taken place.

"After Radcliff died, my brother gave me the land. He felt I deserved my purchase price after enduring my marriage." Her gaze was more direct.

"Is a marriage to be endured then?" he asked, unable to let the curious statement rest.

"Some more than others." Mercy's flat tone startled him.

There was something he was missing, but for the life of him, he couldn't think of a way to politely ask what it was. "I'm afraid you have talked me into a corner."

Faith chuckled. "We Wallflowers of West Lane have a way of doing that, my lord. Let me say by way of apology for our secrets, we have much to hide and have told you more than we divulge to most. That must mean we have some trust in your good nature."

"If that is true, I am grateful for it. However, can you give me a way to ask what you must know I want to know without being rude?" He smiled at each of them in turn.

They burst out laughing. Faith recovered first. "I'm afraid not. Perhaps at some point you might venture just to ask the rude question and let the fates decide if you will be granted an answer."

"Oh, is it up to some unseen deity and not the self-proclaimed Wallflowers?"

Mercy eased forward, which forced her bosom to the front of her pearl neckline. "There are some things one must take a leap of faith on, sir."

Distracted by those pearls, he almost missed what she'd said. He longed to traced a path along those pearl beads with his fingers first and then his mouth. Lord, this was impossible. "May I ask how the Earl of Radcliff died?"

"He cheated at cards or some game of chance and was murdered for the deed." Aurora's tone was flat. Not the slightest hint of emotion laced her description of how her husband had met his fate. There was a lot more to know about these ladies.

"I assume he was not gambling at Whites."

Mercy's eyes lit with ferocity. "Radcliff preferred less lofty establishments for his entertainment."

He met her gaze, looking for the detail he was missing, but he couldn't quite put his finger on it. "It is never wise to cheat, but to cheat in an unsavory crowd is quite foolish."

"As the earl learned." There was that rigid anger again from Mercy. How a woman who could glow with the deepest emotion when playing music could also seethe with such intense anger was a miracle of a kind.

All that bottled-up passion led his mind to baser, more intimate thoughts about Mercedes Heath and what it would be like to be with such a passionate woman.

These women were trying to tell him something more than the words, but either the information was flawed or his reckless desires were keeping him from grasping the detail.

"Wes, come play a hand or two. Mercy has left us one short." Nick's call from the card tables saved him from losing his mind.

Standing, he bowed. "Ladies, if you will excuse me."

* * * *

Wesley spent most of the night trying to figure out what clues were hidden in the information they'd divulged about Radcliff and the rest of the night trying to determine if any of it mattered to him. The answer to the latter was no. He needed to regain control of the land his grandfather had lost and nothing was going to stand in his way.

Half-lidded, he went to the stables. Maybe a good ride would refresh him. The sun rose over the sprawling hills and he was once again reminded of what a fine piece of property Parvus stood on.

Inside the garden, Geb Arafa stood from what appeared to be his prayers. A footman folded the blanket Geb had been kneeling on.

Geb turned. "Good morning, Lord Castlewick. Did you sleep well?"

"I'm afraid not. I had much on my mind." When Geb walked to him, he offered his hand for shaking.

His host's hand was rough but warm. "Something troubles you? Is it something I might help with?"

"I was just going to take a ride. Would you care to walk with me to the stables?" Wesley was eager for some exercise to free his mind.

Falling into step beside him, Geb said. "I too often ride to clear my head. You will find I have some fine Arabian horses. Not as big as your English stock, but what they lack in size they make up for in stamina."

"Thank you. I will try any one you suggest."

Geb wore a turban for his morning prayers and a footman ran to him to collect the coiled cloth. When he saw Wesley watching, he said, "I find my English guests are more at ease if as their host, I am dressed in the English fashion."

"I am not ill at ease, Mr. Arafa. If that were the case, I would not have solicited an invitation to your home." Wesley liked his host and it disgusted him that he worried over such things in his own home.

"You are the exception, sir." He waved off the issue. "What can I do to ease whatever kept you tossing through the night?"

Wesley sighed. "I'm afraid it has to do with the ladies and to ask the question I need answered would not become a gentleman."

"Ah." Geb smiled. "Well, these particular ladies are complicated, to be sure."

"Indeed, they are."

Geb stopped as they approached the gray stone of the stables. Several grooms rushed out to greet them. "Saddle Khamsin for his lordship."

With a nod, the lanky groom ran to do his bidding.

"You will enjoy Khamsin. She is fast and loyal. Her name means wind and she is well deserving of it. Names are a strange thing, my lord. I have often wondered if the name makes the person or if it the other way around. Take the two unmarried young ladies staying here at Parvus. Both are extraordinary. Aurora means dawn and the lady shines brightly with much beauty. The dawn is also life giving. Mercedes or Mercy is benevolence, forgiveness, and kindness. From what I have seen the lady is the embodiment of her name. Always forgiving those around her for slighting her. Always offering kindness, when greeted with prejudice. Perhaps I should learn a lesson from her."

Wesley didn't know what to say. There was truth in the assessment Geb had formed around the ladies and their names, but to say anything could give away too much.

Geb sighed. "I should like to have such a choice before me."

"What?" Wesley suddenly realized Geb's misunderstanding of his situation. "I am not in a position to make any choice, sir. The ladies are both lovely, but I do not court either of them and would never think to court them both."

Brows rising, Geb cocked his head. "I must be mistaken then. You are right about their being complications surrounding these Wallflowers of West Lane. Of course, I am not at liberty to divulge their stories."

"I understand."

"You English never just ask the questions for which you so much need the answers. It makes life quite complicated in my experience." Geb turned and walked back toward the castle.

"Indeed, it does." Wesley agreed long after Geb was out of hearing.

The groom brought a pure white mare to the yard. She was a magnificent beast with clear eyes and a full long main tipped in black.

Taking hold of her bit, Wesley gentled her forward. "Khamsin, you are quite the pretty girl."

The horse nudged him with her nose.

Once he'd checked the cinch and hooves, he mounted and trotted out of the yard and down the road. Before reaching the village, Wesley turned to follow a path along a lush green field. The warm sun reminded him that soon his life would make sense. Things would be settled once Aurora was his wife and her lands merged with his.

So why did his mind continue to return to Mercy and her kind eyes and quick wit? She was far too available was the problem. Perhaps Mr. Colby needed a push toward offering. That would solve two of his problems.

He nudged Khamsin into a canter across the top of the ridge.

If Mercy was betrothed, she would no longer be able to keep him away from Aurora and Wesley would no longer be obsessed with her. It was the perfect solution to his problem.

Slightly nauseated by his brilliant plan, Wesley galloped across the lush green hills until he and the magnificent horse were too tired to continue. Turning toward Parvus, he dismounted and they walked back.

Chapter 11

It was a perfect day for a picnic. They loaded up the carriages and rolled out of the Parvus yard toward the lake. There, tables and chairs had been set up with food as well and blankets for those who wished to sit on the ground.

The sun glinted off the lake like a thousand diamonds and Mercy sat with Faith and Poppy. She'd removed her bonnet and allowed the midday sun to warm her face. She would be pink from the indulgence, but she didn't care. The delight in closing her eyes and letting the warmth infuse her was worth a few days of pink cheeks and a few freckles.

"I thought Aurora would have joined us by now." Poppy nibbled on some cake she'd brought from the table.

Faith shrugged. "Perhaps the problem with her dress was more serious and she had to change."

"I thought it was a torn hem." Mercy sighed as she put her bonnet back on and protected her skin. "Surely Jane would have fixed that by now."

"Mr. Arafa sent a carriage back for her. I'm sure she'll be here soon." Faith picked up a slice of cake from Poppy's plate and popped it in her mouth. "Oh, that's quite good."

Poppy nodded. "You were right about the cook here being wonderful, Faith."

"She's just a girl really. Imagine how good she'll be in a few years." Faith grinned and waggled her brows.

"I can't imagine anything better than this cake." Poppy put the plate aside and rubbed her stomach. "But if I eat any more, I will explode."

Several of the men, including Nick and Rhys, were playing ninepin several yards away.

Mercy was careful not to look at Wesley despite his arriving at the carriages with his hair still damp from a bath and smelling warm and fresh on the ride to the site. Proud of herself for giving no outward indication of the effects his bathing had on her, she still noticed that he spoke in confidence with Mr. Colby throughout the game.

What the two could possibly have to talk about at such length, she couldn't imagine.

"He is quite handsome," Poppy said.

"Who?" Faith's attention returned to the ninepin game.

"Lord Castlewick. It's a pity Aurora has no interest."

"I like him." Faith sounded like it was an apology. "I want to find fault in him, but he's honest and easy to converse with."

Mercy's gut knotted. "He wants to marry Aurora for a plot of land. That does not sound like the kind of man any of us could like."

"People have married for less." Faith was the most practical of the foursome.

"Says the woman who married for a love so pure you were each willing to die for the other." Mercy sat up on her knees and stared her friend down.

Not intimidated, Faith gave a weak shrug. "Not everyone is such a fool, Mercy. I would not expect you to display such an unharnessed bout of emotions over a man."

"A piece of music yes, but not a man," Poppy agreed.

Mercy propped her fists on her hips. "When a man makes me feel as infused with emotions as a well-composed sheet of music, I will be sure to marry him. Until then, I am happy to live as I do."

"Miss Heath?" None of them had noticed Mr. Colby' approach.

"Did you win, Mr. Colby?" Mercy asked as it was the only thing she could think to say.

"No. His Grace won, but we will play again. Perhaps you would care to join us?" He'd taken his hat off and worried the rim in both hands.

When he didn't move off, Mercy asked, "Would you like to sit with us?"

He cleared his throat and his Adam's apple bobbed. "I actually wondered if perhaps you might like to join me for a stroll near the lake, Miss Heath?"

Saying no would offend a man who was mostly nice. He'd even put aside his prejudices and had a lively debate with Mr. Arafa at breakfast. Mercy was impressed that he'd taken her words and actions to heart and modified his behavior. From the corner of her eye, she spotted Wesley's dark green coat, close enough to hear the conversation. Careful not to look at Wesley, she stood. "That would be very nice, Mr. Colby."

She took his offered arm and they walked away from the party toward the sparkling lake. Once there she retrieved her hand and kept her fingers clasped in front of her. It seemed her company was at a loss for words. Mercy searched for something to end the awkwardness. "Do you like the country, Mr. Colby?"

He pushed out a long sigh. "Not overly, if I'm honest. I prefer to be in town where there are concerts and the opera. I'm very fond of Bath. Have you been?"

"I'm afraid not." Surprised by the change of subject, she searched her mind for some information of Bath. "My aunt went when her husband became ill, but I was away at school."

He puffed up like a proud pigeon. "I highly recommend it. A shame that the waters did not cure whatever ailed Lady Mattock's husband. He was Sir John Mattock if my recollection is correct, was he not?"

"Yes. Sir John was my aunt's second husband." Mercy had barely known the man, but he had left her aunt enough money to live on for the rest of her life, so she was happy to have had him as her uncle for a while. Besides, if not for Sir John, she would not have gone away to school and would never have met the Wallflowers.

"Perhaps you might convince your aunt to take you to Bath in the spring. It is a bit rainy, but the opera will be in full swing. I know you would enjoy it as the musicians are exemplary." Mr. Colby grinned and nodded as if he'd had the best idea in years.

"Hmmm…I shall consider it, sir. We have traveled and will travel more this year. In the spring my aunt enjoys her country cottage, and I often go and visit her there." Mercy did not add that if she wanted to go to Bath, she would do so and had no need of her aunt to approve the trip.

He waved his hand as if her words were not important. "Your aunt would do well to take good advice. I always take the advice of those I deem wiser on a subject. Take this walk by this very fine lake, for example."

Either she was missing some bit of information, or Mr. Colby was quite mad. "Whatever do you mean?"

He grinned. "I deem Lord Castlewick to be a man of greater knowledge on the subject of women. He suggested this would be a good opportunity for you and me to take a turn together. As it was very sensible advice and well meant, I took it."

Wesley had prompted Mr. Colby to ask her to go for a walk. Wesley had pushed another man's attention on her. Mercy's head pounded. The blood drained from her head and she stopped to regain her step.

"Are you quite all right, Miss Heath? You look very bad." Mr. Colby stood in front of her and peered down his long nose as if studying an insect in the larder.

"I think I will return to Parvus, sir. Thank you for the walk." Turning, she rushed up the slope toward the others.

"Bath would do you well too, Miss Heath," he said from behind her.

When she reached the gathering, she walked past and stopped only to speak to Aunt Phyllis. "I have a touch of a headache, Aunt. If you don't mind, I'll return to my rooms."

Phyllis cocked her head, looked at Mr. Colby rushing up the slope from the lake and then back at her. "Shall I go with you, dearest?"

"No need. I just need a cold cloth and to close my eyes for a few minutes." Spotting the approach of Mr. Colby, Mercy rushed away to the carriage where Kosey handed Aurora down. "Would you mind taking me back to the castle, Mr. Kosey?"

He handed her up and bowed. "Of course, Miss."

Aurora narrowed her gaze. "Are you ill, Mercy?"

Taking her friends hand, she forced a smile. "No. Just a headache from too much strolling by the lake with Mr. Colby."

"Oh dear." Aurora nodded. "I understand. Do you want me to return with you?"

"No. It's a lovely day and you should enjoy the lake. I just need a few minutes on my own." Mercy was lucky to have such good friends. The Wallflowers were like sisters.

Aurora nodded. "I'll see you later then."

Mercy drew a long breath and climbed into the escape vehicle.

"Bath is just what she needs." Mr. Colby's bellows could be heard over the wheels rolling away from the picnic.

It was a short drive to Parvus and the same thoughts rolled over and over in Mercy's head. Wesley had pushed another man to court her. Of course, Mr. Colby was inclined toward her before he'd ever met the Earl of Castlewick, but he'd never taken any bold measures until today. And he had done so today after being pushed by Wesley. Wesley had pushed another man to court her. There it was again.

By the time they pulled to the front door, Mercy's head really was pounding. How had she let him get under her skin so thoroughly? He never had any interest in her. From that first dance, she had been a means of getting close to Aurora and nothing more.

He must be quite a fine actor to have pretended such passion. "Enough," she said just as Kosey rounded the carriage to hand her down.

"I beg your pardon, Miss?" Everything about Parvus, Geb Arafa, and his staff was comforting.

Just like her, these people didn't fit and somehow that made them familiar. She let out a long breath as her feet touched the ground. "Have you ever had a realization, Mr. Kosey?"

"I'm not certain I know what you mean." He walked slightly behind her as they climbed the stairs to the door.

"I've just realized my own stupidity and I suppose now I must laugh at myself for it." Forcing a smile, she sighed again.

Kosey opened the door. He didn't smile or laugh with her. "It has been my experience that whatever things appear when you first witness them is the truth even if the path alters."

"Here we must disagree. I think people play parts, especially people of rank. They play them so well sometimes that even clever women are fooled." She pulled her gloves off and walked to the large stairs leading to the bedrooms.

"If I may be so bold, Miss. Mr. Colby hardly seems capable of misleading you."

Mrs. Bastian tugged her blue turban into place and rushed into the foyer. "You're early."

"Miss Heath is not feeling well."

"Oh? Shall I bring you some tea, Miss?" Concern and kindness etched across Mrs. Bastian's face. The lines around her eyes deepened as she stepped to touch Mercy's cheek.

Gripping the housekeeper's hand in kinship, Mercy nodded. "Tea would be most welcome."

"You go up to bed and I'll send Jane to help you. The tea will be up shortly." Mrs. Bastian bustled away to have tea started and find Jane.

Giving Kosey a nod, Mercy went to her room.

Once Jane had seen that she was not on death's door, Mercy was able to send her away. When the tea came, she sent Cook away as well and watched some sheep playing in the field while she sipped the strong brew.

Mr. Colby did not like the country. Mercy much preferred the quiet bucolic life to the bustle of town. However, he was right about the theater and opera. Perhaps a life with a man who adored music was not such a bad choice for a girl like her.

A band snugged around her heart, making it harder to breathe.

Hearts were foolish, stupid things. She had to be practical. Perhaps Decklan Garrott with his Sussex parsonage could afford a small pianoforte. Now her stomach heaved and she set the teacup in its saucer.

What was she doing? Mercy closed her eyes and stood. No one had asked her to marry them. There was no need to panic. She had to make certain Aurora was safely out of Wesley's clutches. That was her mission. Once that was done and he moved on to another woman, Mercy would never see him again. There was no sense fretting over a man who clearly would like to rid himself of her through any means necessary, including matrimony.

"Are you all right?" Wesley's soft inquiry came from the open door.

Cook had left it open and Mercy saw no reason to get up to close it since no one was at home besides some maids. She stood. "I'm fine now. Thank you, Lord Castlewick. Has everyone returned from the picnic?"

"No. The weather is still fine and they are gathering reeds by the lake." He gripped the door frame and frowned at her.

Unsure what to say, Mercy pressed her hands together to keep from fidgeting. "You do not care for reed gathering?"

His gaze flitted from the window to the desk and to her bed. He stepped back so that no part of him was inside her room. "I...Not particularly."

Swallowing hard, she kept her voice even. "Shall I come down and have tea with you?"

Again his gaze went to her bed.

Mercy's legs grew weak at the notion of what they might do in that bed.

Licking his lips, Wesley closed his eyes for several beats. "Are you well enough to go out in the garden? There is a hothouse and several paths I have not yet explored."

The wiser Mercy warned her to stay away from a man who first foists another man at her and then comes to find out if she is ill. "You are a puzzle, my lord."

"Even to myself," he said on a sigh.

"You are planning to court my dearest friend. Why should you wish to walk with me in the gardens?" There was no sense skirting the issue. What did she care if he thought her bold or brash?

His smile was entirely too disarming. "It is only a walk, Mercy. If I wanted to ravage you, I could just walk into the room and do so."

"And you think I would permit that?" The words blurted out of her mouth indignantly before she could steady herself. He thought her a trollop. A wave of dizziness washed over her, but she held the back of her chair and kept a steady footing.

"I don't know what you would permit, Mercy." He didn't move. "You are as much a puzzle to me as I seem to be to you."

Stepping forward, she fisted her hands at her sides. "Then let me be quite clear. I am no lightskirt to be toyed with, my lord. I do not give you permission to use my first name. We are not friends. You want to marry my friend and she does not wish to marry at all. She is tolerating you because of her mother and for no other reason. You think your title can buy you anything. You are no different than any other spoiled lord. I let the way you look at me when I play go to my head, God help me. It was foolish and dangerous. Do not seek me out in this manner again." Mercy gripped the heavy oak door and closed it sharply in Wesley Renshaw's wide-eyed face.

For safety against herself more than him, she threw the bolt before she went to the bed and cried into the pillow.

* * * *

Unsure how much time had passed, Mercy startled when a knock came to her door. She went to the wash basin and wet her face and dried it before going to the door.

When she opened it, the hallway was empty. On the stone floor lay an envelope with "Miss Heath" written in a fine hand across the front.

Taking it, she peered down the corridor in both directions and found no one. Mercy stepped back and closed the door. Wesley's fine handwriting lined the letter.

My Dear Miss Heath,

Forgive me. My behavior with regard to you has been abominable. I cannot tell you why you bring out the worst part of my nature, but the fault lies completely with me.

From the moment we danced all those months ago, my mind has continued to stray toward thoughts of you rather than where is should be. Let me assure you, that will no longer be the case.

I have responsibilities to my family and my title. As you know, others in my line neglected their duty and have left me to clean up a rather large mess. I shall not give further detail as it is not possible the gossip of London hasn't set the entire story at your doorstep by now.

I shall tell you honestly one thing and then never speak of it again. If I were free to do as I wish, I would properly court you in the manner you deserve.

My desire to court Lady Radcliff is sincere and without reproach. Forgive me if this information is unpleasant to you. It is a truth and I see

*no reason to keep silent on the matter as it is an amicable match and the
lady is aware of my intentions.*

*You, I am sure, will also make a good match. You are a bright, talented,
and beautiful woman. Any man would be lucky to have you for his wife.*

*As we must remain at this party for many more days, I propose a
truce. I wish you only good things, Miss Heath. You must believe me
when I tell you this. My hope for your continued and future happiness is
in absolute earnest.*

Please accept my apology and request for friendship between us.

With great admiration,

Your friend,
Wesley Renshaw.

Mercy put the letter on the desk and sat back against the hard wood
chair. In one short note, he had said all that she would ever need to know. He
wanted her, but he would not pursue her because she was not rich enough.

Footsteps in the hallway alerted her that the others had returned.
Standing, she folded the letter and tucked it inside her bodice. Later, when
she had the strength, she would burn it and never think of it again.

Yes, that is what she would do.

She pressed her hand against the parchment tucked between her dress
and her chemise and an ache from that constant band tightening around
her heart emanated outward.

The Wallflowers knocked and rushed in.

Mercy attempted a smile.

"Good lord, what's happened?" Aurora flew across the room and pulled
her into her arms.

Poppy closed the door.

Faith appeared ready to do battle.

Mercy let the sobs out again. She pulled the letter from her bodice and
handed it over to Aurora.

Chapter 12

Without a wink of sleep, Wesley hesitated to go below to break his fast. His head hurt almost as much as his stupid heart. He would hold the look of disdain in Mercy's eyes as she scolded him in the hallway for the rest of his life. And rightfully so. He had no business worrying after a woman who was not his concern.

He would never have her and he needed to accept that before he did more damage to his reputation in her eyes. It was bad enough to live with the fact that he'd considered making her his mistress; it was unthinkable for her to know how base he really was.

Her good opinion shouldn't matter. She shouldn't matter. Aurora was the woman he would marry. She was titled, the daughter of an earl, and she held the title to his ancestral home. Nothing would get in the way of his goals, not even his own ridiculous desires.

Steeling his emotions and placing them under tight control, he stepped into the dining room. As the worst possible scenario seemed to always follow him, Mercy sat in the center of the table surrounded by her Wallflower friends.

They all turned to look at him.

Mercy's cheeks were rosy and her eyes clear, with no sign of distress marring those green orbs that haunted him day and night. She raised her brows. "Did you not sleep well, my lord?"

The entire situation was unbearable. "I'm afraid not, Miss Heath."

"That's unfortunate," said Aurora. "Was your bed not to your liking?"

A muffled sound that was half cough and half laugh, if Wesley wasn't mistaken, came from Poppy, who covered her mouth with her hand.

What could he say? "One never sleeps as well when not in one's own bed. At least, that has been my experience."

"You look positively drawn out. Mr. Kosey, bring his lordship some coffee, please." Faith smiled at the butler and then at Wesley.

"Right away." Kosey left in the direction of the kitchen.

"Thank you, Kosey. Ladies, you are all too kind." He took a plate and contemplated the buffet. All his favorites were there, but none of it was appealing.

It wouldn't do to have nothing on his plate when he sat and he couldn't run for the hills no matter how tempting it was. Slopping coddled eggs and sausage on his plate, he gave himself an extra moment to settle his anxiety before pulling back his shoulders and sitting at the table.

Kosey arrived with his coffee and a plate of toast. "I thought some toast, my lord."

"Thank you. This is perfect." Pushing his eggs and meat aside, he took a slice and spread it with butter from a crock on the table.

Faith held a teacup in front of her mouth, but amusement lit her eyes. "My lord, has your lack of sleep damaged your appetite as well?"

"It would seem so, Your Grace."

Mercy watched and kept the slight smile plastered on her lips. He'd noticed she always did this when she didn't want anyone to know what she was really thinking. Despite her efforts, he saw concern in her eyes and longed to know if it was for him or if something else troubled her. Had his letter done more harm than good?

The entire situation was pitiable.

He forced his attention to his toast and coffee and allowed himself to be satisfied that the strong brew was better than any he'd had in his own home and the toast would keep him fortified until his appetite returned.

Aurora dabbed the corners of her mouth and set her napkin next to her plate. "It seems we are to ride out to some caves in the hills today. I do hope you'll be joining us, my lord."

For a long moment he stared back and tried to decide if she was being sarcastic or sincere. Seeing nothing but honesty in her sky-blue eyes, he said, "I wouldn't miss it. This area has not disappointed thus far in its beauty. I imagine today will be as lovely."

An odd noise came from Poppy's direction but by the time Wesley glanced at her, she'd steeled her features into a pretty but passive smile. "We four have decided to ride in the open carriage, but the men were planning on going on horseback. My mother-in-law and Lady Mattock will be using the barouche. We shall be quite the happy party."

While Faith, Poppy, and Aurora all looked as happy as Poppy's tale indicated, Mercy kept her eyes downcast and only glanced up to force her smile. "It should be a lovely day," Mercy said when the table's attention turned to her for no apparent reason.

Sitting back, he took full measure of the ladies and sipped the last of his coffee. "I often find myself wondering if I am the joke or am about to be played the fool when I'm in the presence of you four. Can you imagine why that would be?"

Aurora's grin went from polite to amused. "I have no idea what you mean, my lord."

"Beautiful day." Mr. Colby's bellow filled the dining room, crashing through the levity that was building. "I took a walk and now I understand we're to have a bit of an adventure." He waved a hand at Kosey. "Fix me a plate, will you?"

Rounding the table, Mr. Colby sat across from Mercy. "Feeling better, Miss Heath?"

She pushed her plate aside. "I'm quite well, Mr. Colby. I must change for the day. If you'll excuse me."

Standing as Mercy did, Wesley met her gaze and gave a brief bow. "Miss Heath."

Once she'd left the room Colby continued. "I had hoped she would have played for us after dinner last night, but I suppose her health was paramount."

The other three ladies stood as if strings were attached to their heads. They gave scathing looks to Mr. Colby and excused themselves.

Wesley was standing and shaking. Unable to say anything civil, he remained silent even after the women left.

Kosey placed a loaded down plate in front of Colby.

With great flair, he tucked his napkin into his neckcloth, then fork in hand, he gaped at Wesley. "Fine bit of advice you gave me yesterday, my lord. Miss Heath and I had a nice talk while we strolled together. I think she'll be more than glad when I'm ready to give in and ask for her hand."

"Give in?" Wesley's toast rumbled in his belly.

Mouth full of sausage, Colby nodded. "Women don't like to think you care too much for them. They want it to all seem like a chore. And after all, she'll have my protection and money as compensation and I'll have her musical talent at my disposal."

"Disposal." Wesley stood and tossed his napkin on the table. "Mr. Colby, did it ever occur to you that consistently asking Miss Heath to play for your entertainment is much like asking Kosey to fill your plate when you are fully capable of making your own?"

Colby cocked his head. "He is a servant. It's his job to make the guests comfortable."

Since his wide eyes indicated no understanding that filling a plate and playing pianoforte on command were similar demands to those he found beneath him, Wesley shook his head and asked Kosey, "What time are we meant to ride out, Kosey?"

Kosey's mouth turned up in a knowing smirk. "After the dew burns off a while, my lord. You have time to walk the gardens here if you like."

"Thank you." Wesley went to the back of the house, where a small ballroom gave a fine view of the veranda and the gardens beyond.

Lady Mattock stood near the stone balustrade, her head tipped to one side and her eyes closed.

Careful not to startle her, Wesley opened the French door and stepped out. The sound that filled the air was unfamiliar, but definitely a stringed instrument. Rounded tones rolled into each other in the most sensual way. No violin or cello made such a sound.

Before he reached her, Lady Mattock's eyes opened and she smiled warmly. "You look quite tired, my lord. Are you well?" she whispered.

"I am fine, just a difficult night's sleep." He let the warm sounds fill him. "What is she playing?"

"It's a Spanish stringed instrument called a guitar. My late husband and I traveled there and I brought it back for her. She's far better than the man we heard play it in Spain. I never dreamed it could sound like that when I picked it up. I just missed my girl and thought she would like something different." There was both pain and joy in her memory.

Wesley longed to know more about the time that these women had been together and apart. "You couldn't take Miss Heath with you when you traveled?"

A long sigh and the deepened creases around her mouth made her look her age for the first time. "I was newly remarried. Lord Mattock was a good man, but the notion of raising my niece didn't appeal to him. He did send her to the Wormbattle School. I thought it too far away, but he promised we'd visit often."

"I think Miss Heath would not have traded her experience at school if given the choice."

The darkness lifted from her eyes. "No. She adored being away and the friends she made there."

The song ended and from some place unseen to the veranda, she began another.

"I wonder how she learned to play so well on an instrument I assume she'd never heard played." He mused in a whisper.

Lady Mattock laughed. "She searched out a Spanish musician living in Lucerne. I have no idea how she managed it, and I'm fairly certain I would not have approved of the introduction. However, she did learn to play."

"That much is certain. You must be very proud of her." He looked in the direction of the sound. His heart pounded in his chest so hard. He'd promised her friendship in his letter yet all he could think of was how much more he wished for.

"I must go and rest before our outing." She pushed away from the stones.

"Lady Mattock, may I ask an impertinent question?" He begged himself to keep quiet.

The girlish smile on her lips told him everything. "My favorite kind."

"Why are you so keen to marry Miss Heath off to one of these men like Mr. Colby?"

One curved brow rose over her green eyes. "What is wrong with Mr. Colby? He is wealthy enough and smart in business if not very socially adept."

"He will never love her."

He had meant to say it to himself, but after the long silence, he realized he had said the words aloud.

Lady Mattock stepped closer. "Love is not the only reason a lady marries, my lord, and you should know that very well. Love is a luxury."

Mentally shaking himself, he took a step back and bowed. "Of course. Forgive me."

There was a long moment when she stared at him but said nothing. He waited, expecting her to speak, but she curtsied slightly and walked away. At the French door, she turned back and stared at him for a moment before disappearing inside the house.

Without so much as a thought about whether or not it was a good idea, Wesley stepped into the garden and followed the sultry sounds of the guitar that would lead him to Mercy.

Sitting on a low bench at the base of a tree, Mercy's hair caught the dappled light coming through the leaves. Flowers of white, pink, and lavender bloomed along the path and in the patch behind her, but she was by far the most beautiful flower. *You can like a flower and if you do perhaps you might pick it and put it in some vase for display as Mr. Colby wished to do. This woman should be nurtured and loved beyond all things.*

Lord, he'd become a poet. Closing his eyes, he listened from several yards away.

When the strains stopped, he found her watching him. "My lord?"

"I heard you from the veranda." He couldn't think of anything intelligent to say. "Please don't stop on my account. It's quite beautiful."

A soft blush pinked her cheeks as she tipped her head down toward the instrument. "Some people don't think it's real music, but I love the warm tone of the guitar."

"Anyone who has heard you play it cannot believe it is anything but the finest music." When he reached the patch of grass surrounding the tree, he stopped and waited for an invitation to sit.

Moving over to one side of the bench, she nodded to the other. "Thank you for your letter. It was very kind in light of the situation."

"It was not nearly enough. I feel I've failed miserably in my writing skills. In fact, I have failed in most ways where you are concerned. I shall never be able to deserve your forgiveness." His chest ached and there was no cure for what ailed him.

"It was kind, and in my experience, people rarely bother with kindness." She bestowed a bright smile on him.

"I find myself wishing I had some musical talent to contribute to our friendship, Miss Heath. Your magnificent play makes me want to take up the violin or pianoforte. Do you think me too old to learn?" He touched the arch of the shapely guitar.

Her long fingers gripped the long neck and pressed a sequence of strings while with her other hand she played. "I never think it's too late. If you like, you can come to West Lane and I will teach you. You can then see if you can convince Aurora to marry you and also learn to play, if you are in earnest."

"You would teach me to play?" He'd not meant to sound so surprised, but wondered how she could be so generous to him with all the liberties he'd taken without any right to one.

"We are friends, after all. I don't think you will succeed with Aurora, but you will learn to play music if you apply yourself." The music changed to a slow strum of notes.

"I will think about your offer. Thank you."

She nodded.

"I didn't think you wanted me to marry your friend. You have been intervening at every turn to this point."

Sadly, she put the guitar aside and faced him.

He felt a keen loss when she stopped playing sounds that sang to his soul.

"I want Aurora to be happy. You are not an evil man or a man who would harm her. You are well liked by Nick and Mr. Arafa has shown that he likes you as well. The Wallflowers pledged a few years ago to keep each other safe from men who would do us harm. I can see you would never hurt a woman intentionally. You are a smart, kind man and perhaps Aurora will change her mind. As you wish me happy, I wish the same for you, my lord." Standing, she gripped the neck of the guitar and lifted it.

Rising with her, his pulse pounded like it might jump from his body. "You are far better to me than I deserve, Miss Heath.

"Maybe you are too stern with yourself." She cocked her head and smiled up at him. "I had better change for our little adventure."

He watched as she sauntered down the stone path, her white dress touching the ground behind her, leaving the grass between the stones slightly bent in her wake. She was an angel on earth, but she was not to be his angel. Mercedes Heath was to be his friend.

Wesley's stomach growled. The toast was not going to suffice. He went to the kitchen to beg a few bites before they left.

The cook was a young girl who offered him a seat with a shrug.

Sitting at the long table in the kitchen was not normal for an earl, but Cook didn't seem to mind and kept bringing him meats and other treats as she worked on the luncheon, they were to bring with them to the caves.

"Do you often sit below stairs, Wes?" Nick stood in the doorway with his arms crossed over his chest and a wide grin on his face.

Thea, the young cook, made a quick curtsy and exited the kitchen.

"I had a bad night and an interrupted breakfast. I needed something more to eat if I'm to survive the day."

"Thea is a good girl and loves to feed people." Nick sat across the table. "I understand you're determined to marry Aurora, but what is all this fuss I hear about Mercy?"

He'd almost forgotten what good friends all the ladies were and how good friends often talk and husbands often hear things. "There is no fuss. Miss Heath and I are friends. She is a lovely girl, but I am in need of a landed wife. Lady Radcliff has not told me to trot off, so I continue my pursuit."

Nick nodded. "I see. That will be a difficult goal as I've said before. Aurora is determined never to marry again. Still, I see no harm in you trying. Who knows, maybe you'll land happy somehow."

The possibility of happiness never really occurred to Wesley. Contentment that he had done the right thing was the best he could hope for. "I suppose anything is possible."

Frowning, Nick shook his head. "You might think about the notion that you could live a long life, my friend."

Puzzled, Wesley wasn't sure how to respond. "I hope to."

"A long life where you are not living is a long sentence."

"I don't know what you mean."

"Do you remember Walter Polk?" Nick crossed his arms over his chest. Once Wesley nodded, Nick continued. "He married a very wealthy girl. She's not hard to look at, but not terribly smart."

Wesley sat up. "But Walter is one of the smartest men in England. He took first in several courses at Eton."

"Indeed." Nick sighed. "Have you seen him lately?"

"Not in a while."

"He has a wife who he cannot like and does not love. She spends the money at every turn and does not even offer good conversation. He's aged ten years in the last two and in my opinion the fault lies in a bad match that appeared fine on paper."

"I see where you're going with this, Nick. I appreciate the concern, but Lady Radcliff is a bright, beautiful woman. I don't think your comparison is obvious."

Nick drew in a long breath while nodding. "True. Aurora is a fine woman. But if you cannot love her, will you live or just be alive? And what of her? Will she be happy?"

A heavy weight settled on Wesley's shoulders.

Nick continued with a laugh, "Of course as a man in love, I'm always wanting the same for my friends. Perhaps it's too fanciful."

"It is not the way things always are done. Most people live amicable lives with spouses they respect. Your marriage is an anomaly, Nick."

The weight of his responsibilities grew heavier until he worried the floor would not hold him.

"I'm sure you're right." Nick waved a hand in dismissal and strode out of the kitchen.

Chapter 13

Mercy's boots were wet through after trudging around several caves. Her blue dress was six inches deep with mud and she felt more exhilarated than she had in weeks. Perhaps the answer to the Wesley problem was continued physical exercise. At least it kept her out of Mr. Colby's way as he declared sport of all kind to be wasteful in the extreme and remained enjoying the vistas with Aunt Phyllis and the dowager.

He advised that after Mercy's sudden illness the day before she might benefit from staying behind as well.

Mercy ignored him.

"Can't we stop now?" Faith's whining was followed by a humph as she collapsed on a boulder jutting from the side of the hill.

Nick sat beside her, smiling. "I don't know why you wanted to come along when you hate this type of exercise, my love."

"Because the idea of staying behind with Mr. Colby and her ladyship was less appealing. Forgive me, Aurora, Rhys." Faith gave each sibling a nod of apology for speaking unkindly of their mother.

Rhys laughed and leaned against the rock wall where the cave opening was. "No need to feel badly. Mother is the key reason I am trudging around in the mud. Though I have to say, she has been rather quiet."

"Biding her time," Aurora warned. "She's trying to figure out a way to force me to marry poor Lord Castlewick. Once she finds her means, she'll pounce."

Mercy's banded heart hurt.

Smiling, Wesley raised his brows. "I had no idea her ladyship was so underhanded. She came to me directly in London."

"Ah, but now she has you in her sights." Nick mimicked a shotgun in hand and the jolt of the rapport.

Poppy leaned her head against Rhys's chest. "I'm tired. Can we go back now?"

"We shall have to locate our host. He seems to have been misplaced." Nick stood and stretched his back.

Looking around, Mercy's chest tightened. "I saw Mr. Arafa not five minutes ago up on that ridge." She pointed.

Nick started up the hill toward where she pointed and the rest of the party followed.

Faith made a low groan but took Nick's hand and stomped along with him.

A weariness came over Mercy. The idea of returning to her aunt and Mr. Colby and all the expectations that came with it was an anvil around her neck. She did not want to marry for convenience or the happiness of another. Perhaps it was time to discuss those things with her aunt.

Taking up her damp skirt, she stepped forward. Her foot slipped in the mud.

Wesley took her elbow in an instant, keeping her from falling. "Careful, there, Miss Heath."

Once she was steady, he released her. The warmth of his hand at her bare elbow remained to torture her with the need it left behind. "Thank you, my lord."

"Are you feeling all right?" He should have left her and joined the others, but he remained at her side.

"I'm weary of doing what is expected of me." Why had she said it aloud? It was what she'd been thinking, but she'd not intended to share her thoughts.

A slow sorrow filled his warm brown eyes. "It is part of life, I'm afraid."

"It makes me quite cross, if I'm honest." She still had no idea why she continued to say what she was thinking.

"You are never cross, Miss Heath. I have seen you in a temper but being cross would indicate you take out that anger on those who don't deserve it. I cannot imagine you ever doing so." He met her gaze and the hint of a smile touched his lips.

Climbing the hill, she said, "Perhaps you just don't know me that well."

"I know you, Mercy." His voice was so soft she thought she might have imagined the words.

At the top of the hill the area was laid out before them in rolling hills and pastures. The village lay nestled at the edge of the forest and Parvus stood sentinel on the hillside.

Mercy pressed her hand to her chest. "How beautiful."

"Yes." The same whisper just behind her ear.

A wave of delicious need swept through Mercy and she had to close her eyes and regain her senses.

"Geb, you had us worried we'd lost you," Nick said.

Geb waved from halfway down the hill, then climbed to join the crowd. "I wanted to take a look at the view. Very kind of you all to worry."

Poppy walked next to Geb. "Of course, we worry if you go missing. You are part of our little group now, Mr. Arafa. You'll never be rid of us."

Stopping, Geb turned to Poppy and bowed. "It is my honor to be considered your friend. Thank you, my lady."

Aurora joined them. "You are one of our dearest friends, sir. Never doubt that. And we take our choice in friendships very seriously."

"My deepest thanks."

"I adore you, Mr. Arafa, but can we please go back now and stop all this infernal walking." Faith's whining made everyone laugh.

Nick lifted her into his arms, making her scream. "I shall take you back to the carriages directly, my dear."

Settling into his arms, Faith put her arm around his neck. "This is much better."

"They seem quite happy," Wesley said once everyone was a few yards ahead of them.

Happiness for her friends filled Mercy. "Yes. Both Faith and Poppy have been very fortunate in their marriages."

"Will you marry Mr. Colby?" A stern edge tainted his voice.

Her nerves flitted in every direction. She kept her words even and calm. "I don't see how that is any of your business."

"It is most certainly not my business, but I'd still like to know," he said with a harsh laugh.

She could avoid the question or lie. Yet when she peered into Wesley's eyes all she wanted to do was tell him everything. "As we are friends, I see no harm in telling you that I have no intention of marrying Mr. Colby. He is a fine man, but I do not think we would suit."

The rigidity in his shoulders eased. "I'm sorry I pushed him toward you yesterday. I should have known better."

"Let's catch up with the others, shall we, my lord?"

They approached the carriages and a fierce frown on Jemima Draper's face hid nothing of her anger over Mercy and Wesley walking together. "My Lord Castlewick, I have had the most wonderful idea."

His lips twitched. "Have you, my lady?"

"Aurora and I are going to Cheshire to view her land when we leave Parvus in a few days. Miss Heath and Lady Mattock are joining us for the trip. You know the area; it would be such a help if you came along and gave us the grand tour." Jemima beamed with the brilliance of her plan.

Perhaps she thought to toss Mercy out of the carriage when they reached the edge of some cliff. From the way she glared at her, that might just be the case.

Wesley blinked several times. "That is a wonderful offer, but I shall only accept if Lady Radcliff is in favor of the notion."

Looking shocked with her mouth and eyes wide for an instant, Aurora recovered. She glanced at Mercy before returning her attention to Wesley. "Of course, my lord. You would be most welcome. I'm sure you long to see the property as well."

He stared at Aurora a long beat as if he were defining the truth of her kindness. Finally he bowed. "I would be delighted to accept. Thank you, ladies."

If a rocket had dropped on the road in front of them, Mercy would have been less shocked. Not only was she to spend the remainder of her time at Parvus pretending she and Wesley could be good friends. Now she was to endure another week or more in his company with Aurora's mother's disapproval as well.

Blindly, Mercy walked to the carriage and, not waiting for assistance, she climbed in.

Once they were rolling toward Parvus and the men on horseback were well ahead while Aunt Phyllis and Jemima's carriage was behind, Aurora took Mercy's hand. "Did I do the wrong thing, Mercy?"

Her friend's eyes were full of worry. Mercy squeezed her hand. "What else could you do? It would have been rude to deny his joining us. Besides, you were correct, he probably does long to see that land again."

Aurora sat back but kept her gaze fixed on Mercy. "If you wish it, I will take him aside and ask him not to come."

"No. It will be fine. We are to be friends, after all. If that is true, I will have to learn to be in his company with ease." The notion that at any point Mercy and Wesley could be in the same place together and there be any sense of impartiality was ridiculous, but Mercy kept that to herself.

"So, we are no longer trying to run him off or embarrass him?" Poppy twirled a long lock around her finger.

Faith's hair sprang out in every direction and she pushed it bit by bit into her bonnet before retying the peach ribbon. "He is a nice man. Aurora may not want him, but she can just tell him so. She's a widow not a debutante who can be bullied into marriage. Her mother will have to get over it. I like Lord Castlewick. Don't you, Poppy?"

"Of course I like him. What is there not to like? I just thought the point was to get rid of him so he wouldn't bother Aurora anymore."

Aurora's steady gaze on Mercy forced her to look at her hands. "Lord Castlewick would make a fine husband. Perhaps you should reconsider, Aurora. He might make you happy."

"Do you think so?" Aurora's voice was light and a sense of humor underlined her words.

Mercy looked at her. "I think he is as likely to make you happy as anyone. Do you like him?"

"I do like him, but I have not changed my stance on marriage. However, I think he fits in nicely with our little band of friends. We shall keep him around a while longer and see where it takes us." Aurora glanced from Poppy to Faith and the three nodded.

* * * *

"This is our final evening together." Geb lifted his glass of wine. Though he would never taste it, he always had it filled for such occasions. "Thank you all for coming to Parvus and enjoying all the area has to offer. I could not ask for finer friends. To friendship."

Everyone lifted their glasses and repeated the toast. Even Jemima had grown fond of Geb and his very fine hospitality and warmth of personality.

"I thought as it is our last night, we might relax in the salon with cake. Kosey will play for us and if anyone wishes to play cards that will be possible as well." Geb put his untouched glass down and smiled warmly at the table.

"Perhaps Miss Heath will delight us with her talent as well," Mr. Colby said.

Nick held her chair as they all rose to go to the salon. "Perhaps, Mr. Colby."

Leaning his head near her, Nick whispered. "Don't let them bully you, Mercy."

The warmth of friendship spread through Mercy. "Thank you, Nick. I won't. You know, I don't hate to play for people."

"I know." He offered his arm as his wife walked in with Poppy. "But I also know it is not nice the way certain people think you must always be available to play on command."

"I am lucky to have such good friends as you to stand by me. I think I will play as the wilds of Cheshire are not likely to have any instruments and my guitar is rarely appreciated in the parlor." She allowed him to lead her into the salon and bring her to where the other Wallflowers had collected by the windows.

"Then we shall all have a treat," Nick said. "And Mercy, your guitar shall always be welcomed in the Duke of Breckenridge's parlor." With a smile, he went to stand with Geb by the pianoforte.

"Of course it will be." Faith gaped at her husband's back. "Why on earth would you think it would not?" She turned to Mercy.

Laughing, Mercy waved off her friend's concern. "It was nothing. Poppy, did you taste the cake yet?"

"No, but it looks wonderful, with some berries for topping. Will you have some with me?" Poppy loved her sweets and never let an opportunity to have them pass her by.

"I will." Having some cake would at least give her an excuse to choose the time for her performance. No one will expect her to eat cake and play harp or pianoforte at the same time.

"Is something funny?" Poppy slipped her arm through Mercy's as they crossed the room to where a footman was slicing cake and adding a generous helping of red and blue berries.

"Not really. I was just wondering when my playing music for the joy of it had become a chore for the delight of others. I suppose it's my own fault." Mercy accepted a slice of cake and a fork.

Poppy took a large bite and savored it with her eyes closed for a moment before looking at Mercy. "How is it your fault? It is people like that Mr. Colby who bully you and demand you play at all times who have ruined your wish to play in company."

Kosey played softly on the pianoforte.

"I should have been average."

"Oh, Mercy. Don't be ridiculous." Poppy took another generous bite. Once she had enjoyed it thoroughly, she added, "You could no more hide your talent than I can hide my clumsy nature. We are what we are."

Mercy stepped closer. "You are far more than a torn hem on a dress, Poppy. You are the bravest person I know."

Poppy blushed. "Well, don't tell anyone."

"Everyone who matters already knows." Mercy squeezed Poppy's arm. Taking a deep breath, she ate another bit of cake and berries. Lemon and vanilla along with the sweet tartness of the compote was perfect in her mouth. Mercy left her plate on the table and walked to the harp.

Kosey raised a brow. "What shall we play, Miss?"

"Perhaps you can just play whatever you fancy, Mr. Kosey, and I will follow along." Mercy considered Kosey to be an excellent musician and her curiosity led her to this little test.

He beamed. "As you wish."

The new music that the butler played was fresh and vibrant as the household of Geb Arafa. There were parts that warned of danger and others that spoke of lofty goals and love affairs.

Mercy listened through the first stanza before she followed along with the sultry sounds of the harp, and let them be an undertone highlighting the magnificent piece that Kosey had obviously composed.

When the song ended, Mercy's emotions had gotten the better of her again. Tears rolled down her cheeks without regard for the discomfort it caused some members of the party.

The hum of music had barely silenced when applause rose up from the room and a white handkerchief appeared before her.

Wesley's eyes were full of admiration…or passion, Mercy couldn't tell as she took the offered cloth. Whatever was in them it was not mild friendship; of that she was certain.

Patting dry her face, she handed the handkerchief back. "Thank you, my lord. I'm sorry to be in constant need of a gallant gentleman."

She'd meant it as a joke, but he frowned. "You need not be embarrassed by the passions you display when you play, Miss Heath. Without them the music would be barren and hardly worth listening to."

"That is very kind of you to say. Excuse me." She got up and waited for him to back away so she could retreat and collect herself.

For a long moment it seemed as if he wouldn't move, but then he stepped to one side. "Of course."

In that brief moment as she passed him the scent of soap, cigars, and everything good and familiar filled Mercy's head. Biting the inside of her cheek to keep from grabbing hold and never letting go, she kept her steps steady and excused herself from the room.

In the hallway she leaned against the wall and tipped her head back. The pins in her hair poked at her skull, a good reminder to keep her wits about her. It should be an easy enough thing to stop thinking about a man she had no business dwelling on. He wanted to be her friend and nothing more. He had made that quite clear.

It's just the music. Kosey's composition was too emotional and full of transition. She would give herself a few moments and this would pass.

Aunt Phyllis rounded the threshold and Mercy stood up straight. "Aunt?"

"You really can do anything when given a bit of music. I'm constantly amazed and proud of you, Mercedes." Aunt Phyllis leaned against the wall next to her.

Mercy relaxed. "I'm happy to have you proud of me. I have tried since my parents died to do exactly that."

Stepping in front of Mercy, Phyllis frowned. She put a finger under Mercy's chin and lifted her head. "But, my dear sweet girl, I have always been exceedingly proud of you. I adored the child who came to me so brokenhearted and my heart bursts for the young lady you've become."

Bringing her voice to a whisper, Mercy fought back tears. "But I cannot like Mr. Colby. I know you want me to marry and be settled, but I'd rather die a spinster than marry a man who only really loves my playing and knows nothing of me."

Aunt Phyllis pulled her into a warm hug and chuckled. "Mr. Colby is a good man, but you do not have to marry him. I agree, he seems to have little real feeling for you. However, I seriously doubt you will die a spinster."

Something in her aunt's tone made Mercy step back and look into her eyes. "Why do you say that?"

"Because another man seems quite smitten with you." Aunt Phyllis's grin spread across her lovely face, making her even more so.

"Lincoln Baker is no better than Mr. Colby." Mercy propped her hands on her hips in an effort to be more forceful with her decree that she'd not marry one of these men who loved music and not her.

Aunt Phyllis laughed and threaded her arm through Mercy's elbow. "Oh, my dear, you are precious."

She guided them back into the salon, leaving Mercy no opportunity to ask what she meant.

Chapter 14

It was late when Wesley went downstairs to find something to read. His mind would not put aside the way he longed for Mercy or the way he did not have that same desire for Aurora. It was very much like him always to do everything the hard way.

In the study, he put his candle on the desk and searched the solitary bookshelf for something to occupy his mind. He trailed his fingers along the titles of books he'd never heard of and some in languages he'd never seen. Finally, his hand settled on a copy of *King Lear*. Perhaps a good tragedy would be enough to make him sleep.

He lifted the book but it only rose an inch and then something held it in place. A snick sounded inside the bookshelf.

Wesley stepped back.

The shelving was ajar from the wall on the right side. He gripped the side and pulled. The shelves easily opened to reveal a dark corridor beyond.

A thrill of excitement heightened Wesley's senses. He listened, but the hallway was silent. The air was fresh, which made him even more curious as to where the secret passage might lead.

Taking his candle, he stepped behind the bookshelf, through an opening big enough for one person to pass. The floor sloped down and went straight for about twenty yards before ending at a door. The entire idea was strange beyond anything Wesley had ever encountered.

Wesley pushed open the door and stepped into a surprisingly lit room.

Mercy shot up from a red and gold flowered sofa. "Don't let the door shut."

The heavy door slammed behind him. His imagination had conjured a dungeon or hidden treasures at the end of the hall. A study with Mercy in her nightclothes was the last thing he'd expected.

She ran toward him, her white nightgown and cotton robe billowing around her and her long reddish blond hair loose down her back. Eyes wild, she passed him and grabbed the door handle pulling desperately. "No." Wesley turned and pulled her gently back from the door. He tried the locked handle himself. "How long have you been in here?"

She pressed her head against the wood. "An hour. Maybe more."

"I'm sorry." He wasn't sure what else to say. He would have liked to have been her savior, but he wasn't really sorry to be stuck in a lovely little parlor with her. The dark red rug was thick and two chairs in gold velvet faced the sofa. A small desk sat in the corner and six small tables were arranged with treasures.

She sighed and returned to the sofa. "It's not your fault. The door closes very quickly. It is how I ended up here. I should have walked out of the study when the bookcase opened, but my curiosity was too great."

He sat next to her, but didn't touch her. "What is this place?"

Shrugging she pointed at the tables. "I think Mr. Arafa keeps his favorite treasures here. I'm not sure what else. I thought it would be too rude to search the desk. Since the door has no keyhole on this side, I assume there is some trick like *King Lear* to escape, but I couldn't find it."

The tables held an elaborate gold box with emeralds embedded in the top, a statue of a goddess with six arms, a silver and gold horse fitted with armor, a diamond necklace that the queen would be honored to wear, a scroll with writing Wesley didn't recognize, and a miniature of a woman and man from the East. The man in the picture was an older version of Geb, likely his father if Wesley's guess was correct. "There are worse places to be trapped."

Head in her hands, she tilted to look at him. "I am ruined. You do realize that, don't you?"

He would never allow such a fate to befall her. "Perhaps I will have more success at finding a way out of here."

Turning back into her hands, she sighed. "Be my guest."

Wesley spent the next hour searching every wall in the perfectly square room. He found several sources of ventilation that ingeniously brought fresh air into the underground room. He found a box of candles, so at least they would not be left in total darkness, but he did not find a way to open the door.

Mercy had curled up in the corner of the sofa with her arms wrapped around her knees and her head buried.

Resigned to their fate, he joined her. Leaning in, he kissed her knuckles. "Mercy?"

"Yes, Wesley?" She peaked up, allowing him to see her vibrant green eyes. His name from her lips was like a balm to his soul. "I will find a way to make this turn out well. I promise."

A sad smile pulled at her mouth. "That is kind of you to say."

He wanted to yell to the rafters that he meant every word and ease her worry. He wanted to make her happy, but since they'd met, he had never done so. "I am sorry our relationship has been less than ideal."

The low round chuckle that shook her curls and drew her head up. "That is very gently put, Wesley. Since the moment we met, it has been rather a disaster."

He took one of her hands in his and slid his thumb across her soft palm before feeling the pad of each callused finger.

She drew a long shaking breath and watched their hands intertwine.

"Not a disaster." He couldn't help laughing at the memory of her spectacles being smashed on the dance floor. He loved that she was wearing the replacements now. "Why did you want to put those spectacles on when we danced so long ago?"

Pulling her hand back, she let her legs fall over the edge of the sofa, pressed her hands with stiff arms on either side of her thighs, and faced forward. "I'm rarely asked to dance and certainly not by an earl. It was so lovely, I wanted to see you better. For the memory of the moment. I think the crushed spectacles was my penance. Perhaps we should have heeded the sign."

"I felt a very strong connection to you from the moment I saw you and wanted very much to know you better." Nerves tightened his throat, but it was only the two of them and it was unlikely they'd be rescued before morning. It might be his only chance to tell her these things.

"No. You thought me ridiculous. How could you not? You felt sorry for me and to ease that discomfort, you purchased these spectacles, though how you obtained the right lenses, I do not know." She wrapped her arms around herself.

"I asked Nick if he knew what doctor you used and he gave me several possibilities. The morning after the ball, I sent my valet around to those physicians and obtained the information." It hadn't been very difficult or a secret as to how he'd replaced her property.

"Very clever." She shivered.

It was cool in the room in the ground. He had no jacket to offer her as he'd left his room in only his breeches and blouse. Opening his arms, he said, "May I keep you warm?"

Those expressive eyes stared at him a long moment before she gave the slightest nod that accompanied a shrug as she leaned toward him.

The moment was meant to be savored, as he wrapped his arms around Mercy Heath. She didn't push him away or worry about a crowd of people spotting them. She sank into his embrace, as if it were where she'd always been meant to rest. Her silken hair slid along his jaw where her head tucked against his shoulder.

A low contented sigh pushed from her sweet lips. "Why must this feel so right?"

He'd wondered the same thing about her a hundred times. "Perhaps it is right, Mercy."

"You want to marry Aurora and get your land." Her voice was flat but there was no accusation, just facts.

"Yes. I had a very well laid out plan." He spoke mostly to himself

"Do you think we might not speak? Could you just hold me and forget about good plans and the inevitable morning mess I will be in? For these next few hours might we pretend this is right and good?" Her voice broke just enough for the emotions of her plea to pierce his heart.

"I will do whatever you wish, Mercy." Easing back against the cushioned arm of the sofa, he pulled her with him. Her nightgown was the only thing between his hands and her flesh. The effect made his head spin and other parts of him suffered from heightened awareness as well.

She lay half on top of him, her knee slid along his thigh.

Bringing his legs up, he entwined his bare feet with hers. "Mercy?"

"Yes?"

"I want you more than I ever wanted anything in my life. You must know that. I want to see you cry when you play music. I want to rescue you with a handkerchief. When you feel ill, I want to be the one to see you well again. I want to make love to you and show you all the wonders of what can exist between a man and a woman." He closed his eyes and waited for her to slap him.

She pressed her hands against his chest, and he looked into her curious gaze. "You want to do all of those things while you are married to Aurora and in possession of her lands in Cheshire?"

"I do not want to marry Aurora. She is lovely and bright and she owns the land I need." His heart pounded as he watched his legacy float away.

"Aurora would make a wonderful wife for any man." Mercy continued to watch him. "You would be lucky to have her."

"I am aware of that." His jaw hurt from the strain of clenching his teeth.

"If I made love to you, Wesley, I would have to walk away from my friend. How could I look your wife in the eye after we'd been intimate? Don't you see, as much as I desire you, it cannot happen. I'm not cut from the kind of cloth that makes a good mistress, with secrets and assignations." She drew in a shuddered breath. Her hair fell across her eye.

Wesley tucked it behind her ear. "I will not marry Aurora, Mercy. I told you, I will make this right and I meant it. When we are discovered in the morning, I will tell your aunt of my intentions to marry you."

"Marry me!" She pushed away from him.

The squeal was so out of character, Wesley flinched. He recovered quickly enough to take hold of her wrists and keep her from moving off. "Of course, I will marry you. Do you think I would allow you to be ruined? I may have wished to wed to better my family's position, but I am a gentleman, Mercy."

The expressions in her eyes changed so quickly, he didn't know what he'd seen. Was it fear, worry, anger, or had he imagined an instant of joy? When she spoke, there was something resolute in her voice. "I don't know what to say."

A knot tightened within him. "Say you want to marry me too."

She disengaged her wrists from his hold and sat up. "It doesn't matter what I want. To marry because you are forced into it by an accidental circumstance cannot make for a happy marriage. You would come to resent me for what I'd cost you."

Cost him? Was she mad? He stood. "Mercy, I want you. This…" He waved a hand at the room. "Is just the means of getting me what I want."

Standing, she faced him. "I will not marry because of this odd circumstance, but if you promise not to marry Aurora, we might have this one night together. Anyone else, but not Aurora."

Of all the possible things he'd thought she'd say, that was not even on the list. Never in his life did he expect Mercy to refuse his proposal and offer her body all in one breath. Caught between elation and heartbreak, what did one say? "You do not owe me anything, Mercy. I have realized in the last few days that I can never marry Aurora and see you regularly without touching you. There could be no happiness in that ending."

She moved closer until her body pressed to his ever so lightly. "It is not a matter of debt but a matter of need, Wesley."

The tips of her pert breast touched his chest and her abdomen pressed to his. He longed to grip her bottom and pull her close. "You are killing me. Please, Mercy, do not offer me half of what I want. I am not man enough to resist."

Delicate as a flower, she raised her hand and cupped his cheek. "Why should you resist? I'm not a girl of sixteen who doesn't know what she offers. I may be untried in the bedroom, but I'm old enough to know what happens there. I understand desire far better than I ever have before."

"Mercy." The plea in his voice was unmistakable. He needed her, wanted her physically, but so much more.

Drawing a deep breath, she lifted on her toes and pressed a soft kiss to his lips. "There are two possible ends for me, Wesley. I shall either die a spinster, or I shall marry a man whom I can never love. Personally, I prefer the first. But, tonight, here and now, I can know what it is to be loved entirely. In this room I am the only woman in your world and for a time, I can pretend this is reality."

"Tomorrow, when we are found, I will offer for you. Why can you not see that option?" He slid his hands from her shoulders to her elbows and drew her in until only their lips did not touch.

"There is no tomorrow." She closed her eyes and lifted her chin. Her lips parted just enough for him to glimpse the tip of her pink tongue.

Helpless, he dove in and devoured her willing mouth. Sweet and warm, she was a confection he couldn't get enough of.

A soft moan escaped as she toyed with the hair at the back of his neck.

Rigid with desire, he let his imagination meet reality and gripped her bottom, pulling her hard against him.

She issued a sharp gasp as his shaft pressed against her center. He couldn't blame her; he wanted to call out a hooray at how perfect she felt.

The silken strands of her hair slid over his hand and even that was erotic. He tasted each lip separately then both together. Diving his tongue between her lips, he sipped her essence and the addiction was true and heady. Her tongue touched his with sparks of even finer things to come.

Kissing her and holding her should have been enough, but the promise of more was too great a gift for any man to resist. He gripped her hair and pressed desperate kisses along her jaw and throat. Her pulse ticked against his lips fast and hard. His body thrummed as desperately. "Mercy, tell me to leave you alone. Tell me this is wrong."

Gasping for breath, she said, "I don't want to stop." Those deft hands that breezed so effortlessly against the strings of a harp or the keys of the pianoforte slid down and unbuttoned the fall of his breeches before he could think to stop her.

"Mercy." He didn't know what else to say. Her hand wrapped around his shaft, unpracticed but sweet and deviously delicious.

She wrapped one leg around his, pressing her core to where her hand held him. Her groan vibrated inside him.

Grabbing handfuls of cotton, he worked her gown up until it forced her to release him. She lifted her arms, and he pulled the gown over her head. Her hair fell wildly in her face, and he brushed it back, cupping her sweet face in both of his hands. He kissed those full lips gently. She was his. Let the world and his family be dammed.

He stepped out of his breeches and pulled his blouse over his head. All their clothes lay in a heap on the floor as he wrapped his arms around her back and lifted her.

She wrapped her long legs around his hips and the way their bodies nearly joined made him lose a step. "You are more beautiful than I could ever have imagined."

He eased her onto the sofa and kissed his way down her elegant neck to her chest. Making a pass over one nipple, she arched into his mouth and called his name. Unable to resist, he sought out the other and gave it equal pleasure.

With another cry, Mercy gripped his hair, pressing him tighter to her flesh. He longed to taste every inch of her and continued down her slim waist and hips. He left a trail with his tongue down her inner thigh, bending the knee and kissing the sensitive skin at the back before making his way back up to her sweet center and slipping his tongue inside her.

No honey had ever tasted sweeter. He might never get inside her; his body was near bursting at just the taste and feel of Mercy. It wouldn't matter as long as she had her pleasure. He swirled his tongue around her folds and the sensitive bud above.

Mercy let out the sweetest, softest keels as she pumped her hips against his mouth and found her release.

Holding her close until the waves passed and her breathing softened, he kissed her between her breasts. "You are magnificent."

"I want to give you pleasure as you have given me," she whispered.

Perhaps if she had not offered more, he could have walked away, but he was not a saint. Wrapping her legs around his waist, he lifted her to straddle his lap then rose and carried her to the desk.

Her sultry smile accompanied a raised brow. "Oh, this is wicked." She took her hands from his neck and placed them flush on the desk behind her, leaving herself open to him.

The door lock released.

"Someone's coming." He moved to shield her from the door.

"No. My hand pressed some kind of panel. I think that is what opened the door." She picked up her right hand and after a long moment the door locked again.

It was some kind of sign that he was wrong. He'd never believed in signs before, but all that searching for a way out and now they had found it. Wesley pressed a kiss to her cheek. "You should put your nightgown on and go back to bed. I will stay here and be found in the morning. I think Mr. Arafa would know someone was in here and it is better that they find me alone. Your reputation will remain safe."

Sitting up, she crossed her arms over her chest, hiding herself from him. "You...you want me to go?"

He ran the back of his knuckles down her soft cheek. "I want you safe from any harm. Both the harm I might do and the harm of gossip. Mercy, do this for me. Go back to your room."

Rising to her feet, she went around him, careful not to touch him. She pulled her gown over her head and with a rigid back walked to the door, which had locked again.

"Mercy?"

"Yes?"

"Please don't think I am sending you away because I don't care. I care very much." The pain in the center of his chest was so acute, he wondered if he might be actually dying of a broken heart.

She studied him from across the room. "I understand completely. I'm quite bright, you know."

"Brilliant actually." He smiled and hoped she saw how much he regretted not having the entire night to love her.

Running his hand along the top of the desk, he found the panel and pressed down.

The lock snicked open, Mercy pushed passed it and disappeared down the hall.

Wesley let the door lock, dressed, and sat on the sofa waiting for morning. If he was lucky, Geb or Kosey would find him before breakfast. If not, Mercy would leave him there to rot for all eternity. Who could blame her?

Chapter 15

Mortified by her own behavior and embarrassed that Wesley had sent her away rather than take her virginity, Mercy made sure the last of her things was packed in her trunk.

She had always been told men valued virginity. At least he wouldn't feel obligated to offer for her. No one need ever know what had transpired or what had been said. She would just forget the entire thing.

Oh, but the way he'd touched her, how could anyone forget such pleasure?

Wesley knew as well as she did that he was too far above her station for anything to come of one night of passion. He'd been kind when he'd said he wouldn't let her be ruined, but he must feel the utmost relief that he had avoided being held to that fate.

At least he'd been found late enough that she'd finished breaking her fast before he arrived in the dining room. She didn't know how she would endure the trip to Cheshire. He would return to courting Aurora. There was nothing to stop him.

Though, he had promised not to.

Still, no one knew about the indiscretion and he would likely forget it soon enough. He needed the land to right a wrong done by his grandfather. She understood, but it made her want to cry when she thought of watching Aurora marry him.

Shaking her head, she stood and pushed the lid of her trunk closed and scolded herself, "Aurora is not going to marry him. She doesn't wish to marry again. Stop your nonsense."

"Who are you talking to?" Faith popped her head in the room.

Mercy sighed. "Myself. Did you hear me?"

"Just talking, not the content." Faith put her hand out for Mercy to join her. "Shall we go down so the footmen can get our trunks loaded?"

Taking her friend's hand, she swallowed down her worries. "Yes. Let's go. You have a long trip back to London and I'm off to Cheshire."

"Is something troubling you?" Faith stopped them just three steps down from the upper-floor landing.

"No. I didn't sleep well last night is all. I'm just tired." It was a half-truth and she hated not sharing everything with her fellow Wallflowers, but some things had to remain secrets.

Faith pulled her into a hug. "I suppose you'll tell me the rest when you're ready."

It was no surprise that Faith detected something was missing. They continued down the stairs. Mercy took Faith's hand at the bottom. "I shall miss seeing you every day. It has been a treat for all four of us to be together like this."

Rumple barked and ran through the foyer with Jamie, the house boy, running after him. "Rumple!"

Laughing, Faith smiled. "It was not quite like school or before Poppy married, but it was rather wonderful. Perhaps we shall make a new pact to spend some weeks away together annually until we are all too old to travel."

"That is a marvelous idea." Aurora entered the foyer in her sky-blue travel dress and wrapped in a shawl.

"Ladies, we must be going," Rhys called from outside the open front door.

Nibbling on a biscuit, Poppy arrived and frowned at her husband. "We are saying goodbye. Don't be so bossy."

Mercy loved these women so much it nearly brought tears to her eyes. "A new pact, then. Each year we will promise to spend some weeks away together as a family."

"Oh yes!" Poppy agreed, just understanding the conversation.

"Agreed," Faith said.

"I can think of nothing I'd love more," Aurora said.

They hugged as one, then turned to the door.

Kosey stood just outside Parvus and bowed to them.

"Goodbye, Mr. Kosey. I hope we shall see you again soon." Mercy loved everything about Mr. Arafa's houses, both the one near London and this one in the country.

"That is my wish as well, Miss."

They said their goodbyes to Mr. Arafa and loaded into their respective carriages. Mercy and her aunt rode together, while Aurora and her mother rode in Wesley's carriage. Her ladyship insisted it would be terrible for his lordship to have to travel alone.

Jane and Aunt Phyllis's maid, Helen, shared the carriage with Mercy and Phyllis. Her ladyship's maid traveled in the other carriage, while Wesley's valet rode atop with the driver.

It was going to be a long day for all.

With one last wave, they were on their way to Cheshire.

"Do you think Lord Castlewick is in love with Aurora?" Aunt Phyllis stitched a bit of cloth in a round frame as she asked the idle question.

"No." The ever-tightening band around Mercy's heart tugged painfully.

"Nothing else, Mercedes? Just no?" Aunt Phyllis put her stitching in her lap and looked at Mercy.

Mercy shrugged. "I think he likes her and he needs her Cheshire property. You asked if he loved her, and I do not think he does."

"What makes you say so?" She went back to her needlework.

Mercy wasn't sure how to answer. Obviously, she couldn't tell her aunt about the night before or how he would have offered for her if they'd been caught in a compromising position. She would never trap a man that way. "I have observed in ballrooms and parties that when men are in love, they look at the object of their affection with longing and rush to be near them. I have not detected that kind of attention between Lord Castlewick and Aurora."

Without lifting her head, Aunt Phyllis raised her brows to glance at Mercy. "No. I have not seen that type of attention given to Aurora. How did you like Kosey's composition last night? I thought it remarkable. I wonder how he learned so much as a servant."

The change of subject was as much a surprise as it was welcomed. "He is an excellent musician. I wonder that he wasn't always a servant, Aunt. He seems to have manners befitting a gentleman."

"Is that why you always call him Mister?" Her aunt put her stitching aside as the road became uneven and it was necessary to hold her seat.

"I suppose it is. I enjoy Mr. Arafa's way of life. I like his staff and find his homes comforting in a way I have not since my parents were alive. They were not that concerned with what people outside the house thought." Mercy could almost see her mother standing in the parlor at the house in Grosvenor Square. She was dressed to go out and Father kissed her shoulder when they thought she wasn't looking.

"Your parents were lucky to have security while they lived. It is unfortunate the properties and monies passed to your cousin and even more unfortunate that he married before you came of age. It would have been nice if the two of you could have made a life together with the funds afforded your father." A rare bitterness filtered into Aunt Phyllis's voice. The idea of marrying her cousin Alfred made Mercy a bit ill. "I would not have liked to marry Alfred, Aunt. He has the sweatiest brow and a look that even at fourteen I didn't care for. I cannot fathom why the man is always sweating and thus has a foul odor."

"You would have done very well to have married Alfred Heath. He is respectable and rich. What more could you want?" Her tone scolded, but Aunt Phyllis hid her amusement behind a gloved hand.

"I don't know, Aunt. More." Mercy was a fool and there was no point avoiding the fact. She didn't want to marry for any other reason but love and now she knew she would never have that.

The rutted road bounced them around mercilessly for several minutes before it smoothed out as they climbed a hill.

Aunt Phyllis relaxed against the cushion. "Strange how poor Castlewick got locked into a secret room all night."

"Yes. Very strange." It was a chore to keep her voice disinterested.

"He spoke to me as we broke our fasts. I had the impression he wanted to discuss something, but the dowager arrived and he said no more." Aunt Phyllis gave her a pointed stare.

"What on earth might he have wanted to discuss, Aunt?" Mercy wished the carriage seat would swallow her up, but she had no such luck. She really had no idea why Wesley might want to speak to her aunt. As they were not discovered, no one else knew she had been with him. Certainly no one knew how intimate they'd become. He had no reason to speak to her aunt other than to ruin Mercy's reputation. But why would he do that? It would make him look nearly as bad.

"Is there anything you'd like to tell me, Mercedes? Have you and his lordship been courting right under our noses?"

"Certainly not. He wants to marry Aurora." Mercy answered far too quickly and vehemently. She'd been shocked by the question. Why would her aunt think such a thing? Had someone seen her return to her room early in the morning? Had she looked as thoroughly ravaged as she'd felt? Good lord, she hoped that was not the case.

Phyllis shrugged and picked up her needlework. "Men and women often think they want one thing and sometimes realize they need something else entirely."

Digging a book out of the small bag she'd brought inside the carriage; Mercy gave herself a moment to compose her emotions. She opened the book to where she'd marked it with a blue ribbon. "The Earl of Castlewick would have no interest in a woman of no title and no finance or connections. He needs to marry Aurora or a woman with enough money to allow him to buy Aurora's property. He has not hidden this fact. He told Aurora from the start that he needed the land in Cheshire."

"I'm sure you're right." Aunt Phyllis frowned but did not look up from her work. "Though I do think he's gone about courting Aurora rather passively. I wonder if he would have given up already were it not for her ladyship's constant efforts to push him toward her daughter."

"I doubt he would give up. His grandfather lost his family estate. As far as I can tell, he has no choice but to gather the lands and house back, if he's to restore the Castlewick name to what it once was." Mercy hadn't meant to make such a declaration, but it was all true and all common knowledge. She'd not read one word on the page she'd been staring at, but she turned to the next anyway in hopes her aunt would think her only mildly interested in the topic of Wesley.

A slow smile pulled at Phyllis's lips. "Pickering Renshaw was a rascal."

Mercy put her book aside. "Did you know him, Aunt?"

She nodded. "Of course, I was just a girl and not rich enough to tempt him, but there were many of my contemporaries who were tempted. Renshaw loved to gamble and he loved women. Even after he married, his antics did not stop and, of course, that was his undoing."

"How so?" Mercy sat forward.

"As charming as he was—and mind you, he was all charm—Pickering played the wrong man for a fool." A long sigh pushed from Phyllis and she gave up on her sewing.

"You mean how he lost his estates while gambling?" Mercy asked.

"Oh, my dear, it was quite worse than that. That is true, of course. Pickering loved to gamble but he was not very good at it, and once he depleted his coffers he began losing lands that had been in his family for generations. It was a sad state and would have gotten worse, I fear." Phyllis stared out the window at the passing countryside.

Mercy was bursting with curiosity. "What happened?"

"I told you that Pickering had two vices. Gambling was only the first. Women were his true downfall." She cocked her head. "Though, in retrospect, perhaps what happened saved the rest of the family."

"Aunt!"

Laughing, Phyllis continued. "After his marriage and the birth of his son, Pickering went right back to seducing any woman who would have him. One night he managed to seduce the Countess of Denby. She was a lovely young thing and married less than a year. When the earl found out about his wife's indiscretion, he called Pickering out."

"Good gracious, that's positively barbaric, Aunt."

Phyllis shrugged. "It happens more often than you might think, Mercy. In this case, it was over quickly and Denby had his revenge. Pickering was shot in the stomach and did not survive the night."

It was hard for Mercy to equate the rake her aunt described with his grandson. Wesley gave no indication he might jump from bed to bed. In fact, when she thought of it, since she'd met him, he'd hardly glanced at another woman and that included Aurora. "Something puzzles me, Aunt Phyllis. Why didn't the last earl begin the process of regaining what his father had lost?"

"The last Earl of Castlewick was a nice man. He loved his family and did as much as he could for them, but he had no head for business. He never earned enough from what was left of the estates to buy back any losses, though he did keep them out of debtors' prison." Phyllis picked up her sewing.

Even if Wesley's father had not been capable of restoring what was lost, he had instilled the desire to make things right in his own son. Mercy ached for what Wesley had gone through to gain back so much. He was so close to getting what he wanted. Aurora was the right choice for him and perhaps for her as well. If only Mercy's heart didn't have to be battered in the wake of everyone else's happiness.

* * * *

They arrived in the small town of Plumley near supper hour and pulled into The Smoker, a quaint coaching inn with white exterior walls and a thatched roof. The surrounding countryside was lovely and in the distance the peaks of a large manor house could be seen over the trees.

Mercy stretched her legs with a short walk over to an old oak tree that drifted like a green cloud with one end pointing out to the north. She stayed outside the canopy of its thick leaves. Rounding to its eastern side, she let her bonnet fall to her back and raised her chin to the warm sun.

"This is a lovely spot," Aurora said.

Mercy opened her eyes and looked out over the rough hills of Cheshire. "It's breathtaking."

"Did your aunt make the trip difficult?" Aurora moved to stand in front of Mercy.

"Not really. Why do you ask?"

"Because Mother and your aunt are bickering in the yard and you ran away from the carriages as if they were on fire." Aurora raised her brow and gave her a small smile.

In an effort to see the ladies in dispute, Mercy peeked under the tree's low limbs. "Whatever could they be arguing about?"

"Mother believes Lord Castlewick has lost interest in me and that it is your fault." There was only humor in Aurora's voice, no sign of disappointment.

Unable to catch her breath, Mercy stuttered, "Y...your mother is mistaken. I have done nothing to encourage affection from his lordship, nor do I think his interests have altered." Mercy couldn't bear Aurora thinking that she might be self-serving.

"Of course she is, Mercy." Aurora put her arm through Mercy's and gave her a squeeze. "I know you haven't chased after Lord Castlewick. Though I wouldn't blame you if you had."

"Aurora!"

"What? He's quite handsome and obviously smitten with you." Aurora sounded perfectly happy with the idea of Wesley liking Mercy.

"Everything he's done since Nick's ball has been in an effort to convince you he is worthy of you. It has nothing to do with me." Mercy's heart broke in two, but she knew it was the truth.

"Perhaps at first. But I think he may have had a change of heart."

Mercy scoffed. "His heart has nothing to do with any of this. He is interested in that." She pointed to the majestic spires of the manor house that was likely the ancestral home of the Earl of Castlewick.

Shrugging, Aurora pulled Mercy along toward the inn. "We shall see and, in the meantime, I think this will be a fine adventure. In the carriage, his lordship said there are ruins to explore and Plumbly has an assembly on the first Friday of the month. So we shall go to a ball tomorrow too. I'm happy to be in a place where no one knows anything about me or my past."

"Then you had better swear your mother to secrecy, Aurora. I'm sure she's already explaining to all who will listen your lofty rank." Mercy giggled.

Aurora frowned and sighed. "You're probably right. Still, I think we will have a fine time here in Cheshire."

"I will be happy to just get through the night without being embarrassed beyond my ability to breathe in and out. My aunt and your mother fighting over whether or not Lord Castlewick likes me better than you does not bode well for a quiet evening." Her nerves were frazzled and she rarely felt so out of sorts.

"I will protect you from my mother, but you're on your own with Aunt Phyllis." Aurora laughed as they entered The Smoker's busy yard. "Besides, we have at least a week in this fun place with glorious views and explorations too. Put a smile on your face, Mercy. Don't spoil a fine time away from town."

Her friend was right. They were in a beautiful and new part of the country. There was much to see and do and plenty of space to avoid those whose company was not pleasant. Unable to help herself, Mercy grinned. "You're quite right. Do you think it necessary to dress for dinner?"

Aurora examined their traveling clothes and shrugged. "I think we will be in fine fashion for dinner in a coaching inn. Let's see what the rooms are like."

It turned out that the rooms were plain but comfortable. Mercy and her aunt were down the hall from Aurora and her mother, while Wesley was one floor up and had a suite of rooms. At least that is what the maid who never stopped talking the entire time she fussed around the room said. Jane, Mercy and Aurora's maid practically had to toss the girl from the room to give them some blessed silence.

"Thank you, Jane," Aunt Phyllis said. "That girl is a hazard."

Mercy giggled. "I think she is bored, but I am grateful for the peace."

"Will you change for dinner, Miss Heath?" Jane asked.

"No. I think my traveling clothes are good enough for dinner here." Mercy glanced at her aunt for approval.

Once Phyllis nodded, Mercy continued. "You can go and see if Lady Radcliff needs anything."

With a curtsy, Jane left.

Mercy went to the wash basin and wet her face. The cool water made her feel less covered in grime from the road. A heaviness hung over the room. "I heard you and her ladyship had words when we arrived."

Aunt Phyllis waved a hand in dismissal. "I think Jemima had expectations that she feels are falling apart. I don't disagree with her, but it has nothing to do with you, my dear. You have behaved as you always do, beyond reproach."

"No matter how I behave, her ladyship will manage to find fault. I should have stopped trying to please her long ago." All the wasted moments when she had tried to get Aurora's mother to afford her some respect flooded Mercy's memories.

"Well said, Mercedes. Jemima has long thought herself too grand for anyone's liking." Aunt Phyllis took off her pelisse and checked her hair in the mirror. "Well, shall we go down and see if the inn serves a decent meal?"

Mercy dried her face and tucked a strand of hair behind her ear before following aunt Phyllis out. Her heart pounded with the anticipation of seeing Wesley. Other than a passing glance when they left Parvus, she'd avoided seeing him all day. But as she stepped into the public rooms and dining hall, he was a shiny penny among the tarnished ones. His broad shoulders and crisp white cravat anchored the far end of the room.

The long hall spanned the length of the inn, with rows of tables and benches filling most of the space. At the far end were several round tables for private dining. Diners occupied more than half the tables and many farmers and tradesmen joked and laughed as they drank ale in celebration of the end of a workday.

Mercy looked away from the crowd and once her gaze met Wesley's the other people might have disappeared. Wesley stood at a round table for five and waited as they approached. There was an awkward silence where he dragged his eyes from Mercy to Aunt Phyllis. "Lady Mattock, Miss Heath. I hope the jarring roads were not too unpleasant for you."

"We survived, my lord. Thank you. I hope your journey was pleasant as well." Aunt Phyllis sat in the chair he pulled out.

Mercy made to sit next to her aunt.

In a quick move, Wesley rounded Aunt Phyllis and held Mercy's chair as well. "Are you well, Miss Heath?"

"Yes. Thank you, my lord. I am quite well." It was hard to catch her breath with him hanging over her ear and the warm scent of him flooding her senses.

It would take a miracle to survive the evening.

Chapter 16

Wesley had been a fool to think it would not affect him to see Mercy again. After the torturous ride with Lady Marsden going on and on about how Mercy was little more than a penniless orphan, and he unable to defend her, he'd honestly believed seeing her would be easy.

Aurora scolded her mother several times, but to no avail. The woman was relentless.

Leaning over Mercy's shoulder gave him the heady sense of her. It was an effort not to grab her in his arms and carry her away. "I'm pleased to hear it. I worried the carriage might not be well sprung enough for the rutted roads."

Her throat bobbed in the most delectably alluring way. "It was kind of you to worry over us, my lord. We are of a hardy stock and were not too badly jostled."

"I am relieved." Straightening, he pulled his attention away from Mercy enough to see that Aurora was distracting her mother with some bit of pottery on the banister.

She made a quick glance at him.

If not for his feelings for Mercy, Aurora would be a perfect wife. He liked her tremendously and she was a keen observer. For those who were her friends this was of great value. He wouldn't like to be an enemy of hers or any of the Wallflowers, for that matter.

Rounding the table, he held the remaining two chairs and waited for them to cross the room.

"It smells quite good," Aurora said once she'd thanked him for holding her chair.

"I hope you ladies don't mind, but I took the liberty of ordering for the table. The proprietor recommended the lamb and it seemed a sensible choice." Jemima smiled too sweetly. "That was very kind of you, my lord." Aurora rolled her eyes. "Shall we go and see the manor house tomorrow?"

"If you wish, my lady." Wesley had not been to Whickette Park since he was a boy. "It has been closed up for some time. Hopefully the structure is sound."

"We shall just go and see what it has to offer." Aurora offered a kind smile. He gave a nod. "It might be best to keep your expectations low, my lady."

With a laugh, Aurora said, "I love an adventure. Perhaps not as much as Mercy does, but I'm still excited to see Whickette Park."

Mercy looked as if she would speak, but closed her mouth and stared at the empty place before her.

If he'd claimed that Mercy had said ten words during the meal, it might have been considered an exaggeration. Granted Jemima Draper barely drew breath while she monopolized the dinner chatter. Still, Mercy was disturbingly quiet. He wanted to pull her aside and find out if she was troubled by their intimacy in the hidden office. Had he hurt her in some way? He was sick at the possibility.

Before he had any opportunity to gain a private conversation, the dishes were cleared away and the ladies went to bed, claiming they were tired after a long day.

Wesley went to his room. His exhaustion was welcome and he fell directly to sleep, only waking in the early morning hours. The sun was not yet up, but he washed and dressed and went downstairs to see if a carriage large enough for five could be secured for the rest of their stay in Cheshire.

Her figure was unmistakable. He'd seen it in his dreams for months and held her in his arms just two nights earlier. Standing under the large old oak, Mercy watched as the sun turned the sky a myriad of reds and purples.

Before he could think better of it, he crossed the yard and went to her. "You did not sleep well, Mercy?"

She pulled he shawl tight around her. "Well enough. I love the early morning before the house wakes. I'm in the habit of rising early."

"I too am fond of seeing the sun rise." Letting silence fall between them, he stood next to her as the sky turned orange before showing the blue of a clear day.

Pointing to the rooftop in the hills, she faced him. "Is that your family's estate?"

"It is Whickette Park. It was in my family for five generations before my grandfather's blunder." It took a great deal of control to keep the bitterness from his voice.

"Then you own a great deal of land in this area?" She surveyed the vistas again.

He loved the way her little nose turned up slightly at the end and the smattering of freckles that had spread along the bridge and her cheeks since they began their visit to the country. "A fair amount."

"It's quite beautiful here and the air is so clear." She drew a deep breath. The rise and fall of her breasts were maddeningly distracting. Wesley turned to observe the views, which could not compare to her beauty. "You have spent little time in the country?"

She shrugged. "Some, with my aunt, but most of my time has been in London. Of course, Switzerland was different. The air there was clean and crisp. It was an astounding place to live."

"I'm certain it was."

Mercy looked away from the view and swallowed hard before pulling her shoulders back. "I think I should apologize for my awkwardness."

Stepping until there was little space between them, he shook his head. "No. I was only worried that I had offended you and you might have lost any respect for me."

"No. You were very kind to not tell anyone I had been in that room with you, or about my wanton behavior." She blushed and stared at the ground between them.

"Mercy?"

"Yes?"

Unused to a shy Mercy, he tried to look in her eyes and see what emotions lay there. "Look at me, please."

When she did, tears filled her eyes.

His heart lodged in his throat. "Do you regret our time together?"

"Do you?" A full tear rolled down her cheek.

A horse bolted from the yard, creating a commotion that sent the animal and several stablemen running and screaming. The wide-eyed beast tore off in Mercy and Wesley's direction.

Grabbing Mercy around the waist, Wesley dragged her out of harm's way, deep under the oak.

The horse ran past with men making a commotion that would not inspire the animal to return.

Mercy laughed. "They will do little good hollering like that. If I were that horse, I wouldn't stop until I reached Scotland."

"You would think they had more sense." He grinned and reveled in her warm body pressed to his.

"What on earth?" Lady Mattock stood in the yard with her hand shading her eyes as she watched the chase in the field.

Wesley released Mercy and took a step back. "I suppose we should get an early start if we are to see Whickette Park and be back in time to dress for the assembly this evening."

Mercy curtsied and moved off with her gentle sway. Elegant and graceful, he had never wanted to hold anyone more. It was unfortunate she never answered his question. It would break his heart if she regretted their time together.

* * * *

From the drive leading up to Whickette Park, it was just as Wesley remembered: sandy colored with vines growing around the front door. Though they were quite overgrown, as were the gardens on either side of the gate.

Beyond the gate the oblong yard, with its low garden in the middle and path for carriages wrapping round, was overgrown and wild. The manor and outbuildings followed the arched drive, giving Whickette the feel of a small village rather than a private home.

"Good gracious. It's enormous," Mercy's aunt said.

Lady Marsden clapped her hands. "A fine prospect. Good for you, Aurora."

"What must it cost to heat such a massive home?" Aurora spoke quietly, but Wesley heard her trepidation at the daunting task.

Wesley jumped down and opened the gate. He was glad to have something to do that might hide his apprehension. Heart pounding, he could almost see his grandmother with her hands fisted on her hips calling to him from the front steps. "My grandparents kept most of the house closed up for just that reason, my lady."

Mercy said, "It would make a fine university. I can't imagine it being useful or practical for anything else."

Turning in her seat, Aurora smiled. "Now, that is an intriguing idea, Mercy."

"Poppycock," Lady Marsden said. "You will be a fine mistress of this house, Aurora. You needn't sully your reputation by becoming some kind of schoolmarm.

"It's hardly a house, Mother. It would be prohibitive to live in such a place alone or even with a family. You'd have to move a village inside to make it worth the trouble." Aurora crossed her arms over her chest and stared up at the spires with their rounded caps.

Wesley climbed back into the driver's seat and drove them through the gate. "It's not been tended to in many years, ladies. Are you certain you want to risk going inside? I have no idea what we might find has taken up residence."

Laughter bubbled behind him. Pulling to a stop, he opened the carriage door. Mercy and Aurora grinned, ready for adventure.

"I will remain with the carriage," Lady Marsden huffed, crossing her arms over her chest.

Lady Mattock took a breath and accepted his hand down. "Let's have a look. If it's too unhealthy we can always turn around."

Once only Aurora's mother was left in the carriage, Wesley offered Lady Mattock his arm and they strode up the steps.

Stopping, Mercy patted the head of the great stone lion guarding the house. "Let's hope this fierce beast kept the rats out."

"Mercy, really." Phyllis scolded gently.

Aurora took Mercy's hand and tugged her along before handing the key to Wesley. "I hope this old lock hasn't rusted." He put the key in the lock and turned until the latch clicked and he pushed the heavy door open.

It hitched and creaked but eventually gave way with a bit more force. Wesley's heart lodged in his throat. Light poured in from three flights up. The rectangular foyer surrounded by wooden stairs and ornate banisters was capped by gilt plaster carvings and windows. Dust moats floated in the shards of light like a million fairies awaiting their arrival.

"Oh, my gracious." Mercy gasped, staring up at the sight.

Her aunt touched the dark wood post at the bottom of the magnificent stairs and brushed her hand off. "Could do with a good cleaning."

"Aunt, even you must see the grandeur of this. I've never seen anything like it." Gushing with wonder, Mercy stepped through the arch to the right. She screamed.

Aurora turned to run, but Wesley touched her arm. "I think she's just seen the pianoforte, my lady. I don't believe Miss Heath is in danger."

They walked through the front room with its tall arched window. The alcove formed the ornate rounded face of the house and held an exquisite pianoforte. It was covered with a white sheet, but Mercy was already pulling the cover back to reveal the white paint and gold carvings that had been carefully done so long ago.

She uncovered the keys and played, then winced. With a smile and a shrug she turned to him. "It needs tuning."

"No one has touched it in twenty years, Miss Heath." The joy in her eyes made his heart pound and he felt lighter than he had in a decade.

Steeling himself, he turned to Aurora. "What do you think, Lady Radcliff?"

Out of place among the dust motes and covered furniture, Aurora peaked through another archway into the great hall. "I am overwhelmed, my lord. Your family estates were quite grand. Are you certain you cannot afford to buy it from me?"

Heartsick for his quest, Wesley knew as well as she that there was no other way he would ever own Whickette Park. "I'm afraid that is not possible at this time, my lady. Maybe in a few years, if you were willing to sell."

Her smile was kind and she gave him a nod. "Perhaps it is a conversation that might wait for another time then. I have no use for such an enormous estate. It might be nice to have a small cottage in the country one day, but for now I'm content with my West Lane house."

Mercy and her aunt had disappeared through the great hall and gasps and oh mys echoed through the empty house. "There's a conservatory."

Laughing, Aurora fell in step beside him and they followed the excited sounds of Mercy's exploration. "I think it actually could make a fine school."

Unable to disagree now that he'd seen it again, Wesley nodded. "I'd never thought of it. To be honest, my lady, I've been so determined to get back what my grandfather lost, I hadn't thought what I would do if I succeeded. It's larger than I remember. If you should decide to turn it into a place of education, might I be so bold as to ask you to inform me of the plan before it takes shape?"

The great hall stretched at least eighty feet long and half as wide. In the center of the outside wall, chiseled from granite, stood a huge fireplace with goddesses sculpted on either side of the hearth. Windows lined the walls on either side and, though covered in filth, revealed the lake and park beyond. The ceiling cornices had been intricately carved from the wood and three chandeliers hung between.

Aurora stopped in front of the fireplace and shook her head. "Your ancestor had quite an eye, my lord. I doubt I will take such a step, but I promise you will know if my thoughts wander in that direction."

They walked on to a parlor that overlooked the conservatory. Several windows were broken, but most of the structure was intact. The entire manor was in remarkably good condition considering its disuse. "Thank you, my lady. That is very kind of you."

"May I assume your intentions to woo me have altered, my lord?" She gave him a knowing grin.

Needing a moment to wrap his head around the finality of what he was about to say, he smiled and bowed. "It seems my affections have been diverted. I hope you are not put out."

"Not at all, as I never had any intention of marrying you. It might be best if we kept this information from my mother. I will tell her, when we are back in London. There is no point in ruining the rest of our trip." Aurora peeked under a sheet at a ruby red divan with more gold accents.

"I'm not sure I understand." Wesley had no intention of courting Aurora. His heart would always belong to Mercy. It seemed to him it was best if her mother knew that immediately.

Stepping close enough that her whisper would be heard, Aurora said, "If mother knew your intentions had altered, she would make our lives uncomfortable for as long as she could. Worse, the object of your affection would become her main target. What we endured in the carriage yesterday would be nothing compared to the wrath my friend would suffer."

The notion that Lady Marsden would verbally abuse Mercy set the hair on the back of Wesley's neck standing. "I will not allow that, my lady."

"Nor I, my lord."

He let all the information sink in. "I don't like it, but I can see that a fiction is required. I wouldn't like to come to odds with your mother."

Tipping her head, she raised a brow. "Just the withholding of information, my lord. And frankly, it is none of Mother's business anyway."

"Very well, Lady Radcliff." He offered his arm. "May I escort you out? We shall have to get back to the inn if we're to attend the assembly this evening."

She accepted the offer and they left Whickette Park. As it was likely the last time Wesley would ever see his ancestral home, he held his breath, expecting to feel some sense of loss. However, as he turned the key to lock the house back up, he felt nothing. He handed the key back to Aurora. "Thank you for letting me see it, my lady."

With a nod, she took the key. "No regrets?"

"I had hoped one day to regain the property, but I cannot regret what I feel so deeply is the correct course for my future happiness." Used to keeping everything bottled up, it was odd how freely he spoke to these Wallflowers.

Skirts in hand, Mercy ran around the side of the house. Her cheeks were pink with exertion or excitement as she approached them. "This is the most incredible place. Even the barns are spectacular. I can't believe what great condition everything remains in after all this time."

Her aunt arrived in a much more staid manner. "It is really something."

"No rats then." Lady Marsden made a sour face.

Wide-eyed, Mercy said, "Only one in the barn, but he ran off. I did see several cats mulling about and have a feeling they have been ridding the area of infestation."

Aurora's mother shuddered. "Cats are only marginally better. I'm satisfied having seen the prospect. Can we return to the inn?"

Wesley helped the ladies back into the carriage. Holding Mercy's hand a bit longer than was necessary, he let her warmth seep into him. "As you wish, my lady. Perhaps tomorrow we might venture out to the ruins where my ancestors lived before Whickette Park was built. If my memory serves there are some Roman bits left to observe as well."

Fire lighted behind Mercy's eyes. "Oh yes. Another adventure."

"I've had enough adventure." Everything that came out of Lady Marsden's mouth was either simpering to get what she wanted or sour about something she didn't want. Wesley's patience was waning.

"Perhaps you might prefer to remain at the inn then, my lady. The town has some fine shops so you might enjoy a bit of shopping tomorrow." It might have been more gentlemanly to remain silent, but he'd not regret a day without her company.

Her ladyship appeared aghast before schooling her expression. "I may do just that. I've no great need in stomping around some old rocks for nostalgia's sake."

Aurora looked ready to burst out laughing, but she drew a long breath. "Back to the inn to dress then?"

Swiveling her head from one to the other, Mercy's lips turned up but her eyes held confusion. "Back to the inn."

With a nod, Wesley climbed into the driver's seat and drove them back. It was a miracle he did so without laughing. His fate decided, he only had to convince the lady that he was the man for her.

Chapter 17

Mercy strummed her guitar in her room while her aunt went on some errand. Aunt Phyllis didn't approve of playing the guitar when dressed for the evening. Though she loved to hear Mercy play, she thought the Spanish instrument not elegant for a lady in evening attire.

While she loved the dulcet sounds of the guitar, the fact that she mostly played it when sad or troubled had not escaped her. Sighing, she leaned it against the dresser.

The assembly would be a good distraction from her problems and soon Wesley and she would part company. The memory of his gentle touch would fade as well once things were settled. Then her life would go back to normal and she would be happy again.

Standing in front of the mirror, she brushed out her forest green gown and let her image fade as her sight glazed over. Jane, the maid Mercy shared with Aurora during their travels, had braided and curled her soft strawberry blond hair, leaving several curls to hang around her neck. Mercy toyed with one curl and willed her emotions into submission.

The door opened. Aunt Phyllis stared a long moment. "You look lovely, my dear, but perhaps a smile to complete the fine look."

Mercy put a demure grin in place. It didn't denote any kind of happiness, but she had learned early in life that no one cared if she was happy as long as she didn't *look* unhappy. "Are we ready to go, Aunt?"

For the briefest moment, Phyllis frowned before putting her own contented expression into place. "The others are waiting below. We are to walk as the assembly room is just down the street."

With a nod, Mercy picked up her reticule and followed her aunt downstairs.

Aurora and Wesley stood near the door whispering together while Lady Marsden preened like a cat with a large bowl of milk. When she saw Mercy, she smirked as if the prize were at Mercy's expense.

Aunt Phyllis's expression remained neutral as she passed her ladyship without a glance. "Are we ready?"

Raising an eyebrow without taking her gaze from Mercy, Lady Marsden said, "Everything is exactly as it should be."

In the yard, Aurora took Wesley's offered arm. When he offered Mercy his other, Mercy only gave a quick curtsy and rushed ahead. Wishing the walk was longer did no good as they arrived at the assembly room in just five minutes.

The crowded hall with lively music stilled as they stepped inside. Mercy had hoped to lose herself in the crowd but it seemed she had to be gawked at by the masses first.

For a small town the hall was quite large, with a dance floor taking up the bulk of the main room. Chairs were placed in three rows on two sides and large round pillars held up the high ceiling. Beyond the dancing the room was dimly lit and it seemed refreshments were available in a small room to the left.

At least a dozen couples stood watching from the dance floor, with three times that many milling about the assembly room.

A moment later, the reel continued and a thin man with balding head, warm smile, and a quizzing glass approached. "Welcome to our assembly. You must be the Earl of Castlewick." He offered his hand to Wesley. "We heard you were in the area. I'm so pleased you've joined us this evening. I am Sir William Butler. I serve as the magistrate here in Plumbly."

"We're happy to attend the festivities, Sir William." Wesley grinned. "May I introduce my friends. This is the Dowager Countess of Radcliff, the Dowager Countess of Marsden, Lady Phyllis Mattock, and her niece, Miss Heath."

"Excellent to meet you all. I'm sure the ladies will find many distractions with the dancing. I'm happy to make introductions when needed, though we are not so formal here in the country."

"Thank you, Sir William. We shall manage." Wesley bowed.

Sir William grinned and bid them enter.

Taking the cue, Mercy rushed off to the left. She hoped to hide herself behind some chairs, where she might observe from the shadows and not be bothered by too many strangers.

"It's not like you to be shy, Mercy." Aurora was only a few steps behind her.

Mercy sat in the last row of chairs at the far end where the candelabras and chandeliers barely reached. "I'm not in the mood to meet new people." Aurora sat and smoothed her ruby gown. "I thought you liked places where no one knows you and no one cares about status or family worth." "I do." Mercy sighed. "Did you like the manor house?" With a shrug, Aurora smiled. "I liked your idea of a school. I further liked how perfectly vexed the idea made Mother." Laughing, Mercy nodded. "I thought the place extraordinary. Think of the things we might teach. Shall it be an all-girls school for music and study or shall we make a scandal and mix boys and girls?"

"Lord, wouldn't that turn Mother inside out?" Aurora flipped open her fan to hide her amusement from the crowd watching them.

Wesley approached. "Lady Radcliff, might I have this dance?"

Eyebrows raised, Aurora stood. "A pleasure, my lord."

It was all as it ought to be. Mercy watched as they took to the floor. Despite her own wishes, Aurora and Wesley looked very fine together. If he could make her dearest friend happy, Mercy would never fault him for marrying Aurora or for breaking his promise.

Lost in her thoughts she was surprised when a young man cleared his throat to gain her attention. "I am Jonathan Underhill, Miss. I realize we haven't been introduced, but things are less formal here in Plumbly than you're probably used to in London. I hope you don't mind my forwardness."

Mercy stood. "Mercedes Heath. I'm pleased to make your acquaintance."

Mr. Underhill was extremely tall and as it was rare to have someone tower over Mercy, she smiled. "You find me amusing, Miss Heath. Of course, you do. I am not so grand as his lordship, to be sure."

"You mistake me, sir. It is only that being a tall woman, it is quite nice to look up at anyone. Forgive me if I made you uncomfortable."

His blue eyes and tanned skin were not that of a gentleman but of someone who worked out of doors. His smile was warm and his embarrassment endearing. "Perhaps we might dance and all misunderstanding will be forgiven, Miss Heath." He offered his arm.

"I would be pleased to dance with you, Mr. Underhill." Taking his arm, she let him lead her to the dance floor and they joined a lively country dance where there was little time to talk.

After a second dance with Mr. Underhill, Mercy made a polite curtsy, thanked her partner, and went to find refreshment.

Punch was available at a long table with ale and watered wine. Mercy sipped and hoped to lean on a wall where she could go unnoticed while she caught her breath.

Lady Marsden spotted her from across the room and made a path directly toward her. "That young man seems quite right, Miss Heath. I asked after Mr. Underhill and found that he is a local farmer and very well respected here. You could do far worse."

"He seemed very nice, but it was only a dance, my lady. Do not get your hopes up too high that I might disappear from your world. Who would amuse you should I actually move so far from London?" Mercy hadn't the slightest idea of standing up for herself when the evening started, yet speaking the truth gave her a rare sense of power just as it had at Parvus.

Her ladyship huffed and crossed her arms over her chest with narrowed eyes and pursed lips. "You should be grateful I allow you to touch such expensive pieces of my collection."

Aurora rushed over, ready to battle back her mother.

Before her friend could speak in her defense, Mercy gave a warm smile and cocked her head. "In that case, you may pay twenty pounds to have a master come and play that Stradivarius for you in the future, Lady Marsden. My services have to this point been far less expensive."

"Oh my," Aurora said, but covered her grin with her fan.

Mercy kissed Aurora's cheek. "I shall take some air. I will return shortly."

As Mercy walked away, she heard Lady Marsden say, "Insolent girl."

"Mother, you got what you deserved and it's about time."

Blindly, Mercy excused herself through the crush of people to get to the door. Bumping shoulders with several in her way, she focused on the way out into fresh air. A wave of nausea flooded her and she pressed her hand against her stomach as she stepped into the cool night on the main street of Plumbly.

Like many small villages, buildings lined the main street with several side streets leading to residences. There were shops and homes and it was all neatly kept. Plumbly bustled with droves coming to the assembly and some taking air in the street like Mercy.

Across the wide dirt road, a hat shop displayed a green feathered confection. Mercy stared at the hat until it blurred and she saw only her reflection in the glass, a warped version of herself, fitting with her behavior displaying a complete loss of good sense. Yet it felt so good she could hardly be sorry.

"Are you all right, Mercy?" Concern echoed in Wesley's voice.

Mercy blinked several times until her vision cleared and she saw herself and Wesley reflected in the glass. Turning, she took a deep breath. "I am fine. It seems I've told her ladyship to dig in her pockets and pay someone to play her fine instruments rather than use me as her personal musician at the ready."

"Did you?" There was no mistaking the amusement in his dark eyes.

"I don't know what came over me. I suppose I was tired of her treating me as if I should be honored to be in her presence and the company of her daughter. I think this trip to Parvus and Plumbly have changed me." Unable to look away, Mercy searched Wesley's face for some sign that he agreed with Lady Marsden.

She noted only admiration in his steady gaze. "I would say that conversation was a long time coming, Mercy."

"I suppose it was." Mercy kept her gaze lowered. She'd never liked being the center of attention, though she didn't mind Wesley's attention as much as she should.

He stepped closer. "Are you worried that Aurora will be put out by your standing up for yourself with her mother?"

"No. Aurora will love me no matter what I say or whom I say it to." Warmth spread in Mercy's chest. She could always count on the Wallflowers. They would stand by her no matter what.

"It must be very comforting to have that kind of love from your friends." The distance in his voice drew her attention back to his face.

She lacked the nerve to ask him about his own friendships. "It is. I have been very fortunate in the friendships I have made. I suppose I should return to the ball, but I'd rather not face her ladyship again this evening."

"You could agree to the next two dances with me and by that time it would be acceptable for me to walk you back to the inn. No one would think anything amiss. Unless of course, you would prefer to dance with that nice local fellow I saw you with earlier." Staring with his brows raised, he waited for her answer.

At first, she'd thought him joking about Mr. Underhill, but his expression was so full of worry and hesitation, she knew better. "That gentleman does not interest me, my lord. It was very kind of him to ask for a dance."

"He will be the talk of the town for having danced with the pretty stranger." Wesley's cheeks and neck turned the brightest red.

Watching him, she wasn't sure what to think. "Are you jealous, my lord?"

"It is only the two of us here, Mercy. I don't know why you insist on calling me out so formally." His ears were now as red as the rest of him.

She stepped closer. "Wesley, are you jealous?"

Closing the gap, he didn't touch her, but he could have with little effort. "You're damned right I am. Do you think it's easy for me to watch you dance with other men? To see how beautiful and graceful you are in the arms of another? Then, the way men look at you. The one in there is completely smitten. Do you think it doesn't occur to me that you might be happy with someone who lives in the country, and has a nice home and land, and whose name is not attached to a scandal that forced my current position?"

For a moment, Mercy wondered who had lost their senses. "I am not marrying Mr. Underhill. I barely know him and had only the two dances with him. Why would you jump to such a radical conclusion?"

He closed his eyes and stepped back a few inches. His skin returned to its normal tan before he opened his eyes and took a breath. "Forgive me. Of course you're not. It seems all my good sense and control are lost when in your presence."

It seemed petty to bring up his having danced the first two with Aurora, a woman whom everyone fully expected him to marry. Besides, she wanted Aurora to be happy and Wesley was both kind and thoughtful. She'd not stand in the way of her friend getting what she deserved. "Perhaps it would be best if I went back to the inn now. I doubt anyone would notice."

Before she could take a full step in that direction, he touched her arm. "I would notice, Mercedes. Dance with me?"

It was hard to catch her breath; his gaze was so intense. "Thank you." She didn't know what else to say as she took his arm and walked back into the assembly room just as a waltz began.

He took her hand and glided into the smooth waltz. "How do you like the music?" he asked.

"They are quite good, which is a nice find in a country setting. I suppose it's snobbish, but I expected to find far inferior musicians." Her cheeks heated.

He didn't speak until she met his smiling gaze. "I'm sure you can attest to the fact that we have suffered cruelly at many London balls where the talent has been lacking."

"Sadly, true." She laughed. "Thank you for making me come back in. I am rarely afflicted with malaise and would surely have worried myself into a stupor had I returned to the inn alone."

His thumb caressed the palm of her hand. "Then perhaps I shouldn't tell you that her ladyship and your aunt are watching us rather intently."

Suddenly none of it mattered. "And Aurora, is she staring as well?"

He shook his head. "She glanced over at the start of the dance, but is herself engaged with a partner for the waltz."

"Vexing her ladyship has been one of the pleasures of my life since her daughter dared befriend an orphan. I'll not let her ruin our adventures this week. Not on my account anyway." It felt good to pull back her shoulders and stand up straight. She'd let that woman bully her these last months and all over a man who, while kind, was hardly meant for her. It was enough.

Wesley watched her closely as they whirled around the dance floor in three-step time. "It occurs to me that you never answered my question this morning, Mercy. However, I will answer yours."

Searching her memory, she had trouble keeping calm when she realized he was talking about the question of whether she regretted their night together. She had only responded with the same question to him. Her pulse raced and everywhere he touched her warmed.

He leaned an inch closer. "There is not one moment I have spent with you that I regret, Mercedes Heath. Not an instant I would change or wish away."

Mouth dry, she swallowed several times under his direct stare. "Surely you exaggerate, my lord. You regretted kissing me in the theater almost immediately. I'm sure you were none too pleased with my attempts to distract you from wooing Aurora."

The music drew to a close. The crowd faced the musicians and applauded.

Wesley's lips almost touched her ear. "I never regretted kissing you in the theater. It was the most exquisite intimacy. I have never wished it away and only regretted putting us in a difficult position at the time. I would kiss you anywhere and revel in every moment. Nothing you have done displeases me. I have noticed that you are less eager to run me off these last days."

Pulling away, she faced him. "You...I..." Mercy's heart would not slow and she couldn't catch her breath. "If you can make Aurora happy, I will wish you both great joy. After all, who am I to disapprove of an earl wishing to marry a countess. Aurora will be settled and you will have righted a wrong. Everything is as it should be."

"Mercy, there is much for us to discuss." His whisper and imploring eyes sent a jolt of fear through her. He peered around the assembly. "We cannot talk here."

"I see no reason to discuss anything, my lord." She made a quick curtsy and ran from the hall. Not stopping until she'd reached The Smoker, Mercy held in her emotions until she was safely behind the door of her rented room before she let her tears fall.

It would be unbearable to have him explain to her how he would marry Aurora, or worse, to tell her how much he cared for her, but must do what was best for his family and title. She knew all of those things and didn't need to hear it again. She'd played those words over and over in her own head enough times in the past few months and each time her heart broke a little more.

When no more tears would come, Mercy allowed Jane to help her into her night rail. She washed her face and crawled into bed.

Outside people laughed and talked as they made their way back from the assembly. Mercy kept her eyes closed even when the door to her room opened. She felt her aunt's gaze on her, but made no move to indicate she was awake.

It was childish to feign sleep, but she didn't want to answer questions. Perhaps in the morning, when she was stronger.

Chapter 18

Long after every reveler had taken to their beds, Wesley stood in the stable talking to his horse. "Please tell me I'm not a fool."

Brutus licked Wesley's palm, then nudged his shoulder.

"I cannot seem to convince the lady of my regard. Though I suppose I have been remiss in divulging my true feelings." He scratched the horse's jaw and received a snicker in reply. "I suppose I'll not sleep tonight."

Making to leave the stable, Wesley received a sharp nudge from Brutus.

"You want to walk with me, boy?" He took the harness down from the hook and opened the stall door. Once Brutus accepted the bit, Wesley secured it over his ears.

With the reins in one hand, he led Brutus into the moonlit night. The full moon shone bright but even if it had been full dark, Wesley couldn't have missed Mercy's tall figure staring out over the fields.

Horse in tow, to surprise her was impossible, and she turned before he reached the edge of the tree. "I hope I didn't frighten you."

"What are you doing here?" She looked at the horse. "Are you going somewhere?"

"Where would I go when everything I need is here?" He pointed to Brutus's back. "No saddle. We're just out for a walk."

She turned and gazed up at the bright moon. "Couldn't you sleep?"

Stepping next to her, he let Brutus nibble some grass. "No. I didn't like the way we ended our evening together."

Her eyes wide, she turned toward him. "You cannot sleep because I left the assembly a bit early?"

A stableman yawned and stretched in the yard before looking over at them.

Wesley gripped Brutus's lead too hard and the horse pulled back. Frustration warred inside him as he cooed to sooth the horse. "There was more privacy in a house full of people or in London."

"Do you require privacy, my lord?" With her head cocked and her hair hanging loose around her shoulders, she was adorable. She'd covered her cotton night dress with a heavy cloak and the green of her eyes shone in the light of a full summer moon.

"I require time alone with you." He reached for her hand, but she pulled back.

"Why?"

Two more men who worked around the inn stepped into the yard and chatted as they crossed to the stable.

"Would you ride with me, Mercy? If I asked you to get on this horse and ride out of here for a few hours, would you do it?" He longed to tell her everything, but not in public where they were sure to be interrupted every five minutes by the coming morning and all the activity of inn business. The guests wouldn't wake for several hours, but the staff and servants would be rising with greater frequency as the moon gave way to the sun.

"I don't understand."

He blocked the view of her from the inn. "I need to talk to you. I need for you to hear me. Each time I've tried, I have failed either because I am an idiot, or because the setting was too public. Please, I'm begging you, Mercy."

Her throat bobbed as she swallowed several times.

His hand slid down and he let his thumb caress the soft skin of her neck.

"What are you begging me for, exactly?" She pulled her shoulders back like a warrior queen.

His heart was too full and it was hard to speak. "Just some time. An hour away from everyone and everything."

"My aunt would call it foolishness to tempt a man in such a way." She never let her gaze fall from his.

Of course, she was right. Still, he had to have time before things were so out of accord that he'd never win her. "I would never do anything you did not wish, Mercy. You will always be safe with me."

Wordlessly she nodded.

Before she could change her mind, or he lost his nerve, he gripped her waist and put her on Brutus's back, then swung up behind her. Pulling her tight against him, he wanted to shield her from the horse's back. At least, that's what he told himself as her body molded to his front with maddening perfection.

Once they were out of town, he slowed their pace and continued up the hills to Whickette Park. He thought at some point she might protest, but she sat still, leaning against him without a word.

He jumped down at the gate and immediately missed her warmth against him.

She held Brutus's main as he walked her through to the elliptical yard. She must have tossed her dress over her night rail, leaving white ruffles peeking out at the bottom. She took his breath away.

Reaching up, he helped her to the ground and held her a moment longer than was necessary. Her upturned chin let him see her strength and also her vulnerability.

Reluctantly, he released her and looped Brutus's reins to a ring mounted in the paw of one of the guarding lions.

When he turned, she was beside him. "Are we to talk here? We need Aurora's key to enter the manor."

Wesley took her hand and kissed the back. "Not really. It was just more polite to use her key than the alternative."

Her eyes lit with amusement. "What alternative is that?"

Tugging gently, he led her around to the back of the house, through the overgrown kitchen gardens to a side door that led into the solarium. "The lock on this door has never worked properly. I remember my grandmother nagging Grandfather to have it fixed when I was a boy."

Mercy's laugh was full and joyful. "All this time anyone could have made their home here and only you knew about this silly little unlocked door."

He shrugged. "The people in the village and the neighboring farmers would never have let anything untoward go on at Whickette. It was always safe."

The plants that once filled the solarium were long gone, but two long settees remained in the center of the windowed room. Mercy pulled her overcoat around her and sat. "You have me here, Wesley. Now what?"

His stomach churned with a dozen bumblebees. "I'm not certain how to begin. Things seem to have gotten away from me."

"What things?" She cocked her head.

Pacing was only making his nervousness worse. He sat next to her and stared at his hands in his lap. "I think it's important that we first discuss Lady Radcliff."

Sitting up perfectly straight, Mercy clasped her hands in her lap. "All right."

"I have no intention of courting her ladyship, nor will I ever propose marriage to her." It should have bothered him to say it while sitting inside

Whickette Park. It was, after all, his motivation for getting involved with these Wallflowers of West Lane to begin with. Yet his attachment to the place had waned considerably. It would be nice to reclaim his ancestral home, but other things had taken precedent in his heart and mind.

"What do you find lacking in Aurora? She is perfect in every way." Mercy defended her friend.

The clear effrontery in her tone made him laugh. "She is perfect, just not for me. I might add that she has no interest in me either. Though, as close as you are, I'm certain you already knew that."

Shoulders slumped, Mercy stared at the floor. "Aurora thinks of you with great esteem. That is a pity you two are not suited. I know how much gaining this house back means to you."

"I seem to have lost interest in fixing old mistakes," he said.

Outside light glowed just at the horizon, making the ragged gardens look more fairytale than forgotten. Mercy stood and walked to the window. "You will not marry to gain back what your grandfather lost and you have said you cannot afford to buy the land and house from Aurora. Then you have given up on your dreams."

The sorrow in her voice spoke to him more than her words. "My dreams have altered."

"Oh?" With her long reddish-blond hair loose and the light behind her, she fit perfectly into the fairytale as his warrior queen.

He crossed to her and stopped just before touching her. "I admit I wanted to marry Aurora in order to gain back this place, I never pretended anything else. But standing here now, I only wish I had been less of a fool."

She turned and faced him. "You have been very forthright. Still, I don't understand."

"Don't you?"

Her hair covered half of her face. She pushed her spectacles higher on her nose. "No."

These few days of travel had left the most adorable freckles on her cheeks and the bridge of her nose. He longed to kiss each and every one.

Reaching out, he tucked her silken strands behind her ear to reveal a blush. "I should have known from the moment I danced with you I could never court another."

Her mouth opened as if to speak, but she closed it again.

Open or closed, her mouth was more distraction than any plot or quest he made over his lifetime. "I never quite got over you, sweet Mercy. I tried to like another, but my attraction to you was too strong."

"Perhaps once we are apart, you might find a woman with the funds to afford you Whickette Park. I'm sure Aurora will do nothing but collect the rents for quite some time." Mercy took a step back but the glass wall prohibited her from escaping.

"I'm afraid that won't do either."

"Why not? Once I am not in your purview, I'm sure the attraction will fade and you will be able to get all the things you want. It was kind of you to explain all of this to me, but really quite unnecessary. Men and women make missteps all the time, as we did in that hidden office. No one need ever know and I am unharmed." She scooted to the right and slipped around him. Her back to him, she walked to the hallway that led into the ballroom.

Wesley followed. When she stopped, she leaned her head on the fireplace statue of a goddess.

"Mercy, whatever you think of men and their tendencies to take advantage of young women they care nothing for, may be true, but that is not what happened with you and me." He didn't want her to run from him so he closed the distance but didn't crowd her.

"It was an accident that we were locked in that room together." She took off her spectacles and wiped her eyes before putting them back on.

"What happened in that office was no accident, nor is our being here now. I am at fault for your misunderstanding. Please forgive me."

Finally, she looked at him. "What is there to forgive?"

"I never told you how much I love you. I should have said it a long time ago and there is where I have been a fool. All these months, I thought I could use logic to change what was already right in front of me. I love you, Mercedes Heath. I shall never want another. Tell me you'll be my wife and make me the happiest of men." He spread his arms out and hoped she would see how much he needed her and that nothing stood between them.

Shaking her head, she said, "I have nothing. No money, no relations to speak of. You will never gain what you need if you marry me and one day you will come to resent me as the person who kept you from your dreams."

He closed the gap and took her hands in his. Kissing each one, he took a long breath. "You are my only dream. I don't care about this house or the property or the stupidity of my grandfather. In fact, I think perhaps he did me a favor."

She narrowed those stunning green eyes. "How so?"

"If Grandfather had not acted an ass and lost our ancestral lands and most of our other holdings before getting himself killed, I would not have worked to gain them back, and might never have seen Lady Radcliff's beautiful friend at the ball where we first danced." His gut clenched at the thought that if one thing had been different, he might never have known this amazing woman.

Mercy pulled her hands back and stared at them, then at him. "You love me?"

"More than anything." It took all his will not to pull her into his arms.

Reaching out, she made to touch his cheek, but held back. "You want to marry me?"

Grasping her outstretched hand, he pressed her palm to his cheek and leaned into her touch. "More than I have ever wanted anything or shall ever want anything."

"But you danced the first two with Aurora. You walked this very house with Aurora just yesterday. You were clearly courting her and pulling away from me." She pulled her hand back as if burned.

"Because Aurora said that her mother would make you miserable if she knew my affections were unalterable." He held his breath while this amazing woman decided their futures.

Blinking several times, she walked around him and headed back to the solarium. "You were protecting me from Lady Marsden's wrath?"

"Yes." Where the ballroom had been dim, the solarium was filling with light as the sun crept upward.

"I thought you and she had come to an agreement." A shuttered breath pushed through her lips as she sat on the settee again.

Kneeling in front of her, he said, "We have, my love, just not the one you imagined. Aurora and I acknowledged my affections for you and agreed to put on an act for her mother in order to protect you."

"You might have told me," she scolded.

"I should have gone directly to your aunt and asked for her permission to court you the very morning after being locked in with you. I tried, but it seems Lady Marsden is everywhere. Each time I wanted to talk to you, the dowager was present or we were in a crush of people." He made excuses. "Forgive me. I was cowardly and a fool."

Mercy stared at him unmoving as his heart broke in two. "I do not make this declaration lightly, Mercy. I have never spoke these words to anyone else. However, if you do not share my feelings, I understand."

Leaning forward, her lips turned up in the sweetest smile before she pressed them to his. "I love you, Wesley. I have from almost the moment you asked me to dance at the Duke of Breckenridge's ball. I could have skewered you with my hatpin at the theater, if I'd wished to stop you sooner. But stopping that kiss...I couldn't make myself do it."

Heart soaring up from the pits of Hell to total elation in the span of seconds, Wesley couldn't help noticing the touch of sadness in her voice. "Why do you sound as if this is a bad thing, my love?"

Eyes swimming, she met his gaze. "It will be hard for you to understand."

Rising from the floor, he sat beside her and cupped her cheeks in both hands. Pressing his lips to hers, he felt the salt of her tears touch his soul. "Try me."

"When my parents died, I was happy to have a kind aunt to care for me. When she sent me away to school, I understood her position and made the best of it. It turned out well and when I came back to London, Aunt Phyllis was widowed and things were fine. Fine was good enough. Fine was all I ever expected from my life." Drawing a breath, she shuddered.

"I want you to have far more than just fine, Mercy. You deserve a wonderful and fulfilling life." Parts of Wesley he didn't even know existed ached for this smart, talented woman who set her expectations so low.

"That's just it." She shook her head. "I'm not sure I know how to live beyond fine. I might make you unhappy. I might make a terrible wife."

Unable to help himself, he laughed. "Impossible. Seeing you every day and knowing you love me would be more than enough to keep me happy. However, I have a hunch that you and I will do quite well together. You shall want for nothing and I shall only want for you."

Her curved brows narrowed. "What if there are things I want, which you cannot give me?"

Could he have been mistaken about her desire? Doubt crept into Wesley's heart. "You said you love me, Mercy. Perhaps I've misunderstood. Is there someone else?"

"There is no one. I love only you and I shall always love you, Wesley." The sun gleamed off the solarium windows and Mercy's eyes filled with tears.

"Yet you do not wish to marry me? Is that what you are trying to tell me?" He swallowed down emotions that would bury him if he allowed them to surface.

"There are things I want to do." She pulled her shoulders back. "I always expected to be alone. It is not so bad to think one will be a spinster of sorts. I tuck a few coins away each month in hopes that one day I might open my own school where I might teach music. I have several students now who show some promise. Of course, many would never send their children to learn from a woman, but I expect there are some who wouldn't care if they'd heard me play."

"You want to be a music teacher?" He couldn't hide the confusion from his voice.

"I like teaching." She scrunched up her nose and narrowed her gaze on him. "It is very rewarding to share my gifts with students."

"I'm sure it is."

"You disapprove." She lifted her chin but turned away.

"No. I'm confused."

Looking back at him, she asked, "What confuses you? That a woman would wish to work and make a living of her own?"

"On the contrary. I can see how that would be very liberating. What confuses me is what that desire has to do with your decision to marry me." He held his breath.

"Men do not want their wives to have occupations. They expect their wives to be happy to run the house, keep the servants out of their lord's way, and to bear children." She crossed her arms over her chest.

"Mercy?" He adored every inch of her, from the stubborn tilt of her chin to the way she pointed her toes when she sat looking away from him.

"Yes?"

"If you wish to continue to teach or open a school, I will help you in any way I can. If you do not want my help, that too I will understand. Just look at me and tell me if you want to marry me or not."

Pivoting toward him, she opened her mouth and stared. "I...I do want to marry you." The statement seemed to surprise her more than him and she covered her mouth with her hand.

Flooded with relief, Wesley pulled her into his arms. "Thank God. You can have a school or a dozen schools if that will make you happy, Mercy. I promise you that whatever it is that will bring joy into your life, I will support the project with my whole heart."

She wrapped her arms around him and kissed his neck. "I never dreamed this could happen."

Leaning back, he met her gaze. "Never?"

A blush flooded her cheeks. "Well, maybe in dreams too wonderful to ever believe could come true."

"We shall make all your dreams come true, love." Capturing her lips was like holding the North Star in his hand and letting it carry him home.

Chapter 19

His lips on hers was nothing short of a miracle. He loved her. Mercy didn't know how it had happened, but in the span of an hour, her life had changed and she was happy. Her heart thrummed so fiercely, she didn't know if she had ever been happy before in her life.

Everywhere he touched her skin licked with fire.

"Wesley," she gasped out of breath.

He dotted kisses on her cheeks and eyelids. "Yes."

Sunshine flooded the room as night had given way to morning. Mercy had lost track of the hour she'd allotted him. "Do you think my aunt will wake soon?"

Turning his head, he studied the sun's progress. "It is not yet seven. Is your aunt usually an early riser?"

"Not when she's been out late at a ball. She will stay above stairs until at least ten, and I am always up with the sun."

His hand, stilled on her back. "Then you likely knew the answer to your question. Why did you ask it?"

Mercy turned and swung her leg over Wesley's lap so that she straddled him. He gripped her around her bottom to keep her from sliding to the floor and she clasped her hands around his neck and pulled herself forward. "I was thinking that no one would miss me for some time and we might stay here while the sun warms this room. If you objected, you might have said that my aunt would be awake soon and we should return."

Her dress and nightgown had ridden up around her thighs. Wesley slid his hands down to where the flesh of her knees was exposed then slid them along her outer thighs. "I suppose I might have, but I like the direction of your thoughts, love."

A small tilt back and the release of her hands and her overcoat drifted to the floor. "Do you think anyone comes around here and might spy us through the glass?"

"It is unlikely, but I will take you elsewhere if you are uncomfortable in the daylight." Pushing deeper under the cotton shift brought his hands to the top of her buttocks and he snugged her in close enough that his shaft pressed against her intimately.

Wiggling in tight, she ran her fingers through his hair. "I like the light." It was wicked, but she loved seeing him and the desire in his eyes as he realized she was giving herself to him, both her heart and her body.

He tucked her hair behind her ears. "I long to see every inch of you and kiss my way from head to toe."

Warmth flushed from her chest, up her neck and to her cheeks. She undid the loosely tied day dress and pulled it over her head. "I would not object, my lord."

Cradling her in his arms, he shifted them so that she lay on her back on the settee. Her legs were exposed, but the rest of her was fully covered by either boots or her voluminous nightgown. Wesley slid one hand down her leg to her calf and removed one boot and then the other. As promised, he started at the bottom and pressed kisses from her toes to her knees.

Every kiss was wonderful torture and the skin at the back of her knee sent a shock directly between her thighs. She clasped them together hoping for some relief, but it only increased the tingle at her core.

The kisses he pressed to the inside of her thighs had her arching off the cushion and begging him for relief. "Wesley, please."

"As you wish, love." His mouth covered her and he teased her sensitive bud with tongue and teeth until she tumbled over the abyss and cried his name.

His arms wrapped her in a safe cocoon while waves of pleasure coursed through her and when she could once again breathe, he slid her nightgown up over her torso and her head before placing it on the high arm of the furniture. "You are magnificent."

She pulled him close and opened her mouth on his kiss. It was an intricate dance between tongues, teeth, and lips. Mercy wanted more and scratched at his back to bring him closer.

Sitting back, he studied her. "Are you certain, Mercedes? I can wait."

Bringing his hand to cup her breast, she said. "I want you, Wesley and wanting is not something I do often."

In moments he stood before her naked and leaned down to take her taught nipple in his mouth.

Exquisite pleasure and pain pressed between her legs as he opened her with his hips and pressed inside her.

Mercy bit her lip to keep from screaming against the pain.

Still as a statue, Wesley waited for her to relax. "I'm sorry. I promise there will never be pain again."

Her friends Poppy and Faith had told her as much, but she couldn't help wishing him away as it seemed she was torn in two. As the pain eased, pleasure returned and she lifted her hips, taking him deeper.

A low groan from him was both satisfying and empowering.

His body joined with hers was perfection, and with each press inside her, the friction brought pleasure until she thought she might go mad with it. Clutching for him, she screamed as another wave of ecstasy exploded inside her.

Wesley shuddered and cried out her name.

They lay wrapped in each other's arms while time seemed to stand still and keep them safe.

Kissing her temple and then her cheek, he said, "I think we must dress and get you back before we are missed. I will speak to your aunt today."

Once Aunt Phyllis knew of their love, there would be no hiding. "Perhaps you and Aurora had the right of it."

As he pulled away, she regretted having said anything that would take him away from her sooner. "What do you mean?"

"If you go to my aunt today, she will not be able to keep silent on the subject. She will announce to everyone who will hear her that we are betrothed." It sounded so nice, she blushed despite the point she was trying to make.

He lifted her chin and grinned. "And what is wrong with that?"

As she made to sit up, he pressed her gently back in place. "Let me help you."

Before she could stop him, he'd taken his white handkerchief and wiped between her legs. It was at once sweet, embarrassing, and wonderfully intimate. Despite her mortification, she couldn't take her eyes from the sight of a man tenderly caring for her as if she were his own. He really did love her. She had to concentrate on the issue at hand and not burst into joyous tears.

When he was satisfied with what he could do with a dry cloth, he sighed, but reached for her night rail and handed it to her. "You'll need a proper washing. I'm sorry. I should have thought this through better."

She pulled her gown on, picked up her cloak, and before she could pull it on, Wesley was helping her into it. "Now why don't you want me to go to your aunt today?"

Taking up her boots, she pulled them on and watched as Wesley dressed. She'd never seen a man dress and thought she would watch him often when they were married. "You really want to marry me?" It came out before she could stop herself.

With his breeches on and his blouse hanging loose around him the smattering of hair on his chest could be seen and a day's beard grew on his chin. There was a wildness to Wesley that always lurked under his calm facade. He turned and watched her. "I want to marry you more than I have ever wanted anything in my life. Why do you ask as if it were impossible?"

She shrugged. "Before today, I would have told you it could never happen. I would have told you that men do not marry for love."

"But your Wallflowers have married for love, have they not?" He tucked his blouse into his breeches and secured the fall.

"Poppy and Faith are the daughters of earls."

He took her hand before sitting and pulling her onto his lap. "My love, their titles had nothing to do with their finding love. I'm given the impression that Aurora's marriage was very unhappy, yet she too is the daughter of an earl. Or am I mistaken?"

Why didn't he understand? "Men will marry where it suits them best. It is wonderful that Faith and Poppy found love in their marriages, but they were suitable wives for those men. Don't you see, I will always be thought of as beneath you. People like the dowager will always say I trapped you into an unwanted marriage."

"What do you think, Mercy?" His voice was soft but laced with warning.

"I did not trap you. I tried my very best to send you in another direction. Yet you still say you wish to marry me." It was bewildering.

Tightening his grip around her waist, he drew her attention. "I don't give a damn what anyone besides you thinks. I love you and that is my entire reason for wishing to be your husband. So you may be confounded and if you are set against telling anyone until we reach London, I will comply."

He loved her. He didn't need her as she had nothing to offer save herself and that was enough. Mercy's mind raced with all the consequences to be faced and made her decision. "If the dowager rages, let her rage. I expressed my feelings last night."

He touched the tip of her nose, his grin wide. "And you will be a countess soon enough and there will be no need to listen to her babble ever again. We needn't invite her to our home unless she finds some way to redeem herself to you, my love."

Resting her head on his shoulder, she breathed in the warm scent of him. The band around her heart loosened and warmth spread through her chest. "I don't think I have ever been truly happy before. I have on occasion been content and I did enjoy my time at school, but I actually feel happy."

"My hope is to keep you in this state for many years to come, Mercy." He kissed her forehead and they sat watching the sunrise.

Time ticked away and finally Wesley sighed and kissed her again. "If we don't leave now, the entire party will be awake by the time I take you back and we will have the devil to pay and there is one short stop I'd like to make. If you don't mind."

Mercy stood and pulled her overcoat tight. "Of course."

Taking her hand, he led them out the door with the broken lock and around the manor house. At the front, Brutus waited patiently.

He kept the horse at a walk and on the way back to the village pulled down a short lane. At the end a small cemetery, neatly kept, was surrounded by a low iron fence. Mercy waited with Brutus and watched as Wesley knelt beside the graves of his parents.

When he'd finished, he took her hand and they walked back down the lane. "It's nice that the village kept the graves so neat. I shall have to inquire as to who has done so."

Mercy squeezed his hand. "I'm glad you were able to visit."

"My father wanted very badly to have Whickette back in the family." He grinned. "Father will not mind waiting a few more years. Then maybe we can try to buy the property and perhaps in that time decide what to do with such a mammoth place."

"I'm sorry to have spoiled your plans." It was half a lie. She was sorry for him to fail in what he'd set out to do, but not to be the reason he was not marrying Aurora or anyone else.

Still smiling, he shrugged.

Expecting some regrets for his decision to give up on the lands that would afford him the ability to visit often, she was surprised when he changed the subject.

"Mercy, some time ago the Duke of Breckenridge implied that you might have played some part in the death of Aurora's husband." There was no accusation in his tone, only curiosity.

Nick suspected. How perfectly reasonable. "Did he?"

Wesley chuckled. "Could this be true?"

If she was going to marry him, he should know everything. "I may have sent an unsigned note to a certain gaming hell to keep an eye on the Earl of Radcliff's gambling habits."

Stopping, he turned to look at her. "Good lord. Does Aurora know?"

Lifting her chin, she looked him in the eyes but saw no censure there. "The Wallflowers have never discussed it, but I suspect all three know."

He lifted her onto Brutus's back and blinked. "What an amazing circle of women you Wallflowers are."

Leaning into the circle of his arms, she had everything she wanted. Her heart ached that he did not. "I truly wish you could have Whickette Park back."

He kissed the crown of her head. "What I am getting is far more precious. I think my father would heartily approve."

Having never met the previous earl, Mercy didn't know if he would have been in favor of his only son marrying a girl of no title or wealth. Still, being with Wesley made her happier than she'd ever been.

When they reached the inn, Wesley left her at the back door with a warm kiss that stole her breath and was full of promises.

* * * *

Mercy insisted on being present when Wesley spoke to her aunt. It was nearly luncheon by the time Aurora managed to convince her mother to take a walk. As soon as they were out of the inn, Wesley requested the interview and secured a small private room at the back of the common room at the inn.

"What is this all about, my lord?" Aunt Phyllis sounded stern but her eyes told Mercy she knew what he wanted.

"I have asked your niece to marry me and she has indicated that it would be agreeable." He let out a long breath and sat across the round table from Aunt Phyllis.

Both brows raised, Phyllis studied Mercy. "Mercedes, do you wish to marry Lord Castlewick?"

Surprised by the question, Mercy said, "He is an earl. I would have thought what I want would play little part in your decision."

For a long moment, Aunt Phyllis stared but said nothing. "That does not answer my question." The stern tone now accompanied a harsh stare.

Knowing her aunt was not to be trifled with when in this mood, Mercy swallowed her questions. "I do wish to marry his lordship, Aunt Phyllis. I love him."

Turning back to Wesley, Phyllis said, "I will expect you to treat my niece with utmost respect. The fact that she is not titled might make a man think she does not deserve high regard. If you have a mind to peddle her musical talent for gain, I shall not have it."

Wesley frowned. "Use her...Deserve..." He took a long breath. "Madam, I am perfectly solvent with a good income and several estates. The fact that I am not in possession of Whickette Park as yet should not be taken as a sign of any financial ruin. I can ably take care of Mercedes and have no need to peddle her talents, as you put it. She will play if and when she wishes. I am in love with your niece and intend to marry her. If you disapprove, that will make for an uncomfortable few minutes, Lady Mattock, but it will not change my resolve."

"Pretty speech." Aunt Phyllis fussed with her blue satin reticule. "Pretty indeed. I'm happy to hear that you love her as she is a remarkable woman who deserves nothing less. I give you both my blessing."

"Thank you." His shoulders sagged slightly before he righted his posture.

Aunt Phyllis turned to Mercy. She patted her perfectly coiffed gray hair into place and pursed her lips. "As for your question, Mercedes. I have always wanted you to be happy. When I married Mattock, it was to secure a future where we would be comfortable. You were unfairly judged by him, for which I am sorry. For a long time, I felt bad about him sending you away to school. However, it was for the best. While I did think he would live a bit longer, the outcome was good enough that neither you nor I had to go into service and that was the point. You may think me uncaring, but it was always my intention to see you were secure and my hope that you would be happy. You must forgive me if I failed you in any way. I always had your wellbeing at heart."

Emotion knotted in Mercy's throat as she leapt from her chair and threw herself into her aunt's arms. "You have been a wonderful parent, Aunt Phyllis. I always knew you wanted the best for me. I was content at school and would not change a moment of those years. Forgive me for my callous question. Of course, I know you want me to be happy."

Aunt Phyllis patted her back. "I'm much relieved, my dear."

Mercy kissed her cheek and straightened. Wesley stood near the door smiling at them both.

"I suppose this means we shall have to deal with Jemima's temper for the rest of the trip." Phyllis sighed. "I expect banns to be read for at least three weeks, my lord."

He nodded agreement. "Whatever you ladies wish, I will see it done."

Unable to bear the thought of a big public wedding, Mercy said, "I would like a private wedding with just our closest friends. I do not care for being gaped at when there is no music between me and my admirers." She pushed her spectacles up.

"If at the end of the day you are my wife, I don't care where we marry or how many people witness the event." His eyes sparkled and he never took his gaze from her face.

The joy she saw from him filled her with elation that could barely be contained.

Aunt Phyllis gave a satisfied nod. "You needn't marry at St. Paul's. I would be perfectly satisfied if you married at Grosvenor Chapel, as it is where I attend. Would that be acceptable?"

"I would like that very much." Mercy had always liked the clean white chapel much more than the larger ones in London. It might not be as fashionable, but she would feel more at home.

"Then it is settled." Wesley's grin hadn't faltered since Aunt Phyllis had given her consent.

Never had another person's happiness made her feel so fulfilled. It probably meant that his sorrow would be hers too, but she pushed the thought aside. "Shall we go and see the ruins?"

They walked from the private room. The common area bustled with a luncheon crowd. The mistress of the inn was a stout woman with ruddy skin and bits of brown hair poking from under her cap. Her name was Mrs. Truitt and she ambled over carrying a large basket with a smile that revealed a missing front tooth. "My lord, I've packed a lovely picnic for you and your party. You'll find everything you need within."

"Thank you, Mrs. Truitt. You have been most accommodating." Wesley accepted the basket with a smile.

"I suppose that means we are going to picnic by the ruins as planned." Aunt Phyllis smiled. The breeze blew in from the opened door and her smile turned to a frown. "I believe Aurora has informed her mother of the situation."

Mercy's heart pounded despite her resolve never to let that woman intimidate her again.

The Dowager Countess of Marsden stood arms akimbo, glaring across the common room.

Chapter 20

Wesley stepped between Mercy and the approaching dowager, but there was little he could do.

"I knew I should have tossed you from the house the first moment I saw you all those years ago, Mercedes Heath. How dare you foist your wiles on the earl as if you had any right to him with your low birth." Lady Marsden did nothing to hide her agitation or lower her voice.

The diners and patrons of the inn all stopped and stared.

"Mother, that is enough. You are making a spectacle of yourself," Aurora bit out.

Lady Marsden's bonnet sat slightly askew and her blond hair had come loose, making her look wild and unpredictable. Never having seen the stern lady out of control, Wesley feared there might be real danger. "Perhaps it might be best if we left the inn and discussed this over our picnic lunch."

"Picnic! You want to have a picnic! I demand you marry my daughter and reject this usurper immediately." Her face was bright red and she swung her reticule about like a baton.

It was farcical and Wesley found it harder and harder not to laugh. He looked back at Mercy; her lips twitched and amusement filled her eyes. Returning his attention to her ladyship, he said, "That is not going to happen, my lady. It is unfortunate you have pinned so much hope in that direction and I apologize as it is in part my fault...."

"It is her fault." Lady Marsden pointed a manicured finger at Mercy.

Aurora gripped her mother's outstretched hand and pushed it down from the rude gesture. "Mother, your behavior is unforgivable. Lord Castlewick has been a perfect gentleman and Mercy is not to blame. I was never going to marry his lordship. Never."

"But why? He is rich, you have property he wants, it is a perfect match." Her ladyship's voice took on a whining tone.

"Perhaps on paper, it is a good match, but I will not marry anyone at this time and his lordship loves Mercy." Aurora wrapped an arm around her mother.

"I'm not going on any picnic." Tears pooled in Jemima Draper's eyes. "I'll not be in her presence." She turned a vicious look at Mercy. "I know what you've done, Mercedes Heath, and I'll not forget it."

Wisely, Mercy said nothing. She raised a brow and kept her gaze steady on her ladyship, but she kept her thoughts to herself.

As soon as Aurora had bustled her mother up the steps, Wesley turned to Mercy. "Are you all right?"

Her smile was slow and she shrugged. "It was to be expected. Lady Marsden has never liked me, and she is used to getting what she wants. I'm afraid she will make our lives difficult whenever she can. You may wish to rethink your proposal, my lord. I shall understand if you'd rather not be embroiled in the scandal that will surely follow us back to London."

Lady Mattock huffed. "I most assuredly will not understand. An agreement has been made."

Raising his hand in surrender, Wesley calmed the rising temper of Mercy's aunt. "There is no need to get yourself worked up, my lady. I have no intention of calling off now or in the future. I am honored that Mercedes has agreed to marry me and will do nothing to cloud that path. Rest assured, anything Lady Marsden can do can be thwarted by titles and money."

He offered Mercy his arm and, clutching the picnic basket, they crossed the room to the door.

The carriage waited in the yard. Once he'd helped the ladies in, he stowed the basket in the carriage.

Mercy poked her head out from the window. "I think we might wait a few minutes. I believe once Aurora has settled her mother, she will join us."

It seemed as if Mercy held back more than she'd said on the subject, but she shrugged and hid a smile behind her lowered chin.

"Then we shall wait." He bowed to her and wished they were alone so he could kiss that adorable nose. Leaning against the carriage, he crossed his ankles and waited.

He adored Mercy's optimism, but assumed Aurora would be relegated to dealing with her mother for the duration of the afternoon. However, not ten minutes later, a smiling Aurora Sherbourn, Dowager Countess of Radcliff, appeared in the doorway of The Smoker. "My lady, I'm so glad you could join us."

"As am I, my lord. I love ruins of any kind." Aurora's grin widened. "My mother has decided to remain here in town rather than join us today."

He opened the carriage door and handed her up. "Her ladyship will be missed."

Hiding a giggle, Aurora said, "Indeed."

Looking through the window, Wesley said. "It won't take long to drive there, ladies, and we shall have a fine afternoon in the sunshine."

"Very good." Lady Mattock pulled her sewing from her bag.

He turned to mount the carriage driver's seat.

Inside, Aurora said, "I'm so sorry, Mercy. Mother should not have said those things."

Rather than continue his climb, Wesley was only slightly ashamed of his eavesdropping.

Mercy's calm, round voice echoed from within. "It is no less than I expected when I accepted him, Aurora. I knew there would be consequences and this ordeal with your mother is only the first."

Wishing she was mistaken wouldn't make it so. People like Jemima Draper would stir up a lot of gossip in the weeks before he could marry Mercy and give her a title that would keep the *ton*'s mouths shut. Even members of his own family would voice their objections. He sighed and snapped the reins.

Somehow the ten-minute drive into the hills seemed to take forever as his thoughts grew darker with what Mercy would have to endure in order to marry him. If he could bear the brunt, he would, he must.

* * * *

The ruins hadn't changed since his childhood. All that was left of the medieval castle was the front wall with its two towers and three pillars that likely had once held up the ceiling. They were now covered in moss and overgrown grasses.

They made their picnic under an old oak. Mercy had declined to eat and climbed around in the remains of the old castle.

Wesley couldn't take his eyes off her as, with grace and agility, she leaped and climbed around the old stone fortress. It was impossible not to notice how lithe she was, particularly in the ballroom, and even as she moved from chair to teacart. However, in nature, as she explored the old castle, it was like watching a ballet.

Aurora handed him an apple. "My lord."

Taking the fruit, he kept his focus on Mercy. "I think I shall join Miss Heath in the ruins." Apple in hand, he stood and walked away without waiting to hear what the other ladies might think of his obvious attraction.

Standing on a pier three feet high, she smiled down at him. "Was the picnic not to your liking, my lord?"

"Please don't call me that, Mercy." He handed her the apple.

"Wesley," she whispered before placing her foot carefully on a series of crumbling stones and reaching the ground easily.

"The picnic was very nice, but I find myself distracted." As lovely as she was in a staid bun tucked under her cap, he longed to see her hair flying free in the breeze as it had that morning.

Biting into the apple, she walked toward the standing wall that held the empty arch where an oak door would once have hinged. "I am a distraction? I don't believe I have ever been called that before."

Following like a moth to the flame, he said, "In the time I've known you, you have distracted no less than three men other than me. I think you have been a distraction on many occasions, even if you did not recognize the state of the men smitten by you."

She turned, eyes wide, and blushed the most beautiful pink. "Are you smitten?"

Feeling the eyes of Lady Mattock and Aurora keenly, he stepped closer but not so close as to touch her. "Utterly and completely."

Her nose wrinkled in the most adorable way. "You exaggerate."

As she started through the arched stones, he blocked her path. "No, Mercy. I am quite certain I could never do without you now that I've found you."

Eyes wide, she blushed deeper. "You shall make me cry if you continue these declarations."

"I hope they would be tears of joy and not distress, my love." Holding his ground, he would not let her escape him.

Taking a step forward brought her to mere inches from him. "I have never been happier in my life than I am today. I never dreamed I could feel so much for another person. Never."

He thought the inability to drag her into his arms and kiss her until they were both senseless might drive him mad. "I'm happier to hear that than I can express."

"You do know that the sentiments of the dowager will not be unique, Wesley." Her tone was calm.

"It has occurred to me, but I shan't let anyone ruin our bliss." Wesley hoped he could keep that promise.

Her lips pulled up on one side as if she too knew he had little control over such things. She took another bite of the apple and cocked her head. After a moment she pointed over his left shoulder. "What is that on the hill?"

It was a good time for a change of subject. Not ruining a perfect day seemed far more important than the obstacles they would face when they returned to London. Glancing in the direction she indicated, he said, "Those are ancient standing stones from a civilization before the Romans came to the island."

Eyes bright with excitement, she practically ran past him toward the hill.

When her aunt didn't call after her, Wesley checked back at the picnic area and found it devoid of ladies. Scanning the area, he saw that the carriage stood where he'd left to the far left of the tree. The two figures of Lady Mattock and Aurora walked along a path heading to the west away from them.

Surprised by the trust of Mercy's aunt in giving them privacy, he wouldn't squander the opportunity. He jogged up the hill to catch Mercy just as she reached the ring of standing stones. "Your aunt and Lady Radcliff have gone for a walk."

"I'm sure they think you will steal a kiss." She crossed to the farthest stones.

He stepped just behind her. "Would I have to steal it?"

She rested her hand on one of the tall stones, which stood three feet above her head, and closed her eyes. "No, Wesley. All my kisses belong to you already."

Pressing close, he let her back curve into his front, and placed his hand on top of hers on the warm smooth stone. Under his fingers her soft skin warmed him further and the strange stone seemed to vibrate. "It is extraordinary the way these monuments seem alive."

Sliding her hand out from under his, she turned to face him and pressed her back against the stone. "It's almost as if they want to tell us their story, but we don't know how to understand them."

Her body fitted to his with heady perfection. "I remember coming here as a boy and wishing I knew more about the people who stood these monoliths up. It must have been something to see. I've been to Stonehenge and found the same haunting vibration in the stones."

Capturing her lips, he tasted the top and then the bottom. She sighed into the kiss.

"Do you think they mind our kissing in this ring?" Her hand wrapped around his neck, bringing him closer.

He nibbled on her neck and traced the lobe of her ear with his tongue. "I hope not." He kissed down her neck to her shoulder.

"My aunt will not have gone far." Her voice was breathy and lacked any sign of wanting him to stop.

Still, he took a deep breath, let her flowery essence infuse him, and stepped back, wishing he could return to Whickette Park, where they could be alone. He offered his arm. "Will you walk with me, Mercy?"

She accepted his elbow. "Where are we going?"

"Not far, just to look at the view and then we'll return and you can eat something. You must be famished by now." He led her around the stones to where the hill crested and the rolling land and craggy rocks spread out before them. A mist had settled in the valley in the distance, but the sky was clear and the sun warmed them.

"This is so beautiful, Wesley. Do…" She started to say more then stopped herself.

"What is it?"

"I shouldn't ask questions. I have been told so by many of my mentors over the years. Music teachers, the headmistress as school, Aunt Phyllis, have all scolded me for being too inquisitive for my own good." She pulled her hand away and fisted it at her side.

Taking back her hand, he rubbed gentle circles at her wrist and palm until she relaxed the fingers, then he kissed her palm. "You have leave to ask me anything, Mercy, as I have many questions I will ask over the weeks preceding our wedding. I'll want to know all there is to know about you."

"There is little to know." She stared at where he caressed her palm and her voice was breathy.

"I doubt that very much. Now, ask your question." He threaded his fingers through hers. His hands were big, rough, and tanned, while her long fingers wrapped around his knuckles with strength and small calluses from playing various instruments and were pale in comparison with his.

"I just wondered if you have a house in this area since you own much of the surrounding land." A breeze came up and she closed her eyes. Small wisps of hair fluttered around her face.

"I have a house, Thornsdown Manor in the Peak District. It's about thirty miles east of here. I also have a townhouse in London and a few other manors and cottages. Are you concerned about my ability to care for you, Mercy?"

Her eyes went wide. "Goodness no. I just wondered where we would live."

"You seem to enjoy the country. We could live much of the year at Thornsdown. It's a fine house and you would be comfortable." He liked the idea of her in his house ordering the staff about.

"I'm sure it's very fine, it's only…" She bit her bottom lip.

"Only what?"

"I have lived most of my life in London. I like the country, but it would be difficult to accomplish my goals locked away in an estate somewhere and I would miss my friends." She said the last quickly as if to brush past it.

"I see. If you prefer the city then we can live in town and only winter in the country. I will take you on a tour of the homes available to us and you may pick the one you prefer."

"Don't you care where you live?" She pulled her hand away and gripped both together.

Running his knuckles down her jaw, he relished the soft flesh and the way those green eyes never strayed. "If you are by my side, I shall adore any home you choose."

"You are jesting. I'm sure you have a favorite and will tell me so as soon as we are wed." She crossed her arms over her chest and shifted from foot to foot.

"Mercy, I will never tell you anything that is not entirely the truth." He stepped close and struggled against touching her.

In the distance, Aurora and Lady Mattock were returning and, despite their engagement, he didn't want her aunt to think him ungentlemanly. He was a bundle of nerves for the first time in his life. Now that he'd secured her hand, he would worry until their wedding day.

She pushed her spectacles up and took a deep breath. "I feel like you have more to say, but are hesitant. Have I mistaken your mood?"

He should have known someone who understood emotion as well as she would see his trepidation. He offered his arm. "There are some things on my mind, which I'd like to share with you and hear your thoughts."

Taking his arm, she raised a brow. "Tell me."

"My cousin Malcolm is currently the heir to the earldom. He is not a bad sort, but he is a bit of a snob about certain things." Even through the fabric of his coat, he felt the heat of her touching him.

"You think he will object to you marrying me." Her tone was matter of fact and held no anger, only resignation.

"Mercy, whatever Malcolm thinks will not change anything in our lives. I just want you to know that when we return, you will meet him and he may say things that are abhorrent to you and certainly to me."

She cocked her head. "You're the head of your family, so why would he say anything with regard to your choices?"

It was a fair question and Wesley laughed. "I haven't any brothers. Malcolm and I were very close growing up. Still, he can be very difficult and opinionated. I have told him on more than one occasion that he's a snob. And of course, there are my sisters, though I'm sure they will love you."

With a shrug, she sighed. "I suppose there will be a lot of people who will think the worst of me when they hear of our engagement, so your cousin will be in the majority. I am looking forward to meeting your sisters. What are they like?"

"Charlotte and Ester are twins." Thinking of his sisters always brought him joy.

"Oh! I didn't realize. How old are they?" Mercy smiled and the expression lit her green eyes.

"Just seventeen. My parents thought they could not have any more children after me and were quite surprised when the twins came along ten years later." The memories of coming home from school to those two tiny bundles of cooing and crying flooded him.

Mercy's gaze was distant and a line formed between her eyes. "You never mentioned when your mother passed. I know your father has been gone a few years, but when did you lose your mother?"

"Mother died of a fever ten years ago. My father passed almost three years ago now." Missing his parents was part of Wesley's daily life and he rarely gave it any thought, but now a sadness washed over him. He would have liked his mother and father to have met Mercy and seen how amazing she was. His mother would have doted on her and Father would have hidden his feelings but loved her just the same.

She touched his arm. "I have made you unhappy with my incessant questions. I'm sorry, Wesley."

Taking her fingers, he forced a smile and kissed them. "No. I was just thinking about how much my parents would have loved you. Charlotte and Ester will adore you."

Lifting her chin, she said, "We have much in common. I too was young when I lost my parents. They were lucky to have you to care for them."

He stopped her progress to where her aunt and Aurora now waited under the tree. "Will you mind the twins staying with us, Mercy? I would hate to have them live apart from me until they have found husbands."

Eyes wide, Mercy stepped back. "Of course, they must live with us. Do you think I would put them out or send them away?"

Shame washed through him. "To be honest, I hadn't given it any thought at all. I am so caught up in loving you, I didn't give the effect on my siblings and Malcolm any thought. It was reckless of me."

Her hand dropped away and she put even more distance between them. "Are you having regrets? I would understand if you wished to rethink your offer."

Closing the distance, he wished her aunt and Aurora were not so nearby. "I may deserve a strong word or two for some selfishness and impulsiveness, but I regret nothing and it changes nothing. I love you, Mercy. Nothing will change that. I hate that there will be gossip. I shall protect you from as much of it as possible. My cousin will get over any pride he might experience and my sisters will be thrilled to have you in our family."

A sad smile played across her lips. "London is nothing without some gossip. I shall survive if it means that in the end we are together."

Longing to pull her into his arms, he glanced at her aunt and bowed instead. "Once we are married and you are the Countess of Castlewick, no one will dare say a word to disparage you."

Her laughter rang out on the clear day. "Of course they will. They shall just do so when I am out of earshot."

Chapter 21

Having left Cheshire early, Mercy and Aurora were back in London in time for Tuesday tea. "There really was no sense in staying any longer. Her ladyship was so vexed about my engagement she would give no one peace," Mercy said.

Aurora sighed. "Mother was petulant for the entire trip back to London. At least you could escape her during the carriage rides, Mercy. It was such a blessing whenever she fell asleep and stopped her nagging."

Faith shook her head. "Didn't you tell her that her hopes of a match between you and Castlewick were unfounded, Aurora?"

"Of course, I did. I could never love him, though I think him a fine man. I'm so happy for you, Mercy. You and his lordship make a perfectly splendid couple." Aurora's smile lit her eyes as she leaned forward to pour more tea.

Heat rushed up Mercy's cheeks. "Thank you. I wish I could be sorry it didn't work out for you, Aurora, but I'm so happy to have secured Wesley's love, I can feel little else."

Poppy had been particularly quiet during the tea. She leaned forward and placed her cup and saucer on the table before taking a biscuit and sitting back. "Do you love him, Mercy?"

"Of course, I do. I would not have agreed to marry a man I do not love." Mercy couldn't keep the surprise from her voice. "Why would you ask me that, Poppy?"

Standing, Poppy fisted her hands. "Please don't misunderstand me, Mercy. If you are happy, then I am happy for you. It's only that this feels very sudden. You must know you needn't marry if you do not wish to. You have the three of us to support any endeavor you should pursue. I would not like to think you married because you felt you needed a husband to keep you safe."

Perhaps Mercy should have been angry at her friend's notion that she was desperate, but knowing Poppy's worry was based on her love, she stood and hugged her. "Poppy, I love him. I never believed it would be possible to love any man based on the callers I've had over the years. And most of them were perfectly respectable men who sincerely wanted to marry me."

"So you could play music for them every day for the rest of their lives," Faith added with little attempt to hide her contempt.

Mercy laughed. "Perhaps. Still, Mr. Colby and his ilk were all fine choices and would have afforded me safety if not happiness." Sighing as Wesley's strong jaw and kind eyes flitted through her mind, she said, "Wesley has pushed aside his dream of restoring his family estates to marry a woman of no means or connection. Though I think he will continue to look for a way to purchase the final piece of land from Aurora. He put those things aside for me. I am overwhelmed with emotion, but I loved him long before he did this. In fact, I think I loved him from the moment I met him, but I had just determined that since I could never have him, those emotions should be held back and I tried to bury them. Unsuccessfully, I might add."

All three of her friends listened with wide eyes, without interruption.

Aurora grinned and nodded.

Faith's soft smile accompanied a sigh.

Poppy shook her head and dragged Mercy into another hug. "Then I am overwhelmed with joy for you. Wesley Renshaw is a lucky man, and I shall be sure he knows just how lucky on our next meeting."

Squeezing Poppy, Mercy giggled. "I'm certain you will."

Faith poured the last of the tea. "Will you continue giving lessons now that you have no need to work?"

"Oh yes." Mercy accepted the tea. "Though I might be choosier about my students and allow another teacher to instruct the novices. Then I can focus on serious musicians and gifted children. I would enjoy that much more and so would my ears."

They all laughed.

Poppy asked, "How does his lordship feel about your working after you're married?"

Just the mention of Wesley, even in title only, warmed Mercy from the inside out. "He said he would support any venture I took on. I shall hold him to his word."

"The way he looks at you tells me he would give the moon if you asked for it." Aurora's eyes glittered the way they had years before. It was wonderful to see her becoming more herself with every day that passed since her horrible husband's death.

"Then it's a good thing I have no use for a celestial globe. His love and affection will do nicely for a start." Mercy folded herself into the chaise and curled her legs beneath her.

Always worried, Poppy asked, "And where will you live? I should not like for him to curry you off to some country home several days from West Lane."

"I would not like to be far from the three of you either, which is why we shall live most of the year in London." Mercy raised a brow to see if Poppy had any other concerns.

From behind her teacup, Poppy said, "I am satisfied for the present."

"Thank goodness." Faith put her cup down. Are you all attending Savington's ball on Friday? "Nick wants to go because Mr. Arafa was invited and he's worried Savington might be up to something."

"What do you mean?" Poppy sat up straight ad narrowed her eyes. She and Rhys had become good friends to Geb Arafa over the past year and she was fiercely protective of her friends.

Faith shrugged. "I'm not sure. It is unusual for Mr. Arafa to receive invitations from *ton* members outside of our group. Savington has never struck me as a dishonest person, but the invitation is unusual. Perhaps he is just in need of information and wishes to speak to Mr. Arafa."

"Or perhaps he has something more dire in mind." Poppy frowned. "I will speak to Rhys. He had a meeting with a ship's captain this afternoon, but he will come to collect me. I'm sure he will wish to attend on Friday. I'll not have anyone embarrass Mr. Arafa if that is Savington's plan."

"I shall write Lady Savington today and tell her I will be at the ball," Aurora agreed.

They all turned and gaped at Mercy. "I was going anyway. I'm to meet Wesley's sisters and his cousin, Malcolm Renshaw, on Friday."

"Why should that make you look queasy?" Aurora and all Mercy's friends were often too observant.

"Wesley warned me that his cousin is a bit of a snob and will not approve the match." Mercy wiped her hands on her skirt as they started perspiring. "I shouldn't care, but I hate the idea of his relatives disliking me."

Poppy made a scoffing sound. "Firstly, no one who truly knows you could possibly dislike you. And secondly, if he dislikes you based on something monetary like a piece of land or a large dowry, we have no use of this Mr. Malcolm Renshaw anyway."

"Perhaps not, but I still would like to make a good impression. I'm glad you will all be there. We shall support Mr. Arafa as a group." Mercy gave a nod that was more assured than she felt.

Aurora nodded back. "And we shall all support you as well. Malcolm Renshaw does not know the Wallflowers of West Lane and therefore is already outnumbered."

"Indeed." Faith gave a smile.

Poppy crossed and sat next to Mercy on the chaise. She took her hand. "Not to worry, Mercy. Shall we call for more tea?"

The knocker sounded from the foyer and Poppy went to the window facing the street. "Rhys must have arrived early from his meeting. Oh, it's two ladies."

"I wonder who that could be." Aurora stopped her progress to call for tea and turned toward the door.

A moment later, Tipton opened the salon door. "My lady, the ladies Charlotte and Ester Renshaw to see Miss Heath. I have asked them to wait in the grand parlor."

All eyes turned toward Mercy. Wesley's sisters had come to call. "Is Lord Castlewick with them, Tipton?"

With no sign of thoughts or emotions, the butler said, "The young ladies are unattended but arrived in a carriage with driver and footman."

"But they are only seventeen. Surely they have a governess." Mercy worried for their safety and couldn't imagine what Wesley was thinking not having a chaperone for his sisters.

Poppy came back to the seating area and grinned. "I'm liking these sisters. Do send them in here, Tipton. We shall need more tea as well."

"Yes, Lady Marsden. I shall inform Cook." Tipton backed out of the room.

Aurora said, "I assume you didn't expect a call from your future sisters-in-law, Mercy."

"No. As I said, I expected to meet them on Friday at the ball." Mercy held her breath and stared at the door.

Tipton returned, flanked by two girls with dark blond curls and bright brown eyes. They looked like sisters but were not identical. One had a rounder face and dimples; the other had a stronger chin like her brother. "Lady Charlotte Renshaw and Lady Ester Renshaw."

Once the butler had left and closed the door, the wide-eyed Renshaw twins made their curtsies, as did the Wallflowers of West lane.

The slightly taller twin spoke first. She had very similar features to Wesley. "Please forgive me, which one of you is Miss Heath?"

Mercy had to hold back her giggle. They were adorable. She stepped forward. "I am Mercedes Heath."

The rounder-faced twin rushed forward and grabbed Mercy's hands. "I am Ester Renshaw. Our brother has told us all about you. Though only yesterday. I know we were supposed to meet on Friday, but I hate to meet at a ball where we will have no chance to talk. It seemed better to come and call on you and Charlotte agreed. Of course, Mrs. Manfred would never have agreed, so Charlotte had to convince our driver to take us. I thought we should hire a hack, but this was better." She turned to her sister. "You were right about that, Charlotte."

Charlotte approached. "I hope you are not too put out by our coming. You are to be our sister and we knew nothing about you until yesterday. I further hope we are not intruding on a private tea. Though I fear we are."

Both twins stepped back and stared at the other three ladies, who were close to laughter.

Aurora, always the most contained, steeled her features and stepped forward. "You are most welcome. I am Aurora Sherbourn. Please come and sit. I have called for tea."

They glanced from Aurora to Mercy.

Mercy, who had not been able to get a word in thus far, said, "Please, join us for tea. These are my closest friends, the Dowager Countess of Radcliff, the Duchess of Breckenridge, and the Countess of Marsden."

"Gracious, you have lofty friends, Miss Heath." Ester fussed with the trim around the bodice of her peach gown.

Poppy laughed. "You'd not have thought so if you would have met us some years ago."

Faith sat and giggled. "That is certain."

Opening the salon door, Mercy called, "Tipton."

A moment later the butler appeared. "Yes, Miss Heath?"

"Will you send word to Lord Castlewick's home that his sisters are calling here and quite safe?"

"Of course."

Ester appeared sheepish, at their planned escape from whoever Mrs. Manfred was.

Charlotte just shrugged. "Perhaps it's inappropriate, but we just couldn't wait for the ball."

"It wouldn't do," Ester agreed.

Mercy sat on the chaise. "I couldn't agree with you more and I'm delighted to meet you both. However, if I caused your brother worry, it would pain me greatly. It's better, at this point, to send word that you are safe."

"Besides," Poppy said. "If your Mrs. Manfred comes to collect you it will still be a while and we'll have had time for a short visit."

"So true." Aurora sat and smoothed her gown. "Now, who is Mrs. Manfred?"

Ester cleared her throat and pulled at her lace again. "Our governess. She has been with us since our mother died when we were quite young."

They were sweet girls. Mercy could see that right away. They might share a birthday, but that was where the similarities ended. Where Ester was talkative and gave her opinion freely, Charlotte was thoughtful and careful with her words.

"My brother tells us that you are a musician, Miss Heath." Charlotte cocked her head to the left.

Ester cocked her head to the right. "We love music. I hope you will play for us soon."

Mercy liked them. "I will play so often that you will soon tire of my music, Miss Renshaw."

The tea arrived and conversation ceased until the maid left.

"I do not think that is possible." Charlotte accepted a cup from Aurora.

"You are correct." Aurora poured a cup for Ester. "We have been blessed with Mercy's music since we were girls of just fifteen and we have yet to tire of hearing her play."

Faith declined another cup. "That is an understatement. Her play is remarkable."

"Do either of you play?" Mercy wanted to move the conversation away from herself.

A huge grin spread across Ester's sweet face. "We both play the pianoforte, though do not practice as much as we should."

"Then I look forward to hearing you both play. Perhaps I will accompany you on another instrument."

Charlotte's eyes widened. "How many do you play?"

Somehow Mercy had misspoken and brought them back to her. "A few."

Laughing, Poppy said, "We don't even know the answer to that question. It seems whatever you hand her, she can play."

"Then she'll come back a month later and be an expert on the flute or oboe." Faith shook her head, but her eyes sparkled with mirth.

"I do not play the oboe." Mercy said.

Aurora sipped her tea. "Only because you have yet to try it."

Ester put her cup on the table. "You four have been friends a long time."

"We have," Mercy confirmed.

Charlotte put her own cup down and smoothed her periwinkle day dress. "Ester and I have had each other since birth. We were born friends. I cannot imagine finding such a close bond with anyone else, but I can see you have something quite similar here."

The sisters gazed at each other with sadness.

"What's wrong?" Mercy asked.

Ester sighed and looked at Mercy. "We didn't know about you until our brother came home from the country and we were quite excited to have a new sister. Now we can see you do not need us as you already have sisters."

It took a bit of energy not to chuckle at the sweet notion. "But my dear, Ester, you should know that when you become family with one Wallflower of West Lane, you gain them all."

Ester gaped at Poppy who nodded. "We shall be a fine party whenever we're together."

While Charlotte tried her best to be calm and refined, her elated expression hid nothing when she looked at Faith. "But you are a duchess."

"That is only a title, my dear. Besides, marrying a duke has its advantages." Faith waggled her brows.

The twins giggled.

"It does come in handy," Mercy agreed.

"If we are truly to become sisters, we must confess." Charlotte fidgeted.

Heart jumping to her throat, Mercy put her tea aside. "What must you confess?"

Charlotte and Ester exchanged a silent look and agreement. Ester said, "It was not completely our idea to come here today."

Shocked, Mercy didn't know what to think. "Wesley sent you?" A million thoughts ran through Mercy's mind and none of them made any sense as to why he would have sent his sisters to see her without a chaperone.

"No." Charlotte stared at her shoes. "Wesley doesn't know we are here. He left early this morning on some business."

"Who sent you?" Faith's voice was soft and reassuring.

Ester pulled too hard on the lace she'd been fussing with and it came free of her gown. She smoothed over the fabric that would have to be mended. "Cousin Malcolm came and was in a bit of a snit over you becoming engaged to Wesley. He said you must have tricked him. He distracted Mrs. Manfred while we slipped out of the house. He'd gotten us into a bit of a panic but then on the carriage ride over, we talked and realized we had never seen Wes so happy. He never smiles so easily. If you had tricked him, he must have needed tricking if you make him that happy. Then we thought Malcolm might have other reasons for being mistrustful. He can be quite suspicious. So we decided to meet you first before we decided if we should like you or not."

"And there you have the whole story." Poppy hid her amusement behind a bite of biscuit, though not very well.

Charlotte said, "I hope you are not too angry with us. We should have told you the entire truth as soon as we arrived, but if Mal was right…"

"And are you certain your cousin is not correct about me?" This cousin Malcolm had not yet been introduced, but Mercy already disliked the way he had manipulated his young cousins.

"Oh yes. We are very good judges of character. You are not prideful or sneaky." Ester beamed.

She was glad that despite Mr. Renshaw's plans, these young ladies had made their own decisions rather than come to West Lane with bad intentions. "Whatever your reasons were for coming, I am pleased to meet you both."

The twins' shoulders relaxed as one and conversation returned to music and then books.

Mercy forced herself to concentrate on the moment and not think about Malcolm Renshaw and whatever he might have hoped to gain by coercing these girls.

Chapter 22

By Friday afternoon Mercy's nerves had gotten the better of her. She went downstairs to the pianoforte at the West Lane house and played for over an hour, only stopping when Aurora warned her she would not have time to dress. The idea of meeting another relative shouldn't be so daunting, but knowing full well that Malcolm would not approve made her uneasy in the extreme.

Wesley had described his cousin as a snob but he had also said they were like brothers. She wanted her new family to like her and she wanted to like them. Charlotte and Ester were both dears and she couldn't have been happier about that.

Taking a deep breath, she bolstered her courage and tried to be more like Poppy.

Jane, her maid, helped her into a ruby gown that she had never been brave enough to wear before. If she was going to be scrutinized by a stranger, she was going to look her best. The gown was cut lower than she normally wore and it fell straight from just under the bust, leaving little room to hide her figure. She put on her mother's pearls and allowed Jane to curl and pin her hair for over an hour. The tiny braids and pearl-tipped pins made her look far more elevated than was her station. She smiled at herself in the glass and felt pretty. Sliding the Wallflowers essential hatpin into the coif was the final step in dressing for any event.

With thirty minutes left before Wesley came and collected her and Aurora, Mercy returned to the music room. She played an old piece from when she had tried her hand at composing. It was a sweet tune but had turned dark with her mood and the addition of a minor key.

"I don't know that piece," Wesley said from only a few feet away.

Mercy rushed to close the key cover. "Just something I used to play with long ago."

He stepped closer and sat on the bench beside her. His warmth infused her. "I didn't know you compose music."

Touching the dark wood of the instrument, she said, "I haven't bothered in a long time. My skill is in playing. I never had much talent for composing."

"You may say what you wish, but I thought that was quite beautiful. However, if you take no joy from creating your own music, then you shouldn't do it." He wrapped his fingers around hers, lifted her hand, and kissed her knuckles. "Are you ready to leave, Mercy?"

"Of course." She made to pull away and rise, but he held her in place.

"I'm sorry I could not call more often this week. My solicitor and secretary had collected a great deal of work that needed my approval after being away so long." His voice was soft and he stared at their joined hands.

"I understand. You sent several letters. I was happy to hear from you." She'd not worried overly about his lack of availability during the week. "I had students to teach and a lot of time visiting with the Wallflowers. It was nice to meet your sisters. They are darling."

"I'm happy to hear that. I wouldn't want you to worry over anything, least of all my affection." Keeping her hand in his, he threaded their fingers together and placed a kiss on the sensitive pad of her thumb before giving the same attention to each digit.

Mercy closed her eyes as a wave of desire swamped her. "I think we had better go, Wesley. Aurora is waiting."

"First, tell me why the music you chose was so somber and grew angry at the end." For the first time, he turned his head and met her gaze.

"Balls and gatherings where I might conjure attention always make me nervous. I suppose the music is always telling." It was only half a lie, she comforted herself.

"I will remain by your side," he promised.

"Of course." Pulling her hand away, she rose. "We should go now."

Pretending she didn't notice his concerned expression as they climbed into the carriage, Mercy kept her breathing steady and her eyes focused on the street speeding by in the window.

Aurora carried the conversation for the ride to the Savington townhouse. She smiled and went on about Mr. Arafa and the note she'd received from him about his devotion and appreciation of her and all the Wallflowers.

Mercy had received a similar letter. It had been kind that Mr. Arafa, upon hearing that the Wallflowers would all be at Savington's to support him, had offered advance thanks. Though he assured them that it was not necessary and he would not be in any danger from the earl.

Before Mercy had too much time to worry, they arrived at the extravagant home and Wesley handed her down. Making their way up the steps together, Mercy took Wesley's offered arm.

Aurora leaned over and whispered, "Mercedes, you shall have to breathe, if you are to survive the night."

"Perhaps I should have worn a demurer gown." Her pulse pounded in her chest.

"You are stunning, Mercy. There is no need to doubt yourself." Wesley wrapped his hand around her for a quick squeeze before returning to a less intimate public display where her hand gently rested atop his arm.

"Lord Castlewick is right." Aurora stepped in front of them as they reached the door and plastered a soft smile on her face. It was a familiar expression and one worn by most ladies of the *ton* when in company.

Mercy expected that her own expression was quite similar as she and Wesley entered the grand foyer of Savington's townhouse.

Lit by several candelabras, the tall stairs set a gilded backdrop to the receiving line where Wesley greeted their host and hostess. "Savington, may I present my fiancée, Miss Mercedes Heath?"

Tall and austere, Savington glared down his pointed, thin nose at Mercy. "A pleasure, Miss Heath." He exaggerated the Miss as if it were a vulgarity.

Lady Savington grinned, showing large front teeth. "Miss Heath, how lovely you look. Your dear aunt arrived only moments ago. I'm sure she awaits you in the ballroom."

Mercy took pains not to show either surprise or relief at knowing Aunt Phyllis was in attendance. "How nice that she arrived before us. Thank you, Lady Savington."

Mercy spotted Aunt Phyllis standing with a group of her friends on the far side of the ballroom.

Aurora disappeared into the crowd.

At her side, Wesley leaned in. "Shall I escort you to your aunt, Mercy, or would you like to dance?"

As much as she longed for the safety of her aunt's company, dancing with Wesley sounded heavenly. Besides, it wouldn't do to hide for the entire ball, as tempting as it was. "A dance would be lovely."

The other dancers were setting up for the Boulanger and Mercy followed suit to stand in a group of six with Wesley to her left. Mr. Arafa stood to her right and she greeted him. "It is good to see you again, Mr. Arafa."

"Miss Heath, the pleasure is all mine. You are a vision as always."

The lady beside him was Miss Wallthrop, whom Mercy had known for many years. She was a very kind woman who some people called dim, but Mercy had always found her timid, yet bright if one paid attention. Miss Wallthrop smiled. "How do you do, Miss Heath?"

"Very well, Miss Wallthrop." Mercy returned the smile before the frown of the tall gentleman next to Miss Wallthrop caught her eye.

Wesley said, "Malcolm, I didn't think you cared for dancing."

"You are mistaken, Castlewick. I am fond of the dance if the company is preferable." He barely gave his partner a glance, though the petite brunette blushed dark red. Instead, he narrowed his gaze on Mercy. His dark blue eyes were framed with thick, dark lashes and dark brows, while his hair was lighter with a slight curl. He was handsome, but in such a different way that many in the crowd stared at him.

The music began, precluding a proper introduction to Wesley's cousin. The lump in Mercy's throat grew and it took her a full turn to find her place in time with the dance. She took pains to keep her smile in place.

"Miss Heath, I believe," Malcolm said when they were forced to touch gloved hands.

"Indeed, sir. And you are Mr. Malcolm Renshaw." She impressed herself with the steadiness of her voice. Her knees might be quaking, but he need not know that fact.

Wesley smiled at her and the circle turned again. The lively music was well played and gave Mercy little distraction. If the musicians had been bad, she could have focused on their mistakes and taken her mind off the constant scrutiny of Wesley's disapproving relative.

Mr. Arafa took her gloved hand. "You look ready to do battle, Miss Heath. Is something amiss?"

Immediately calming her nerves and plastering a pleasant smile on her face, Mercy said, "Thank you for telling me, sir. I shall endeavor to keep my expression more guarded. You needn't worry."

"I am pleased to hear it." He gave her a knowing glance and relinquished her partnership to Malcolm.

"I understand we are to be cousins. My felicitations, Miss Heath." If anything, he sounded sarcastic rather than felicitous.

Having spent so many years with Poppy as a friend, Mercy was quite comfortable with sarcasm. "And I have heard that being your cousin shall be joyous to be sure."

A moment of surprise crossed his face before he had no choice but to release her hand as the music and dance required.

Relieved not to have to speak to Wesley's cousin again, Mercy kept her smile in place and sank her attention into the dance. When the final strains petered out, she applauded the musicians and immediately sought out her aunt and was happy to find her standing with Faith and Nick.

"You look lovely, Mercy." Faith kissed her cheek. Faith's deep rust gown was a perfect complement to her golden eyes and light brown hair.

"As do you. I don't remember this gown," Mercy said.

Faith tipped her chin up. "I have ordered a new wardrobe. It seems I am a duchess and can afford to have new gowns from time to time."

Mercy laughed. "It sounds to me like you are quoting your generous husband."

"Perhaps, but it was fun to go shopping. I dragged Poppy with me and she was miserable the entire time, but she made me go for several walks in the park while you and Aurora were away, so I feel the score is even." Faith and Mercy both giggled.

She'd almost forgotten the unpleasant Mr. Renshaw, when he appeared behind Faith. "You ladies seem to be enjoying the ball."

Faith turned and stared up at him. Despite her petite stature, she was formidable with her hands fisted and a severe frown. "Have we met, sir?"

Bowing, he apologized.

Wesley stepped closer, a frown tugging at his lips. "Your Graces, Lady Maddock, Miss Heath, may I present my cousin, Mr. Malcolm Renshaw."

Once curtsies and bows were made, Wesley leaned against the doorframe of the French door leading out to the veranda. The open door allowed a light breeze to enter the overcrowded ballroom. It was rude to lean so casually, but Mr. Renshaw seemed unconcerned with the slight as he studied Mercy.

In an attempt to ignore Wesley's cousin, Mercy turned to Nick. "Are you satisfied that Mr. Arafa is in no danger, Nick?"

Nick nodded. "It would seem that while our host is a snob and disapproves of your engagement, he came to the knowledge that Geb is from a wealthy family in Egypt and therefore deserving of his respect."

Stepping so close that his front touched Mercy's back, Wesley said, "I'm glad for your friend, but Savington's opinions of my choice in bride are irrelevant."

Malcolm scoffed, straightened, and stepped away without a word.

"His opinion doesn't matter either." Wesley lifted Mercy's hand and kissed her knuckles.

Wishing that money was not important in people's opinion of her would not make it so.

A harried-looking woman of perhaps forty rushed over. "Oh, my lord, thank goodness we've found you."

Behind her tall figure the Renshaw twins grinned happily. They wore matching pale yellow gowns but Ester's gown had a blue ribbon at the high waist and Charlotte's ribbon was green.

Ester rushed forward and took Mercy's hand. "You look so beautiful, Miss Heath."

"Thank you. You both look stunning and I'm delighted to see you again."

Wesley frowned but laughter lit his eyes. "I had a mind to make them stay at home for running off the other day, but Mrs. Manfred took the blame for their bad behavior."

"I am Mercedes Heath, Mrs. Manfred. It is a pleasure to make your acquaintance." Mercy liked the chaperone for her loyalty to the girls alone.

Red faced and in a dour gray gown, Mrs. Manfred fanned her face with one hand while reaching out to Mercy with the other. "You are an angel for sending word that the ladies were with you on Tuesday. I was near panic and Mr. Renshaw was of no help."

Since Malcolm knew full well where the ladies were, Mercy found it disappointing he would allow Mrs. Manfred to worry. She tucked the information away for a later date. "It was no trouble, madam. I was happy to meet the young ladies and they were a delight at tea on West Lane."

"Miss Heath," Charlotte said, "our brother told us of your habit of keeping a hatpin handy." She pointed to a gold butterfly resting at the back of her carefully coiffed golden hair.

Mercy pointed to the largest pearl in her hair. "They can come in quite handy, Charlotte. I never leave home without one." She gave her future sister-in-law a wink.

Charlotte blushed and Ester giggled.

The conversation turned to the theater and a waltz began.

"Miss Heath." Malcolm appeared from behind her.

Heart in her throat, Mercy turned. "Mr. Renshaw. I did not see you approach."

His smirk hid a dozen questions. "May I have this dance?"

Her traitorous brain could think of nothing to occupy her as an excuse not to dance with him. With a nod, she took his arm and they moved to join the other dancers.

She kept an arm's distance between them as he moved them around the floor. "Do you have a house in town, Mr. Renshaw?"

"My parents have one and rarely come to town. They prefer the country house. I use their house as it is generally empty." His stare made her uncomfortable.

When he made no further comment, she felt compelled to continue some kind of conversation. "What do you occupy yourself with? Are you involved in politics or shipping?"

"I help my cousin with his investments and act as a steward of sorts for some of his properties. I am well compensated if that is your concern. Or are you worried I might be taking some funds away from the family that you had your eye on, Miss Heath?"

Dropping his arm, she stopped mid-dance. She had to force her gaping mouth closed. "Frankly, that never occurred to me, Mr. Renshaw, but clearly it has occurred to you. I thought perhaps we could be friends as we are going to be related, but it is possible I have enough friends already."

He pulled her back into the dance. "Come now, Miss Heath, you of all people know that more is always better. You will find me very accommodating in all things if you are nice to me."

"I find you repulsive, sir." Pulling harder to free herself, she stalked away.

Halfway to the entrance to the ballroom, Faith touched her arm. "Is something wrong?"

Flustered and angry, Mercy didn't know what to say. "I'm going to the ladies retiring room for a moment."

"Shall I come with you?" Faith asked, her eyes filled with concern.

Forcing a smile, Mercy shook her head. "No. Stay here and wait for Poppy to arrive. Aurora may need a rescue from Lord Postmore as well." She pointed to where an elderly gentleman was lecturing Aurora, complete with a finger in her face.

"Oh dear." Faith sighed. "I shall intervene sooner rather than later, if you are certain you will be all right."

"I'm fine." It was only a small lie. She would be fine. Excusing herself, Mercy wound around the thick crowd and slipped out the ballroom door and up the stairs. A long hallway would take her to a ladies' retiring room. Several candles had gone out, leaving the hall dark, but Mercy had been to the Savington townhouse before and felt sure she knew the way.

An arm came hard around her waist and Mercy was pushed against the wall. Hot breath blew on her cheek as Malcolm cupped one of her breasts "Perhaps you can show me exactly how you convinced my cousin to marry you rather than do his duty by his family. I'd be very curious about what talents you possess to accomplish such a feat."

Mercy struggled to free herself, but with no success. "Unhand me. I didn't convince Wesley of anything. He proposed and I said yes."

He pressed his wet lips to her neck. "Oh, I think you're lying. I think you very much swayed him from his goals. You have harmed the family beyond repair if you go through with the marriage, so I'll offer your fortune hunting heart another opportunity, Miss Heath. I will marry you and set you up in a very fine home in the country with everything you could ever want. All you have to do is tell my cousin you've had a change of heart."

His knee bruised her as he forced her legs apart and he squeezed her breast painfully.

Fear rocketed through Mercy. She lifted her hand to her hair, found the larch pearl at her crown and stabbed Malcolm in the shoulder.

He screamed an obscenity she'd never heard before and stepped back. With no room to run, she stepped in and thrust her knee between his legs. Gripping himself, he tumbled to the floor, cursing her.

Mercy ran down the hall to the stairs and rushed down them as quickly as she could.

At the front door, she rushed outside and directly into Poppy and Rhys.

"Zeus's beard, what's wrong?" Poppy gripped her hand.

Hugging Poppy tight, Mercy said. "Can you take me home?"

Rhys scanned the area for danger. "What happened?"

"Oh, Rhys, don't ask me that. Can you just take me home?"

His jaw ticked and he searched Mercy's face before looking to his wife. "Of course, we will drive you home."

Chapter 23

Wesley had left the ball shortly after learning Mercy had gone home. He wanted to go directly to West Lane, but Poppy and Rhys assured him she was feeling ill and needed to rest.

He arrived home to his butler, Peters, and a message waiting on the silver tray on his desk. Wesley had noticed the lovely handwriting from the messages that had accompanied her paying him back for her spectacles. He would know her scrolling hand anywhere, it was as willowy as the lady.

Heart pounding like a boy in love for the first time, he broke the seal. She had thoroughly woven her way into his heart and he longed for even this small note from her.

Dear Lord Castlewick,

This evening has proved very upsetting. I have not enjoyed a proper family life since my childhood, and perhaps am misguided in my beliefs. However, I think of my friends from school and my aunt as family and they would never wish me harm for any reason. Yet your cousin seems to have little regard for your happiness. I'm sorry to deliver this type of news and it might have been better to wait until the emotions of the evening had subsided, but my impulse aside, it seems our marriage will create a deep rift in your family. There is also some indication that your entire family will be irreparably damaged by our union.

You were kind enough to inform me of your close relationship with your cousin. I do not wish to be a barrier between you. However, I refuse to ever be in his presence again. If you wish to alter your desire to marry me, I will be disappointed, but understand.

Forgive me for wanting a life without drama and relations who wish to do me harm. I know you wished only good for me.
With sincere regret,
Mercedes Heath.

Fury seethed through Wesley to the point where he had difficulty focusing his vision. He crushed the letter in his hand, then thought better of it and smoothed it out before reading it again.

"Peters! Call the carriage back." He stormed into the foyer. The urge to smash the entry table into the scrolling baluster and stairs had to be wrestled down.

With his coat unbuttoned, Peters appeared, eyes wide. "You are going back out, my lord."

"I'm going to pay a call on my cousin." Wesley waved Mercy's letter in the air as if that were all anyone needed to see. "Never mind the carriage, a brisk walk will do me good."

The experienced butler bowed and backed away.

The night air did little to cool Wesley's fury and he arrived at Malcolm's townhouse even more irate than when he'd left home. He pounded on the door.

In his robe, the young butler opened the door, saw who it was, and pulled it fully open. "My lord, Mr. Renshaw was not expecting company at this hour."

Malcolm stepped from the study to the right. "It's all right, Ward. My cousin is the head of my family and has every right to call no matter the hour."

Ward stepped aside, allowed Wesley to enter, and closed the door before making himself scarce.

"I suppose she told you." Malcolm limped slightly and went back in his study. He stepped to the glass table, where he poured two draughts of brandy.

"What did she have to tell me, Mal?" Wesley narrowed his eyes.

Turning, Malcolm gave back a similar look. "I assumed you had a conversation with Miss Heath and you are angry at me. Am I mistaken as to the nature of this visit?"

"Miss Heath is my fiancée and she wrote me to tell me that she doesn't think she wishes to be a part of my family. Why would she say such a thing, Mal?" Wesley took the brandy and downed it.

Malcolm stared into his glass, then at the floor. When he looked up, he appeared genuinely bewildered. "She didn't tell you of our conversation? She ended your engagement?"

"Don't get yourself too excited. She left it to me to end our betrothal and I have no intention of letting her go. I would sooner let you disappear from my life, Mal, than her. Do I make myself clear?" Pain at losing his close friend and cousin battled inside Wesley. However, it paled in comparison with his need for morning to come so he could beg Mercy to reconsider.

After drinking most of his brandy, Malcolm rounded his desk, put the glass down, and leaned both hands on the surface. He stared long at the polished wood before finally looking up. His eyes showed pain and regret in their depths. "I tested her, Wes."

"You did what? How?"

Malcolm shook his head. "I shouldn't have done it. I thought she had bewitched you with her wiles and tricked you into proposing. I knew it would take something really terrible to force you to put her aside, so I tested her."

Never having seen his cousin contrite, Wesley took in the new emotion. In doing so, he also noted that his white blouse had a bloodstain on the left shoulder. "From the look of you, I'm guessing Mercy passed your abhorrent test. Would you care to tell me the nature of your pursuit?"

Shaking his head, Malcolm said, "I fear doing so would only embarrass the lady and I have done enough of that for one evening. If she wishes to tell you, I will leave it to her."

"You will apologize to her and, if necessary, beg her forgiveness." Still seething, Wesley saw his perfect life with Mercy slipping away over the stupidity of his cousin.

"I will do what I can to make amends." Malcolm sank into his chair.

Wesley stepped to the desk and put down his glass. "I shall go at ten as the household rises early on West Lane. I expect you there at eleven, Mal."

"I am sorry, Wes."

"I do not require your contrition. Save it for Miss Heath and pray she is benevolent." Wesley stormed from his cousin's townhouse and didn't bother to close the front door as he struggled to catch his breath.

* * * *

Wesley bathed, dressed, and waited for the appropriate time to pay a call at West Lane. He was tempted to ride over at dawn since he knew Mercy would likely be awake. It would have been rude and impertinent, but it took all of his willpower to continue to shuffle paper on his desk while the bells on his hallway clock chimed the hours.

He checked the damned thing twice to make sure it had been properly wound, only to find the hateful thing ticking away.

Finally, nine forty-five rang out and he donned his coat and hat. His horse was brought around and he mounted without a word to his footman as he rode away.

It was a few minutes before ten when he arrived and knocked on the West Lane townhouse door.

Tipton opened the door, raised a brow, and waited more beats than were comfortable. "My Lord Castlewick, the hour is quite early. The ladies and Lord Marsden are breaking their fasts."

"I intend to enter regardless of anyone's meal being interrupted, Tipton." Wesley kept his tone flat. The butler was doing his job. There was no sense creating a scene in clear view of the street.

"I see." Raising his brow, Tipton stepped aside. "Follow me, my lord."

The dining room doors were left open and two footmen flanked the wide entry.

Tipton preceded him in. "The Earl of Castlewick for Miss Heath."

Mercy was the only one of the four people at the table not to turn her head. She put her fork aside and clung to the napkin in her lap.

Wesley bowed. "I apologize for arriving so early, but I was met last night by a disturbing letter upon my return home. It was all I could do not to come directly here at that time."

Marsden stood. "You might wish to come back another time, my lord. Miss Heath is quite upset and does not wish to see anyone outside of family."

Taking a step forward, Wesley pulled her letter from the inside pocket of his coat. "Mercy, if you wish for me to go, I will, but this letter has shattered my world and I would like an explanation."

Her eyes swam with unshed tears and her nose was red and swollen. "The letter explained my position."

"I understand my cousin did something that upset you. I have already been to see him and he refused to tell me what exactly he did. He said telling me would embarrass you further and he had already done enough." Wesley shifted his weight rather than drop to his knees and beg her to take back the things she said in the letter.

"You went to see him?" She dabbed at her tears.

He knelt beside her anyway. "Of course. I went directly after I got home and read this." He shook the sheet of parchment.

Turing away, she said, "Why would he care about my feelings? He didn't care about them last night."

"What did he do, Mercy?" Holding his temper was becoming more and more difficult.

Fire snapped in her eyes. "He inferred that my only goal was to gain your money. He said I was ruining your family for all time. He treated me like a woman of low values."

Biting down a curse, Wesley knew he should have beaten Malcolm when he'd had the chance. "I am sorry, but it does not explain why you would walk away from what we have. I would sooner disown Malcolm than lose you. We shall have our own family just as you have made a family here at West Lane. You need never worry about Malcolm again if you cannot forgive him."

"Forgive him!" Mercy stood and backed away.

Getting to his feet, Wesley opened his arms in surrender. "I told him to be here at eleven to formally apologize to you."

"Oh, Hades Gate." Poppy tossed her napkin on the table. "I suppose that means he's recovered from his injuries."

Aurora snickered. "Poppy, now might not be the time for sarcasm."

Rhys sat back down. "In my world, there is always time for sarcasm."

"Injuries?" Wesley asked.

Aurora slid her hand up to her bun and withdrew a long hatpin. "Wallflowers always keep a hatpin or two available in case some man forgets he's a gentleman."

Poppy slipped a similar weapon from the sleeve of her gown.

"You stabbed Malcolm." Wesley had a hard time keeping a straight face.

With her hands crossed over her chest, Mercy faced him. "To get him to release me, but that wasn't enough to give me an escape, so I did what Aunt Phyllis always suggested in such cases."

Before he could ask after her aunt's instructions, Mercy stormed from the room. He turned to Poppy as she was generally the most direct of the Wallflowers of West Lane.

"She struck him with her knee in a delicate area." Poppy smirked and raised a brow as if to issue a challenge.

Wesley didn't know whether to be mortified that she was put into such a position by his relation, or to be proud that she defended herself so admirably. "He deserved far worse."

"On that point we are in agreement, my lord." Aurora stared at him.

The pianoforte strains echoed through the house.

Turning, Wesley stepped toward the hallway.

"You may as well wait until she's played herself out," Poppy said.

"My wife is right, Castlewick. It is Mercy's way." Rhys put his napkin back in his lap and turned toward his plate.

Wesley exited, walked down the hall, and stopped just a few feet inside the music room.

The fresh, bright room must have been recently redecorated as it, and many of the rooms in Aurora's home, were a juxtaposition to the gloomy exterior typical of these older London townhouses. In contrast, the piece Mercy played was dark and full or pain. The minor key gave a dirge-like tone, yet the emotion put forth to produce such emotions was remarkable.

This was her escape from the world. She played out her feelings and he was blessed to stand in the room and listen. Unable to bear the idea that this might be the last time he was so fortunate, Wesley's gut twisted. If he had to return to West Lane for the rest of his days, he would convince this spectacular woman that they were meant for each other.

The sound of footsteps in the hall forced him to turn.

Wide-eyed, Malcolm stood in the doorway. His voice was hushed. "Dear lord, she's a miracle on the pianoforte."

Wesley narrowed his gaze on his cousin. "She's a miracle in all things, Mal."

With a nod, Malcolm took a deep breath and crossed the music room to where Mercy played.

Wesley remained near the door, but kept still. He would protect her, but forgiving his cousin would be her choice alone.

Stopping about five feet from her, but in full view, Malcolm stood with his hands behind his back and waited. When she played the last note and put her hands in her lap, he bowed. "Miss Heath."

"I am at a loss for why you are here, Mr. Renshaw, beyond the fact that the head of your family commanded you arrive this morning." Her voice held strength and assuredness that the somber composition of the music had not.

"My appearance this morning is at my cousin's command. However, I would have sought you out at some point to make a formal apology. I expected a woman of little morals when I approached you last evening. I had no evidence beyond gossip about you're having secured my cousin's affection. I know better than to believe such things. Had you purred and simpered or taken a haughty turn, I would have guessed the gossips were correct. However, you did neither. You pushed me aside and defended yourself, quite amply too." He rubbed his injured shoulder.

Mercy stood and rounded the bench. "You were testing my worthiness for Wesley?"

"I was worried that my cousin had been pushed into proposing by a seasoned woman of persuasive charms. I find I was mistaken. I deeply regret my behavior and am ashamed." Malcolm opened his arms, palms up in defeat.

Turning away from him, Mercy surveyed the garden. "I had hoped we would be as family, Mr. Renshaw. I do not know if I can ever forgive you. You made me feel unsafe and a victim. I love your cousin and therefore I will not allow him to disown you after our marriage. Perhaps one day we might become friends, but that day will not be today."

She was going to marry him. Wesley's heart, which had clutched tightly, began to beat again.

Malcolm bowed. "Of course. I understand. I will await the day when I have proved myself worthy of that forgiveness."

Head held high, she gave him a nod and watched as he walked away.

With a brief bow to Wesley, Malcolm left.

As soon as he heard the front door close behind his cousin, Wesley went to her. Even as tall as Mercy was for a woman; standing alone beside the large pianoforte and tall windows, she appeared lost.

When he reached the end of the instrument, he stopped, unsure what she needed. Her eyes glistened with emotion. She had been made to feel small by his cousin and Wesley was to blame. Again, he had not protected her as he should.

Hopeful but uncertain, he opened his arms.

Mercy rushed into his embrace. Her head tucked into his chest and her arms came around him.

Folding her in his arms, Wesley breathed in her essence. "I don't know how you will ever forgive me, but I am begging, Mercy. I have failed time and time again to protect you. I shall never atone for my stupidity."

Muffled by his coat, her voice was soft and tight with emotion. "Just hold me, Wesley. I always feel safe in your arms. Besides, I have long taken care of myself. Surely you don't think your cousin is the first man to feel the point of my hatpin."

He wished he could have seen Malcolm's face when he realized a woman had stabbed him. "You nearly skewered me once. I would never have underestimated your abilities."

Snuggling in closer, she sighed. "I dare say your cousin shan't do so again."

Holding her by the shoulders, he eased her far enough away that she could see his face. "You never have to worry about Mal again. I'm shocked by his behavior, but I really don't believe he would have harmed you. In any event, you will never be left alone with him again. I will see to it."

Mercy relaxed against him. "I shall always be ready to defend myself should he or anyone forget their manners."

"I will disown him if that would make you more comfortable with our marriage." A knot formed in his gut.

"No. We shall give him the opportunity to make amends. He told me he helps you with the family estates and investments. Perhaps he meant to protect you. I don't know. I'm sorry about the letter I wrote."

The air went out of him at the mention of that letter. Releasing her, he sat on the bench. "Your words tore my heart out. Never say you would leave me, Mercedes. I cannot bear the idea of living without you."

She stepped between his knees. "I promise, I will never leave you, Wesley. Not in this lifetime or the next."

The ache in his heart eased and he pressed his forehead to her abdomen. Her hands threaded through his hair and she held him.

Heaven.

Chapter 24

Mercy should have been exhausted after the day she'd had, but she was too happy and excited to even think of sleep. She touched the family brooch at her neck, a gift from Aunt Phyllis, and thought of her mother.

After the small wedding and a lovely breakfast, which had been hosted by Aunt Phyllis, Wesley had whisked Mercy away to a lovely manor he owned near Oxford. She ran her hand along the delicately carved mantle in their bedroom and looked forward to exploring the rest of the house. "This is lovely, but we could have stayed in London, Wesley."

He wrapped his arms around her and kissed her neck where it met her shoulder. "My sisters and Mrs. Manfred are in London. I wanted you to myself."

His lips set her afire. Turning into his embrace, she wrapped her arms around him. These warm hugs were even better than kisses. There was nothing to compare with being wrapped in Wesley's arms. No fireplace was warmer. No blanket more comforting. With her head resting on his chest and his heart beating beneath her ear, it was perfection. "Now that you have me to yourself, what will you do with me, my lord?"

With a chuckle he kissed her forehead. "I plan to ravage you thoroughly, but first I have a wedding gift, my dear sweet Mercy."

She watched him and the love shining in his beautiful brown eyes. "A gift? But I have everything I could possibly want. There is no need to give me more."

"I think you should be showered with gifts whenever possible, but we can disagree on this point if you wish." His grin was full of mischief.

"What are you up to?"

With a step back he touched his chest with both hands. "Me. Up to something? Come now, my love, what could I be up to?"

Mercy searched the room. It wasn't exceedingly large and the bed took up most of the room. A small table with two chairs sat in a windowed alcove. It would be a lovely place to take her breakfast. She imagined Wesley sleeping in with her, and Jane setting out their meal. Jane had decided to come with Mercy after the wedding. It had been a lovely surprise not to have to find a new maid and have a familiar face in her new life.

Despite the early autumn date on the calendar, the weather was still too warm for a fire in the hearth. Two overstuffed chairs and a thick aubergine rug sat before the fireplace. The walls were cream, papered with the palest stripe.

Everything was lovely, but she saw no gift beyond the perfect life she'd been given. "Is not all of this your gift to me?"

"I can see I shall always be forcing you to act like the countess you are, Mercy. You deserve to be showered with jewels." He backed away several steps.

"Come back here and shower me with love; that will be more than enough." Suspicious, she kept her gaze on him.

"Don't move," he commanded.

Unable to keep from laughing, she said, "Where would I go?"

Wesley stepped to a door that likely led to a dressing room. He went through and disappeared.

"What are you up to?" She stretched her neck trying to see where he'd gone and what he could be hiding.

"Just stay where you are," he called from the dark doorway. A moment later, he stepped out, carrying a very fine wooden box. Crossing to the bed, he lay the box atop the mattress. His eyes were full of love and trepidation when he turned. "Don't you wish to see what it is, Mercy?"

"You told me not to move." Her cheeks hurt from smiling.

Holding his hand out to her, he said. "Come and see."

Rushing over, she took his hand and studied the rich wood of the carefully carved box. "What is it?"

"Open it." His voice was breathy and oddly nervous.

Two small leather latches kept the box closed. Mercy slipped the knots through the loops and lifted the lid. Lying on a red velvet cushion inside was the Stradivarius, its rich wood gleaming up at her in perfection. "How? Where did you get this?"

He took her hand and placed it on the neck of the extraordinary instrument. "From the Dowager Countess of Marsden, of course. I bought it for you. Are you pleased?"

"Pleased?" Tears flooded Mercy's eyes and she caressed the scroll, then the tuning keys. "Why would she sell it to you? She hates me."

"I can be very convincing." Wesley dabbed her tears with a soft handkerchief. "Do you want to play it?"

Heart in her throat, she lifted the violin from the cushion and rested it on her shoulder. Picking up the bow where it rested at the side of the box, she pressed her chin to the chin rest. As she ran the bow over the strings, she had to close her eyes. The perfect tone of such a wondrous instrument went right to her soul. She played it gently, reverently, and then she let the music take her to another place.

As she drew the bow over the strings with the last note, it struck her. "This is mine?"

When there was no reply, she opened her eyes. Turning, she found her husband watching from one of the chairs near the hearth.

Handling it like delicate bit of china, she eased the Stradivarius back into the box. As soon as it was safe, she rushed to Wesley and dove into his arms. "Is it really mine?"

He kissed her cheek and squeezed her to him. "You never have to play if for another soul should you not wish to. You never have to play on command ever again, Mercy. No one shall ever hold an instrument just out of your reach again and you will never be bullied into preforming for a crowd. From this day on, you can play a magnificent instrument at your leisure or not at all. If you play for friends, it will be your choice. You are the Countess of Castlewick. I hope you will always remember that."

The implications were too great to contemplate after the emotion of playing a master's violin. Mercy had to draw several breaths and let the sound of Wesley's heartbeat calm her. "It's a kind of independence. You meant to buy my freedom."

Wesley cupped her face in his hands and kissed her nose. "You were always free, my beautiful, sweet, talented angel. I only purchased the violin so you would see that freedom made real. You are magnificent and I expect the world to see that as clearly as I do."

She straddled his lap and threaded her fingers through his thick hair. "I don't care what anyone else sees."

Easing forward, he pressed his lips to her and coaxed them open. The kiss went right to her heart and expanded until she couldn't get enough of him.

Pushing at his coat, she longed to feel his skin against hers.

He tugged on the stays holding her wedding gown in place and soon the laces were loose and she stood quickly to step out of the garment. Mercy pulled the ties at her shoulders and let her chemise fall to the floor.

Standing with her, he took her hand and walked to the bed. He closed the lid on the violin and carried it to the table near the window before returning to her.

Mercy climbed on the mattress and pulled off her stockings. Unable to take her eyes from him, she watched as he divested himself of his cravat and blouse. At the bed, he removed his boots and breeches.

He climbed up and pulled her on top of him.

Every inch of him was hard and chiseled. She ran her hands along his ribs to his arms and shoulders. "You didn't have to buy me such an extravagant wedding gift. I was remarkably happy just to be your wife."

"I have a plan." His mischievous grin was back.

She pressed her pelvis against his shaft and moaned at the pleasure the friction caused and the desire reflected in his eyes. "What plan is that?"

"I want to see you look as you did when you first heard the tone of that violin. I long to watch you transform into the goddess you are when you play. I plan to make you deliriously happy every day of your life. Anything less just won't do."

Mercy adored him through watery eyes. "How shall I make you as happy as you've made me?"

He brushed her hair out of her eyes. "You are my angel of mercy. You fill my heart to capacity, my love. I cannot be any happier and as long as you are mine, I shall continue to be spoiled with delight."

"I shall always be yours."

Tears and love merged as she pressed her lips to his. A life filled with unhindered emotions was his true gift. Mercy silently vowed that she would spend her lifetime trying to match such a perfect present.

Keep reading for a special excerpt of Faith and Nicholas's story in MISLEADING A DUKE *by A.S. Fenichel.*

Chapter 1

The home of Geb Arafa, a mile outside of London

The last person Nicholas Ellsworth expected to find at his good friend Geb Arafa's dinner party was Lady Faith Landon. Yet there she was, Nicholas's fiancée, maddeningly pretty and equally aggravating. She fit perfectly with the lush décor and priceless artifacts in Geb's parlor. "Lady Faith, I had not expected to find you here. In fact, you and your friends' presence is an astonishment."

"I hope you are not too put out. It seems Lord and Lady Marsden have become fast friends with Mr. Arafa, and that friendship has extended to the rest of the Wallflowers of West Lane." Despite his desire to be rid of her, Faith's soft voice flowed over him like a summer stream and he longed to hear that voice in the dark, in their bed. The way her curves filled out the rose gown set his body aflame and there seemed nothing he could do about it.

He shook away his attraction, reminding himself that this was a sneaky, manipulative woman whom it had been a mistake to attach himself to. The fact that he longed to find out if her honey-brown curls were as wild as they promised, despite her attempts to tame them into submission, shouldn't matter. Nor should his desire to get lost in her wheat-colored eyes and voluptuous curves. This was a woman made for loving.

Lord, he hated himself. "I wonder that your being here with those friends is not some dire plot in the making."

He had reason to be suspicious. When he'd first arrived home from France, in the spring, she and her friends had engaged in spying on him and trying to ferret out his past. It was intolerable. He should have called off the engagement, but the thought of ruining her for good society didn't sit well with Nicholas. Instead he'd offered her the opportunity to set him aside, but she had refused to do so as of yet.

She frowned, and was no less stunning. Her full lips longed to be kissed back into an upturned state. "We are here because Mr. Arafa invited us. He's your friend. I'm surprised he didn't mention it."

Nick was equally bewildered by Geb's silence on the matter of Faith and the other members of the Wallflowers of West Lane. He had met them on several occasions during his feeble efforts to get to know Faith. Her instant suspicions that he was hiding something might have led to her friends' actions, but he still couldn't let the slight die. Though he did admire the strength of the friendship between Faith and the three women she'd gone to finishing school with. They were as close as any soldiers who fought and died together. Even if they called themselves "wallflowers," there was nothing diminished about any of the four.

"He is not required to give me his invitation list." It pushed out more bitterly than intended.

Those cunning eyes narrowed. "I think you would like it exceedingly well if he did."

That she wasn't wrong raised the hair on the back of Nick's neck. He had not been able to keep many friends over the years. His work for the Crown had made that impossible. Now his friendship with Geb Arafa was in jeopardy as well.

He bowed to her. "I do not always get what I want, Lady Faith."

Head cocked, she raised one brown eyebrow. "Don't you, Your Grace?"

Geb chose that moment to stroll over. His dark skin set off his bright tawny eyes, and though he dressed in the black suit and white cravat typical of an Englishman, there was no mistaking his Eastern background. "Nicholas, I'm so glad you are here. I thought you might be held up with politics."

Nicholas accepted his offered hand. "I finished my meetings and came directly."

Smiling in her charming way, Faith's golden eyes flashed. "I shall leave you gentlemen to catch up."

Both Nicholas and Geb bowed and watched her join her friends near the pianoforte.

"She is a delightful woman, Nick. You should reconcile and marry her." Geb ran his hand through his black hair, smoothing it back from his forehead.

Not willing to let his attraction to Faith rule his decisions, Nicholas forced down the desire seeing his betrothed always ignited in him. "She is sneaky and devious. I shall wait for her to give up and call off."

"I would have thought such character traits would appeal to you." Geb lowered his voice. "After all, you are a spy with much the same qualities. You might consider speaking to the lady and finding out the details behind her actions."

"Why don't you just tell me what you know, Geb?" It was obvious his friend knew more than he'd disclosed thus far. Nicholas asking for more was futile. If Geb was going to tell him more than he already had, he would have done so months ago when he'd first informed him that Poppy and Rhys, now the Earl and Countess of Marsden, were investigating his character. Being spies meant that Geb and Nick kept their own counsel most of the time. As an information broker, Geb was even more closed mouthed than most spies. He only offered what was necessary to complete a contract or in this case, informing a friend of something less than critical.

"I am not at liberty to divulge that information." Geb's white teeth gleamed.

"I didn't realize you were so keen on keeping a lady's secrets," Nicholas teased.

Grabbing his chest, Geb feigned a knife to the heart. "I would never tell tales of a good woman. There have been a few ladies of our acquaintance who were not reputable, and those who are part of our line of work whose secrets I had little scruples about divulging."

"Indeed." As much as he wanted to be angry with Geb for befriending Faith and her friends, he couldn't manage it. The truth was, Geb was quite discerning about who he called friend.

During the time he'd spent with them, he couldn't help but like them as well. They were the most spirited and brightest women he'd ever known. He recalled a beautiful blonde in Spain who had tried to put a knife between his ribs, and shuddered. At lease he didn't think these Wallflowers were out for his blood, just his secrets. What he didn't know was why they were so keen on divining his past. He might be a fool to think them innocent. His trust of a sweet face in the past had nearly gotten him killed.

Geb nudged him out of his thoughts. "Talk to the girl."

Glancing at where Faith stood drinking a glass of wine and talking to Poppy Draper, Nicholas mused over whether they were plotting their next attempt to invade his privacy. "Perhaps later. First, I would like a glass of your excellent cognac."

"Avoiding her will not make your situation better," Geb warned, his rich Egyptian accent rounding the words and lending a sense of foreboding.

"The lady will decide I am not worth the trouble and find herself a less complicated gentleman to attach herself to."

Nodding, Geb said, "I'm certain that is true. She is too lovely for half the men in London not to be in love with."

Nicholas wished that thought didn't form a knot in his gut. He also longed for a day when Faith wouldn't enter his mind a dozen times. She had gotten under his skin before he'd even met her, and he couldn't rid himself of her spell. Even knowing it had been her mother and not the lady herself who had written to him when he was in France hadn't dulled what he knew and liked about Faith Landon.

"One day you shall have to tell me how you came to this, my friend." Geb signaled for Kosey, his servant.

The extremely tall Egyptian wore a white turban and loose black pants and a similar blouse. He carried a tray with two glasses of dark amber cognac. "Dinner will be ready in ten minutes, sir. Will that please you?" Kosey spoke English in an Eastern way, which made the language warmer and less harsh to the ear. It gained looks from some of the other guests, but Nicholas liked the formal, old-fashioned speech.

"Very good," said Geb.

Nick observed the gaping of the other guests. "Why have you invited these snobs to Aaru, Geb?"

"Flitmore has some items I wish to obtain and Humphry has proved to be a good source of information about certain parliamentary discussions."

"I trust you would never use such information against my beloved country." A knot formed in Nick's gut.

"No, but I might try to sway other members of your government. I like to know what is happening in my adopted country, Nicholas. That is all. As a foreigner, I have no say. This gives me some needed control." Geb grinned.

Nick held back a scolding that would do no good.

"Do not look at me so ill. I merely use information to my advantage just as everyone else does. I will share bits with them or buy back pieces of Egyptian art. It will harm no one."

Kosey moved to the door, where he waited for word from the cook that dinner was ready to be served.

Lord and Lady Flitmore gaped at Kosey. Perhaps it was his height as he towered over everyone in the room. It might have been his odd clothes. Whatever it was, their shocked regard needled at Nicholas.

Faith stepped between him and the couple. "Lady Flitmore, it's nice to see you again. I heard your daughter Mary would be here tonight, but I've not seen her. I hope nothing is wrong. I know how she can get into mischief."

Lord Flitmore coughed uncomfortably. "Mary had some trouble with her gown and is coming in a later carriage. She will be here any moment."

As if on cue, a footman announced the arrival of Lady Mary Yates.

A slim woman with red hair and flawless skin sauntered into the room. Pretty in the classical way, her long, thin nose appeared in a perpetual state of being turned up at everyone and everything. Hands folded lightly in front of her, she walked directly to where Faith stood with Mary's parents. In a voice without modulation, Mary said, "Mother, Father, I'm sorry to be late. I hope no one was waiting on me."

The lack of any emotion in Mary's voice made it difficult to tell if she was sincere or just saying what was expected of her. "Thank you for sending the carriage back for me."

Lord Flitmore pulled his shoulders back and beamed at his daughter. "Dinner has only just been announced, my dear girl. Please say hello to His Grace, the Duke of Breckenridge."

Mary made a pretty curtsy and plastered a wan smile on her rosy lips. "How do you do, Your Grace?"

Bowing, Nick couldn't help but notice the look of disdain that flitted across Faith's face. "A pleasure, Lady Mary. I'm pleased you could come tonight. Do you know Lady Faith Landon?"

Another curtsy and a smile that likened to a wolf, and Mary said, "Lady Faith and I went to the Wormbattle School together. We have been acquainted for many years. How are you, Faith?"

Faith raised a brow. "Very well, Mary. You are looking fine. Your parents tell me you've had some issue with your gown this evening."

Mary's gown was dark blue and threaded with gold. It pushed all her assets up to the breaking point of the material at her breast and flowed down, showing off her perfect figure. She blushed. "Just a small issue that my maid and a needle and thread resolved easily enough."

The ladies leered at each other.

Clearing his throat, Lord Flitmore said, "Mary, let me introduce you to our host."

"Of course," Mary agreed, and with a nod to Nick, all three Yateses left the circle.

Faith watched after Mary but had schooled her features to a pleasant expression that no one could have noted anything amiss from. Nick had many questions, but none of them were any of his business.

"Shall we go in to dinner?" As they were officially engaged, Nick offered Faith his arm and they preceded the others into the dining room.

The long table had rounded corners and was draped in white linen. Fine china leafed with gold, and highly polished crystal and silver, made the setting gleam under three fully lit chandeliers hanging overhead, and with four standing candelabras placed in all corners of the room. The high-backed, dark wood chairs were cushioned with a pale blue damask. It was decidedly English, and extremely elegant, to appeal to Geb's guests.

At the head of the table, Geb welcomed everyone formally to his home, Aaru, before launching into a story of being on a sinking ship, and the diners were riveted despite the fact that most of them would not invite an Egyptian man of no known rank into their own homes. Faith smiled warmly at Geb, and Nick wondered if she were different. Would his friends, regardless of their origins, be welcomed to her table?

He shook off the notion. He would not be going through with marrying Faith Landon, no matter how much he desired her or how kind she pretended to be. She had betrayed him with her spying, and he wouldn't have it.

Another exception to the apparent prejudice against Geb were Rhys and Poppy Draper. The earl and his bride genuinely liked Geb and had become fast friends with him after being stranded at his house in a storm.

"Did you swim to shore from that distance, Mr. Arafa?" Poppy's blue eyes were wide and her dark hair and lashes made the color all the more demonstrable.

Geb's cheeks pinked and he laughed. "I'm afraid nothing so heroic, my lady. I was hauled out of the ocean by a small fishing vessel. My lungs were full of water and I caught a terrible ague and spent three weeks in a Portuguese hospital."

They all laughed with Geb.

Rhys Draper took a long pull on his wine. "I would be willing to bet you were the most interesting thing those fishermen plucked from the Atlantic that day. And you were damned lucky. Not only could you have drowned, but if this had happened a year later, you might have been caught up in Napoleon's invasion."

"Indeed, luck was with me that day and many others." More sober, Geb gave Nick a knowing look.

Nick noted his friend's careful use of *luck* rather than invoke the name of the Prophet in a room full of Christians. Knowing how religious Geb was, Nick knew what he was thinking. They had experienced many adventures together, and luck, Allah, or God had seen them through some things that at the time seemed impossible.

The footmen served the soup.

Nick noted that many of the guests poked at the fine broth, vegetables, and bits of tender beef, but didn't eat. The Yates family were among those who would not eat from the table of an Egyptian but would be happy to attend, since Geb was a good resource for many business dealings. Not to mention the depth of Geb's pocketbook.

Faith, Poppy, and Rhys ate with gusto. Perhaps more than was natural, and Nick decided they had also noticed the rudeness of the other guests.

Besides the Yateses, Sir Duncan Humphrey, his wife, and two sons, Montgomery and Malcolm, were in attendance, as well as William Wharton and his wife. All were well respected among the *ton* and had obviously not come for the food or company. They didn't speak other than the occasional thank you.

On Nick's right, Faith sipped the last of her soup and turned to Mary. "You didn't like the soup?"

"I'm not hungry. I'm certain it is quite good." Mary narrowed her eyes at Faith.

"It's really too bad, it was the best I've tasted." Faith smiled warmly and turned her attention back to Geb. "Poppy told me how wonderful your cook is and now I can taste the truth of it."

"You always did have a great love of food, Faith." Mary's voice rang with disdain and she peered down that thin nose at Faith's curvaceous figure.

Poppy looked ready to leap across the table and do Mary physical harm.

A low laugh from Faith calmed the situation. "I suppose where I am fond of a good meal you are fond of a good bit of gossip. We each have our hidden desires. Don't we, Mary?"

It was a warning, but Nick didn't have enough information to know what was at stake.

Mary bit her bottom lip and narrowed her eyes before masking all emotion and nodding. "I suppose that's true of everyone."

A flush of pride swept over Nick. He had no right to feel any sense of esteem for Faith's ability to outthink another woman and put her in her place. Yet he couldn't help liking that she had not been bested by a bigoted daughter of parents who would attend the dinner party of a man they clearly didn't like, but wanted something from.

Turning his attention back to Geb, Nick noted his friend's amusement at the social volley going on at the table. Geb smiled warmly at Poppy as she changed the subject to the delectable pheasant and fine wine.

By the main course, Nick had given up on the other end of the table and was ensconced in a lively conversation among the four people around him. Rhys was well versed in politics and they discussed the state of coal mines. Faith and Poppy both added their opinions, which were well thought out and more astute than he would have thought for ladies of their rank. Perhaps he should rethink his views of what ladies ponder in the course of a day. Clearly it was more than stitching and tea patterns.

Geb, too, ignored the reticent group at the far end of the table and joined the banter. When Kosey announced that cake and sherry were being served in the grand parlor, Nick was disappointed to leave the conversation.

As soon as they entered the parlor, Flitmore cornered Geb about the sale of several horses, and Sir Duncan wanted to know when the next shipment of spices from India would be arriving.

Stomach turning at their duplicity, Nick escaped to the garden.

Geb had torches lighting the paths. The gardens here were one of Nick's favorite places in England. They were orderly and wild at once. White stones lined the lanes meant to guide one through the low plantings. It was a maze but without the threat of becoming lost. The fountain at the far end broke the silence of the pleasant autumn night. Soon winter would turn the garden into a wasteland and a good snow would give it the feel of an abandoned house.

Nick sighed and walked on.

"Are you determined to be alone, or might I join you, Your Grace?" Faith called from only a few feet behind him.

He must be losing his training for her to have sneaked up behind him without notice. "Is there something you wanted, Lady Faith?"

She stepped closer. Several curls had freed themselves of her elaborate coif and called out to Nick to touch them. "It is a lovely garden." She glanced around and smiled.

"Yes. Geb has taken bits from all his travels and placed them in his home and this garden. I think it brings him comfort."

Faith's golden eyes filled with sorrow. "Do you think Mr. Arafa is lonely here in England?"

"It is never easy to live amongst a people not your own." Nick considered all the time he'd spent in France, Spain, and Portugal and how much he'd missed the rainy days in England and people who understood his humor.

"The Wallflowers are very fond of Mr. Arafa. We have not entertained much, but I will see that he is added to our invitation list. Perhaps a circle of good friends will make him feel more at home." She'd placed her index finger on her chin while she considered how best to help Geb.

Adorable.

He needed to be free of this woman. "You didn't say what it was you wanted, Lady Faith."

Frowning, she walked forward and down the path. "Must I have a reason to walk in the garden with my fiancé?"

Leaving her to her own devices and returning to the house flitted through his mind, but it would cause gossip and he was curious about her reason for seeking him out. "We are hardly the perfect picture of an engaged couple."

"No. That is true. I wanted to apologize for any undue strain I may have caused you by trying to find out what kind of character you have."

"Is that your apology, or shall I wait for more?" he said when she didn't elaborate.

She stopped and puffed up her chest. Her cheeks were red and fire flashed in her eyes. "Why must you be so difficult? Even when I'm trying to be nice, you find fault. The entire situation was mostly your doing. If you had been open and honest, that would have been an end to our query and none of the rest would have been necessary."

She was even more beautiful when she was in a temper. He longed to pull her into his arms and taste those alluring lips. He was certain just one tug would topple all those curls from the pins that held her hair in place and he could find out if they were as soft as they appeared. It was maddening. "I hardly see how it was my fault. You and your friends spied on me and involved Geb, which is unforgivable."

As soft and lovely as she was, a hard edge caught in her voice. "I suppose, then, you will not accept my apology. I see. Well, in that case, I'll leave you to your solitude." She turned to walk away and stopped, eyes narrowed into the darkness beyond the gardens, which were surrounded by tall evergreens.

Following her gaze, Nick saw nothing, though the hair on the back of his neck rose. "What is it?"

"I felt eyes on me, as if someone was watching." She shivered and continued straining to see in the shadows.

"I'm sure you are imagining things." He dismissed her worry.

That hateful glance fell on him before she plastered false serenity on her face. "Perhaps."

He preferred the disdain to the untruthful agreement. Why he should care when he wanted nothing to do with her, he didn't know. "Shall I escort you back inside, Lady Faith?"

"You are too kind, Your Grace, but I can manage the journey on my own." With a curt nod, she stormed away from him toward the house.

Unable to look away, he admired the gentle sway of her hips until she climbed the veranda steps and went inside. Lord, how he longed to hold those hips and slide his hands up to that slim waist, and so much more. He shook away the wayward thoughts before he embarrassed himself with his desires.

One thing was certain, Faith Landon would be his undoing.

Look for **MISLEADING A DUKE** *on sale now!*

Meet the Author

A.S. Fenichel gave up a successful IT career in New York City to follow her husband to Texas and pursue her lifelong dream of being a professional writer. She's never looked back. A.S. adores writing stories filled with love, passion, desire, magic, and maybe a little mayhem tossed in for good measure. Books have always been her perfect escape and she still relishes diving into one and staying up all night to finish a good story. The author of The Forever Brides series, the Everton Domestic Society series, and more, A.S. adores strong, empowered heroines no matter the era, and that's what you'll find in all her books. A Jersey Girl at heart, she now makes her home in southern Missouri with her real-life hero, her wonderful husband. When not reading or writing, she enjoys cooking, travel, history, puttering in her garden, and spoiling her fussy cat. Be sure to write visit her website at asfenichel.com, find her on Facebook, and follow her on Twitter.

Printed in the United States
by Baker & Taylor Publisher Services